# PRAISE FOR *CHICK MAGNET*

"Emma Barry has been one of my favorite authors in the world for many years now, and *Chick Magnet* only deepens my already fervent love of her writing. Her books are always crafted with exquisite care and thoughtfulness, abounding with graceful prose, extremely likable characters, rueful humor, and a thorough grounding in how good people think, work, and love. Plus, her writing is simply *fun*, not to mention sexy. With the release of this book, I expect new hordes of fans to join the Emma Barry Stan Club, but rest assured: I will always be the club's president and most enthusiastic member."

—Olivia Dade, national bestselling author of *Spoiler Alert* and *All the Feels*

"One of the chief pleasures of being a romance reader is getting to watch Emma Barry's complex, honorable characters forging themselves into stronger, happier versions of themselves. *Chick Magnet* is Emma Barry at the peak of her powers: hilarious and humane, it will restore your faith in the power of love."

—Jenny Holiday, *USA Today* bestselling author

"I could tell you all the reasons *Chick Magnet* is spectacular—the nuance of the emotional arcs, the witty dialogue, the delightful characters, the endearing small town—but really, all you need to know is that Emma Barry is about to become your new favorite contemporary romance author."

—Therese Beharrie, author of *A Ghost in Shining Armor*

"Intoxicating and deeply romantic, *Chick Magnet* delivers a riveting opposites attract, slow-burn-with-the-hot-guy-next-door small-town romance. I fell in love with Will Lund from the first grumpy meeting."

—Zoe York, *USA Today* and *New York Times* bestselling author

# chick
# MAGNET

# chick
# MAGNET

# EMMA BARRY

 Montlake

Text copyright © 2023 by Emma Barry
All rights reserved.

Published by Montlake, Seattle

www.apub.com

Amazon, the Amazon logo, and Montlake are trademarks of Amazon.com, Inc., or its affiliates.

ISBN-13: 9781662505010 (paperback)
ISBN-13: 9781662505003 (digital)

Cover design by Elizabeth Turner Stokes
Cover photography by Michelle Lancaster
Cover images: ©Foxys Graphic, ©Miro Novak / Shutterstock

Printed in the United States of America

# chick
# MAGNET

# CHAPTER 1

The tiny dinosaurs surveyed Nicole Jones hungrily. One scratched the ground. Another squawked.

Nic rolled her eyes. "Come on, ladies. We've been through this a bazillion times. I can't get into the coop if you crowd the doorway."

Her words fell on feathered ears. Feathered gallinaceous ears, those belonging to her backyard chickens. They moved with none of the coordination or grace of a school of fish. Heads bobbing to individual rhythms, they kept bumping into one another, seemingly unable to get out of each other's way. One managed to shake the group. She celebrated by snipping at the fabric of Nic's skirt, which she found inedible . . . and then tried to eat a second time.

"Oh, you clever girl." Nic *tsk-tsk-tsk*ed her way between the birds and hung the feeder on a hook. "There you go. Plenty to eat now."

She dropped back a few steps and watched the flock peck greedily at the pellets of grain and meal. Nic still had to paint the coop and plant its rooftop garden bed with herbs and flowers, a process that she would document in extreme detail for her loyal fans, who'd give her clicks and subscribe to her Patreon and otherwise keep Nic's career simmering— especially after the disaster of six weeks ago.

As she'd been dumped by her boyfriend and rejected by her best friend and then had driven across the country in a car jam-packed with chickens, the only thing Nic had been able to think was "Granny would've seen this coming."

She would've sized Brian up with a glance, something Nic hadn't managed to do in years of close observation, and she never would've let Nic forget that she hadn't fallen for his act.

*That one's a dud, darlin'.* She would have known it instantly.

Nic had flaws, of course. She scribbled in her books and left her socks on the floor, and she cared entirely too much about what people thought of her. But she'd never suspected she was a poor judge of character.

There was no escaping what you'd hatched.

But speaking of chickens: "Where's Mitzi?" Nic asked.

The flock just kept eating, of course. The absent one was probably laying, grateful to finally have an egg box and some privacy again. That Nic completely understood. She was looking forward to alone time herself.

Rain splattered across Nic's face. The black clouds that had been hanging heavy in the sky all afternoon while the movers finished their work were finally spilling over. At least it had held off that long.

"I'll check on you in a bit," Nic said to her birds. Then she hiked up the skirt of her maxi sundress and dashed across the yard to her back porch. Several raindrops ran down her back before she got through the screen door and into the house.

The atmosphere inside was heavy and still. It had been too long since Nic had been in the South, and she'd forgotten how the air was different here than on the West Coast. More present, never letting you forget about it. Air that demanded things from you.

Nic dodged through the piles of boxes and the maze of the unfamiliar layout. *Move to a new town,* they said. *Get a fresh start,* they said. *Nothing like a thousand miles to put your breakup behind you,* they said. They left out how much damn work it would be.

She threw herself into the first chair she could find. But the instant her butt hit the seat, before she'd even finished exhaling all the way, a knock sounded on the front door.

Nic didn't want to get up, not now and maybe never again. She was *exhausted*. But it was probably a curious neighbor who'd seen the moving truck, and Nic needed to make a good first impression. She slid her aching feet back into her flip-flops, forced a smile onto her face, and dashed down the hallway.

The hello died, or more precisely evaporated, in her mouth when she opened the door. An enormous, wide-shouldered, sandy-blond-haired, broad-faced man—good looking in a pillaging-Viking sort of way—stood on her steps. He had been smiling, a polite, neighborly sort of smile, but as soon as he and Nic locked eyes, the corners of his mouth fell, and crisp parallel lines appeared across his forehead.

"Um, hey. What can I do for you?" Nic asked after an almost inappropriately long pause. He was just so good looking, and he appeared to be so annoyed, and she was so tired. Too tired for the puzzle this was going to be, for whatever apology she was going to have to offer. For what, she didn't even *know*.

"Do you have chickens?" His tone wasn't rude, but it was curt.

For a minute, it was all Nic could do to blink at him. Did *she* have chickens? But this wasn't about Nic at all. The guy probably hated chickens, assuming they'd be smelly or loud and bring down his property values somehow. The kind of person who lobbied cities to keep the poultry laws strict and punitive.

She knew all about how to handle that type. She needed to be charming and to promise him some eggs, and he'd fade into the background.

"Yes, I do," Nic said. "But they won't bother you. In fact, I—"

"One of them is loose."

The grumpy Viking was wrong. He had to be. "That's impossible. I was just out there."

3

"She's about this high." He held his hand about a foot and a half off the ground. "Golden. Sort of . . . curvy."

He was describing Mitzi, the hen Nic had assumed was laying.

"Son of an amorous Zeus, how is that possible? How did she get out?"

"Chickens can fly."

Normally, Nic would *eat* anyone who tried to mansplain chickens to her—but she didn't have the time just now. She had a bird to catch.

She stepped onto the stoop and scanned the yard. It was poultry-free. "Where did you see her?"

"In those bushes." He pointed to the large holly hedge that separated Nic's house from the one next door, maybe his place.

No—nopity, nope, nope, nope. The last thing she needed right now was some silly crush. The best way to avoid landing on TMZ again was not to fall in love, and, at this point, that seemed a small price to pay.

"Hubris," she muttered as she marched away from the man whose hotness she wasn't going to notice again.

"What?"

Obviously his granny hadn't gifted him d'Aulaires's *Greek Myths* for his fifth birthday. "That's how people offend the gods. Like Arachne, bragging about how she could weave better than a goddess. I'd just been thinking I could relax—that was hubris. I need to atone, make an offering. Roasted meat is traditional." Maybe she ought to barbecue a certain chicken.

Nic lifted a branch to the side, but no bird was visible in the thick hedge. Her neighbor had no reason to lie to her, though. He wasn't Brian. She moved another branch, and bingo. A small dark figure stood in the midst of the bushes. It shifted its weight from one foot to the other, the universal signal for chicken guilt.

"Mitzi, come out here right now." Nic's hens responded only to treats in her hands, but a sharp command was worth a try.

The figure shifted again.

This wasn't going to be easy. Nic got on all fours and began crawling into the hedge.

"Flush her toward me." The Viking's voice came from behind Nic and down a ways. From there, he'd have a perfect view of Nic's ass hanging out of the bushes.

Sweet salami on a cracker. She had bad luck.

"I got this." Nic had been aiming for a breezy and confident tone, but she'd hit "gritted out between her teeth" instead.

"It's raining." He didn't sound happy about it. All this just seemed to annoy him, which raised the question about why he'd bothered to knock on her door at all. Was it really a random act of kindness if you were growly about it?

Except it had really started to come down. It wasn't cold—thank you, southern June weather—but Nic's dress suddenly seemed hopelessly thin and increasingly damp. She might need some help.

*Swallow your pride and then ignore him forever.* That was what Granny would say if she were here, anyhow, and Nic could at least pretend to follow her wisdom.

"Okay. I'll try to shoo her out. If you sort of . . . loom over her, she'll probably squat down, and you can grab her."

Nic edged into the bushes. As her eyes adjusted, she could see Mitzi clearly. The hen flicked her head from side to side, likely trying to decide which way to run.

"Go out toward the large man. Better yet, you could let *me* grab you." Nic wasn't certain whether she could get them both out even if she could get a hand on Mitzi, but it would do wonders for her ego. Maybe then she'd ask for the Viking's name, see whether she could get him to smile, though that might crack his stern face in half.

"You want to get out, don't you?" Nic tried to make her voice soft and nonthreatening as she inched forward. "We're going to help you. We'll get you back to the coop, and you'll feel so much better with your flock and some dinner."

Nic lifted up one hand and slowly extended it toward Mitzi's foot. "I'll give you a big handful of—ack!"

Mitzi made a distress call as she rushed *toward* Nic, and then feinted and dashed out of a small gap in the branches. Outside the bush, there was a rustle of wings, a few choice curses, and then a thud.

Nic backed out of the holly as quickly as possible and found an irate Viking on his butt in the grass without a feather in sight.

"She eluded you?" Nic scrubbed at a scratch she'd gotten down one arm.

"Yup. I slipped and—" He gestured to finish the thought, and he was such a picture of grumpy disappointment that Nic wanted to giggle.

She didn't want to be rude, though. For all that he was aggravated, he was helping her. "I'm sorry. Just so sorry. I appreciate you telling me she was out, but you really can go. I won't be offended." Actually, Nic would prefer it.

"Nah," he replied dryly, "I'm curious how it'll end. What's her name?"

He hadn't asked for Nic's name, but she tried not to let that bother her. "Mitzi."

"Houdini would've been better."

Probably when he wasn't wet and being bested by a lawn dinosaur, the Viking was charming. But it was the charming ones who hurt you the most.

"Believe it or not, she's never escaped before. The move upset her. Do we have any leads?"

"There, I think." He pointed toward the landscaping in front of the house, a whimsical mix of flowering bushes. They looked impossibly deep and as if a chicken might find shelter there indefinitely.

Nic really hadn't spent that much time, make that any time, in front of her new house. She'd bought it almost overnight after browsing on Zillow. Ninety-some years ago, Granny had been born in Yagerstown. It hadn't mattered that she'd moved away at fifteen and Nic had never set foot there in her life. It had seemed like Brigadoon, hidden and waiting for her and disconnected from the rest of the world. *Yagerstown, I should move to Yagerstown.*

When an adorable bungalow with a massive porch and yard and a nice kitchen had appeared, it had been the real estate answer to her prayers.

Now, the dream had collapsed, a Jenga tower five minutes into the game after all the easy moves had been taken. Because of a tangential connection to the town and a porch, Nic had actually bought a house over the phone.

She was definitely suffering from hubris.

"Mitzi, you better not be eating that hydrangea, or so help me." Obviously Mitzi wasn't taking Nic's advice, but some lines were worth defending.

The Viking nodded. "It's toxic."

He must have pets of some kind to know that. He seemed like a dog person. He'd have something massive and manly, maybe a Danish wolfhound.

So she shouldn't get a crush on him. She shouldn't get a crush on anyone. But she could ask. It would be neighborly. It wasn't as if she had many friends these days, seeing as her best friend wasn't speaking to her. Who didn't want to be at least friendly with their neighbors? "Do you have a dog, or—"

"You take that side," he said, ignoring Nic's question. "I'll look over here."

Okay, then.

A few moments later, Nic called, "She's here."

Mitzi stood behind an azalea with one foot stretched out behind her, the same posture as a ballet dancer about to launch herself across the stage or the Road Runner about to smoke Coyote for the hundredth time.

"I'll flush."

"Right. It's a plan." In some other time, she would have offered a halfhearted cheer. That was the sort of thing Brian was always trying to get her to do and always putting on his or her YouTube channel when she complied. The reflex almost reemerged now, but then she remembered she didn't have to do that shit anymore. She could be herself without any need to perform. No one was filming this. It wouldn't be on the internet later.

The Viking crouched down, disappearing from sight.

A beat passed.

Then the hen exploded from the bush, a storm of clucking and flapping wings. Mitzi was incensed. For a second, her feet touched down on the banister, but then she was off again, across the yard in the other direction.

Chickens couldn't so much fly as they could leap and use their wings to extend their distance. They were basically the best long jumpers of all time. While Mitzi was drenched, her feathers deflated, she still crossed a good twenty feet of the yard before Nic had made it three strides.

"You saucy minx," Nic shouted as her flip-flops lost purchase on the wet grass, and she had to windmill her arms to stay standing.

Mitzi had come to rest on the low-slung branch of a small tree.

"You sure she's never done this?" Nic's Viking neighbor was out of breath, his chest working like a bellows and straining against his damp T-shirt. It wasn't checking him out to note that that was objectively a lot of muscles. Was he a jogger? Or maybe he carried Thor's hammer around or something?

*No. Damn. Men.* She resolutely trained her attention on the hen. "Not her, but the others. Somewhere, I have a hook I use to catch them"—though Nic had only ever used it to snatch one out of the flock for a nail trim—"but everything's still boxed up. I could get some treats, but honestly, she's so worked up, she's not going to eat out of our hands right now. We could leave her for a bit, hope she finds her way back to the coop, but—"

"That's not safe."

"Nope."

"Excuse me, but—this blows."

Nic had to laugh. "I've been using way stronger curses, at least in my head, for the last five minutes." She'd become pretty good at not uttering profanity out loud; Chick Nic had to keep it clean for the kids, or she'd lose some portion of her audience.

"I didn't want to presume."

"Presume away." Oh, she wanted that back. It was far more of a come-on than she'd intended.

But it was too late. He gave her a long look . . . and then his eyes glided down her body, as if her sopping curves were the Slip 'N Slide they no doubt resembled.

If his scowl were anything to go by, he didn't seem to approve. Because she'd sworn off men, this shouldn't bother her. She certainly didn't want her neighbor to leer at her, but surely there was a happy medium between skeevy and disdainful. Why did she seem to bother him so much? And why was he helping her if he couldn't stand the sight of her?

"Hey, I didn't, I mean—"

He turned from her with a grunt. "Try again?"

Because she just wanted to get this over with, Nic echoed, "Try again."

Their third attempt resulted in Mitzi dashing wildly across the yard, back into the holly. When they managed to get her out of there again, she flew over the picket fence into Nic's backyard. But rather than heading for the safety of the chicken run—and her flock mates who were watching with concern from the other side of the wire fence—she flew over the back privacy fence and into a small easement between Nic's yard and that of the neighbor behind her.

"I'm beginning to think we're not good at this," Nic deadpanned as they regarded the space: it was about two feet wide and overgrown with soggy plants. It was probably filled with snakes. Wet, tropical snakes. Pythons. "I guess I'd better go after her."

The Viking made a rough noise. He'd become less and less vocal as the ordeal had dragged on, and he hadn't exactly been chatty to begin with. The idea of him crashing down the easement was impossible. His shoulders alone were twice that size.

"I'll try to herd her toward you." That was all the strategy Nic had. Mitzi might have a brain the size of a ripe green pea, but she was canny and bound and determined not to be caught. "If worse comes to worse, I guess I'll try to keep her going. You could meet us on the other side, on—what's that street called? Mason?"

Her neighbor gave a brusque nod. "Can't wait to see how the chicken will defeat us."

Nic began inching down the alley sideways. "Please let there not be snakes." There weren't enough . . . stones. Or sunlight. Snakes liked stones and sunlight, right?

Once Nic had made it about twenty feet, Mitzi materialized under a large fern frond. She made a bobbing twirl that carried the air of *nanny nanny boo boo*. But all the bravado was hollow because Mitzi's feathers were sodden. Nic only had to get on the other side of her and drive her toward the Viking.

"You're a damn nuisance."

Peck, peck, peck.

"You can make it up to me, though. Let me get past you."

Peck, peck, peck.

"Okay, do we all understand our roles here? Peck if you do."

Peck, peck, peck.

"Let's go, then."

Nic made to grab the chicken's feet, but Mitzi dodged. Then Nic made the best squall she could. Mitzi's eyes widened at the sound, and she tossed her head to one side and then the other and began to run.

"No! No! Up!" Fast as she could, Nic lunged forward and down. One of her hands brushed a claw, which drove the hen up. The ground was slick, and Nic powered . . . straight under her. For a long second, Nic slid on the wet ferns and grass and weeds, but she finally managed to grab the fence on either side—that was going to give her splinters—to stop herself before pivoting and starting toward the hen and the Viking.

Having completed the biggest, or at least the highest, flight of her life, Mitzi was completely disoriented. She was making the raptor call she uttered when you opened the egg box and she was laying. All rage and confusion and ancestral swagger.

Mitzi leaped again, smacked into Nic's fence, and landed on the ground. Without pausing to recover, she started down the alley in earnest toward the wet waiting neighbor.

"It's working," Nic bellowed. "We're—"

But before she could get the rest of the sentence out, the Viking came crashing into the alley.

Mitzi squealed, and then she launched herself straight into his chest.

Which was when something extraordinary happened.

He caught her.

Those enormous hands of his wrapped tightly, securely, perfectly around the hen. Mitzi let go of a huge breath and sagged as if to say, *Thank goodness. I'm so relieved. I was wondering how long it was going to take for you to get me.*

Nic pushed her stringy hair out of her face. "Holy crap, you did it. You did it!" Now she actually felt like doing some cheering. "I thought we were going to have to put her on the FBI's most-wanted list or something."

"Let's get her caged."

They edged out of the easement—he honestly didn't fit into the space at all—and then into Nic's backyard. When she opened the gate to the chicken yard, he released Mitzi before snapping the door closed with almost comic haste. Nic snorted, though obviously neither of them wanted to risk a repeat performance. The flock immediately surrounded Mitzi, clucking loudly, no doubt asking for every detail of her walkabout.

"I can't see how she got out," Nic said. The run was fully enclosed, there was even chicken wire on the ground, and there weren't any gaps or tears in the fencing. Nic had sent a detailed plan to the contractor she'd hired, and he'd done a good job.

The Viking shrugged. His expression was shuttered, his hair plastered to his head, his shoulders sagging, and his shirt almost black. Well, at least she knew Brian hadn't broken her totally. She could still notice an attractive man and feel as if someday she'd like to tangle with one of those again.

But she merely said, "I really appreciate you helping me. Especially since . . . just thank you."

The polite thing would have been for him to respond *you're welcome.* Or even *no problem.* Hell, she would have taken a shrug.

Except Vikings weren't people pleasers. After a few seconds that could best be described as aggrieved scowling, he took his fine wet butt across her backyard to the gate and away from her.

"Good riddance," she whispered after him. Nic had had quite enough arrogant men for a lifetime. From now on, she was going to stick to chickens.

# CHAPTER 2

Will Lund, doctor of veterinary medicine, was having a bad day. No, scratch that. He was having a bad half decade.

The bloodhound General Zod, reclining on the exam table, looked as forlorn as Will felt. The bags under his eyes were as droopy as his ears. Even his tail hung listless and limp.

"Mrs. Benjamin, I mean, Leonie," Will asked, "have you been feeding him pork chops again?"

"No, Will! I haven't." Leonie Benjamin, Will's former preschool teacher and Zod's owner, shook her head earnestly, her brown eyes a picture of innocence—and likely deceit. "We talked about that."

He'd told her a dozen times to stop feeding Zod human food, but he'd bet the last dollar in his pocket, and he was almost down to it, that she hadn't listened. This was their third visit in as many months.

"I'm glad, because if you had, that might explain his intestinal distress."

From the depths of Zod's abdomen came a noise halfway between a rumble and a peep, as if a squeaky toy were caught in a bread machine.

Will raised his brows and looked down at Mrs. Benjamin. This was one of those rare occasions when he was grateful for every one of his six feet two inches.

She quailed under his gaze but didn't crack. "Nope."

Except there was the diarrhea to explain. From a certain perspective, Will *loved* poop. Poop told you about diet, about stress, about behavior. It could reveal illness, and it didn't lie, unlike the pet owners who were the most difficult part of Will's life. Sometimes poop didn't have all the answers, sometimes Will couldn't find the answers, but poop was a gift to vets everywhere.

Will waited. Waited until he began to think that his big trick was going to fail and that Zod's owner was going to keep what had happened to herself, and then Leonie looked away, down at the floor, and muttered something.

"What was that?" he prompted.

"Maybe Bob slipped up." Oh, throwing the spouse under the bus. That was a common one. "But whoever heard of a dog with a pork allergy, anyhow?"

There was Zod's problem, revealed. Probably a few scraps of pork chops had sent this one-hundred-pound lapdog into fits.

"It's more common than you might think." Will tried to make his voice gentle, though he knew he mostly sounded gruff. He didn't want to punish Leonie or make her feel guilty. He was relieved she'd told him the truth, even if it had taken some coaxing. Now he just had to help Zod.

"We'll start him on antihistamines, and there are supplements that might help. But the main thing is controlling his diet."

Mrs. Benjamin gave a big, defeated sigh, and it was music to Will's ears.

While Will might have, did have, complaints about his practice, his family, and the state of the world, he knew that his former teacher was a good pet owner. That was rarer than Will would have predicted back when he'd graduated from vet school seven years ago. Then, he'd been naive, assuming everyone was doing their best. Even more importantly, he'd had no sense of *why* someone might choose not to seek care. Not from not knowing they should or by accident, but more often because they thought it was silly to see a doctor for an animal, or, even more heartbreakingly, because of inability to pay.

Will knew that he and what he did were luxury goods in a world where people could afford few extravagances. The margins of his practice were already thin, already close to falling from the black into the red. He didn't blame everybody for buying their dog's heartworm medicine or cat's allergen-reducing food online, where it was cheaper, but he hated what it did to his balance sheet. He hated how much time he spent thinking about his balance sheet, not to mention that other b-word: bankruptcy.

As they were wrapping up, Mrs. Benjamin, who'd stopped being chastened a while ago, leaned against the counter and gave him a long assessing look. "Did your new neighbors move into the Davises' house?"

"Um, yes. And I think it's just the one."

At least, Nicole Jones wasn't married and didn't have kids as far as he knew, and he knew an astonishing amount about her.

It had been shocking to see a chicken strolling around the front yard of the house across the street from his, but that was nothing compared to when the new neighbor had opened the door and been Nicole Jones.

For the shortest second, he'd thought he'd been imagining things. As if maybe he'd conjured her doppelgänger by watching one too many of her TikTok and YouTube videos. Without the perfectly distressed plaid shirt and Daisy Dukes, artfully tousled hair, and shiny lipstick, he hadn't been certain whether it was Chick Nic or someone who bore an eerie resemblance to her.

As soon as she'd opened her mouth, however, he'd known it was the real Nicole Jones.

Gobsmacked. That was the only word for how he'd felt.

His, um, obsession had started during quarantine, when he'd been bored and stressed out of his mind. He'd run across her name on some list of trends and remembered that multiple patients had mentioned her. And then he hadn't been able to stop watching.

It wasn't that he liked chickens—quite the contrary. It was that Nicole Jones was magnetic.

She worked hard enough at it, he could tell, with the hair and the makeup and the fancy production values and the self-promotion. But she had the kind of charisma that couldn't be faked.

Hate-watching, was that what he'd been doing? Maybe.

Especially when she'd given reams of medical advice and never once mentioned vets. Most of what she'd said had been fine, but it had given him heartburn. At least until that ex-boyfriend of Nicole's had broken up with her, which had left Will feeling all kinds of ways, mostly sympathetic for her . . . and then concerned that he cared at all about what the obviously fake people on the internet were up to.

Now Nicole was his neighbor. She and her chickens and her sexy underwear.

He'd barely slept a wink last night because the sight of her in a sopping wet yellow sundress was branded on his cerebellum. The way the lace of her bra had peeked out here and there, basically winking at him. The way the fabric had been clinging to the swell of her stomach, outlining the dimple of her belly button, before adhering to the curves of her thighs. God, her thighs left his mouth dry. By the end of the chicken chase, her dress had gone translucent, and he'd been able to tell that her panties were navy.

Before yesterday, he wouldn't have said that dark blue was an erotic color. He would have been totally wrong. The vision wasn't ever going to fade. He'd tried not to look at her, but he'd failed, and what he'd seen was seared on his retinas, like a burn from a solar eclipse. He'd close his eyes last night, and there it would be. The shape of her body, and the *tick tick tick* of hunger it set off inside him.

All night, he'd tried to reason with himself. To remember that they'd both looked like half-drowned dogs, their hair sodden and their skin clammy . . . but that just reminded him that he'd wanted to tumble her into the grass and warm them both up. Soft kisses. Heated kisses. Kisses that made promises, and kisses that kept them.

He was being a goober. All the lusting had been on his part, and besides, she was a menace. A chicken-hawking menace.

"Single man?" Mrs. Benjamin asked, entirely too casually.

"Single woman."

"Interesting." She was smiling as if she knew what he was thinking, but, thankfully, she couldn't. "Did you meet 'er?"

"We waved hello." That stretched the truth further than Mrs. Benjamin had when he'd asked about Zod's diet.

"This town could use some more single women." The look she gave him needed no interpreting.

The thing about living in the town where you'd grown up, where you and your parents and your family had at least three decades' worth of history with everyone, was that a river of subtext ran under everything.

Mrs. Benjamin thought it was time for Will to get married. She was not alone. Everyone under forty who wasn't partnered, didn't own a house, didn't have kids faced the same pressure. The town would survive only if the young people would stay. And they'd stay only if they had thriving businesses or families or both. But what the older folks didn't get was that there wasn't a lot of choice involved. Will had tried to make a life here, he'd bought the house, he'd run the business, but he was sinking all the same.

"Only because you keep turning me down," Will told Mrs. Benjamin seriously.

"William Lund!" She slapped him on the arm and let out a whoop of laughter. "You're incorrigible."

He really wasn't. He was practical. He was serious. He was dependable. And now, or very soon, his practice would be belly up.

How surprised everyone in Yagerstown was going to be when it all went down. No one would expect it of him, not that financial ruin happened only to people who made bad choices. Shit, Will definitely knew that wasn't true now. But everyone in the county thought his practice was doing fine, and the shame, when it all came out, was going to be scalding.

Mortifying. He'd avoided all social events, quit being an assistant youth soccer coach, and hid in his house long after lockdown had ended, all because of the shame he knew was coming. He'd probably always been quiet and grumpy, but he was on the edge of hermit status here.

Well, he *did* need a new career.

If only the pain were going to be limited to him, because as he and Mrs. Benjamin finished their visit and headed up to the reception desk, there was Marsha, his administrative assistant, and Kim, his vet tech. They were his family, as important to him as his parents, his sister, and his brother. More supportive of him, when it came down to it, than most of the people with whom he shared DNA. When his practice ended, it wouldn't just pull him under; it would swamp their boats, too, and it would make it harder for everyone in town to get good veterinary care.

The shame of it made eye contact, let alone conversation, with anyone in Yagerstown hard. So he stayed quiet in his house, cut himself off before anyone could do it for him.

"Don't you think, Doc?" Marsha asked.

Will had to blink, hard, to bring himself back into focus. "Sorry, I was distracted."

"Probably by that new neighbor," Mrs. Benjamin muttered, and Marsha and Kim giggled.

*"No."* At least not right then. "She has chickens."

He said that as if it explained his objection, and the three women stood blinking at him because of course it didn't.

He didn't want to get anyone started on Chick Nic. Once word got out, everyone in town was going to become obsessed, and then, inevitably, they would watch her get dumped. It was impossible to watch just one of her TikToks; you'd end up watching them all, and that would lead to her terrible ex. No matter how much of a menace she was, Nicole hadn't deserved that.

Will's own coming shame was unavoidable. Hers might be avoidable.

"Chickens, the fluffy things? Lay eggs? Say *bok-bok*?" Marsha asked.

"Yes," Will gritted out.

"Well, what's wrong with that? You like animals, don't you?"

Did he like animals? Liking animals had practically ruined his life and would soon steamroll over theirs. Liking animals wasn't his problem.

"Chickens are trendy."

"Aren't dogs and cats? Or at least Bengal cats and cockapoos?"

That was true, though they didn't see many designer breeds in Yagerstown. It wasn't that flavor of place.

He could remind Marsha and Kim about the chickens they'd euthanized, the bad chicken ownership they'd seen, but he'd probably just sound bitter, which he kind of was.

"It's different." Will sounded grumpy and petulant and all the things he knew he was but didn't want to be. "Chickens are farm animals. Would you be thrilled if Dan got a cow?"

Dan was Marsha's neighbor. He hadn't gotten so much as a new car since George Bush had been president, but if he ever got a cow, he wouldn't take care of it, and it would be disastrous, which was Will's point.

"Not about a cow, no, but maybe some of those fainting goats. That would be something."

Will huffed out a laugh. Marsha had texted him a steady stream of goat videos, trying to keep his spirits up. He was going to miss her so much when this place folded.

"I don't dislike chickens. Just the people who make them look glamorous."

"I told you she must be pretty," Mrs. Benjamin said, and all the women dissolved into more giggles while Will slipped out to his private office to brood.

Nicole Jones might be pretty, but pretty solved none of his problems. Nothing and no one could.

# CHAPTER 3

Nic flew down Route 74, the back wheels of her Subaru 4x4 leaving the road when she hit bumps. "Please be open."

She turned off into an empty parking lot, and scree shot out from her tires, a spray of stone confetti. She'd set a new land-speed record for the poor hen on the passenger seat. Nic pulled her keys from the ignition, threw them into her purse, and softly, so very softly, gathered up Camilla.

"You'll be okay." That was the sort of meaningless dribble that easily spilled from Nic's mouth because she couldn't not say *something*. Running a YouTube channel had turned her into a constant monologue-er. She was basically the badly written friend character in a Hallmark movie who was there to provide the exposition, except that woman didn't have a seriously ill pet and Nic, sadly, did.

Yagerstown Veterinary Clinic, the words on the door read. Open 8 a.m. to 5 p.m. Monday, Tuesday, Wednesday, Thursday & Friday. They had some weekend hours, too, but Camilla didn't have that long.

But it was 4:51 p.m. on a Friday, and the door wouldn't budge. Nic rattled the handle again, careful not to disturb Camilla. What kind of jerk vet closed nine minutes early? Camilla needed those nine minutes.

Okay, Nic probably should've called before coming over, but she'd been so scared. A broken egg in a hen's body could be fatal. Nic hadn't even really believed what she'd seen—the obscene yellow of a yolk pooled in the egg box—so it had taken her far too long to realize what was going on and then to locate the closest vet.

Her past experiences with veterinarians and chickens hadn't been good. The only other time she'd taken a hen in, the vet had chided her about her overreaction and insisted everything was fine. Then the hen had died a few days later from what Nic now suspected was a tumor, probably caused by a virus. Nic's guilt had been crushing, and she'd decided then and there that she had to learn everything about chickens and to share it with as many people as possible.

But this, this was a situation when she needed the kind of help only a professional could provide, and the only professional in the county wasn't anywhere to be seen.

Nic cupped her hand against her face and squinted against the glass. The lights in the lobby were off. "Argg."

Against Nic's chest, Camilla shuddered with every exhale. When Nic switched the bundle to her other arm to try the door again, the hen quirked her head, trying to turn her face to the light. Her dark-gold eyes blinked, but they were duller than they should be. Even her comb was pale against the revolting mint green of the towel, a relic of the 1970s Nic had found when packing up Granny's house and had kept for sentimental reasons.

Camilla gave another minute rumble, something Nic felt more than heard. In her "Top Ten Chicken Noises (and What They Mean)" video (830,000 views and counting!), she had explained this precise noise. The hours Nic had spent awkwardly crouching in the coop to capture all those different squawks and cries, which had been followed by the hours Nic had spent editing—she hadn't been as good with tech then—had resulted in one of her more punchy, informative videos. She'd said this sound was a difficult one to parse. This purring could mean distress or deep contentment. It was obvious which this was.

Nic had been distracted with unpacking and juggling appointments, and she hadn't paid enough attention to her flock. This was her fault. More so than the messes with Rose and Brian, more even than Mitzi getting out the other day, Nic should have handled this differently. Should have handled it better. Camilla was paying the price for Nic's mistake.

For lack of anything better to do, Nic pressed the small black button by the door frame. A mechanical buzz sounded in the lobby.

"I'm sorry," she whispered to the hen, jamming the button a second time. "I'm sorry, I'm sorry, I'm sorry."

A light flickered on the hallway visible beyond the lobby, and an absolutely hulking mass came into the glow.

"Hello! Are? You? *Open?*"

The mass unlocked the first set of doors, entered the breezeway, and stopped being an undifferentiated colossus. It was a he, and he was the neighbor who, two days prior, had chased Mitzi with Nic in the rain.

Nic gasped. Stupidly. Loudly. If it had been Brian, if it had been Santa Claus, she would've been less surprised. The Viking worked at the vet's?

"You." He sounded even more unhappy than he had the other day.

"Me." She tried to dispel the shock with a toss of her head. The power of her hair didn't extend that far, though. She wasn't She-Ra. "I need some help." Surely it was obvious she wasn't selling Tupperware.

"Another chicken problem?"

Nic bristled. She'd been chastising herself—she knew she was responsible—but she majorly disliked him pointing it out.

"Yes." She boosted up the bundle, tipping it so that he could see inside. "She's egg bound. Or maybe the egg's already broken, I'm not sure." Camilla could be bleeding internally, she could have an infection . . . and Nic needed to stop jumping ahead to the worst-case scenario.

"Since when?"

Nic didn't want to get into the full history before crossing the threshold of the practice, especially if he wasn't going to treat her bird. "Awhile. Are you still open?"

While she could put on an imperious tone, Nic didn't have a lot of cards. What was she going to do if he said no? There wasn't an emergency vet for fifty miles. Camilla might not have fifty miles.

"Yeah," he finally said. "We are."

He unlocked the front door, and Nic followed him inside. She was suddenly, sharply aware that no lights were on save for in the hallway and no one else was around. She and this massive guy were probably alone. Unlike two days prior, they weren't out in public now, with whatever measure of safety that might offer. Her well-honed alarm bells weren't going off, but they likely should be.

"So are you the vet? Or is, um, the vet here?" she asked. "Because she might have internal injuries, and—"

"What happened?" As it had the other day, his voice had absolutely no softness, which would make him perfect for raiding coastal villages and whatnot.

It was comforting that he led with rudeness. The people who meant you harm, who did the most harm, were often charming. They lured you in with sweetness, and then they pounced. This guy had no sweetness, hence he wasn't a threat . . . she hoped.

"I checked the egg box around lunchtime, and I saw some yolk—"

"You knew this might be a problem hours ago?"

Shame crackled through Nic, and even though she wanted to do nothing more than look away, she forced herself to face his look of derision. She'd earned it.

"I know. But I have eight hens, and some of them are older. It's not unusual to find the occasional shell-less egg." Nic should've been more vigilant, though. She should've done more to check it out. "At first, I didn't know it was serious, so I—"

He cut Nic off. "How old is she?"

"Three."

"What's she been doing since you found the discharge?"

"She's been in the box pretty much all day. Even before I found the yolk. But as you know, I just moved, and the girls are . . . spooked. They've all been acting abnormally. Sniping at one another, escaping. I thought this was that."

The Viking frowned. He moved around the reception desk, wiggled the computer mouse, muttered something that might be a curse, and then pressed the power button on the computer. Presumably the receptionist had shut it down whenever the office had, prematurely, closed.

That was why they should stay open until five.

"Did you take her temperature?" he asked.

"No, but she feels warm to me. And she's definitely lethargic."

That had been the scariest part. Nic had seen injured chickens, many injured chickens. They were normally beating like hell around the yard and raising a ruckus. Camilla's quiet and stillness were part of what made this scary. Ginger, Nic's bird who'd died of the tumor, had also been lethargic at the end.

"I tried to get her to leave the box to eat and get some water, and when I picked her up, that's when I realized the yolk was draining out of *her*. That was about ten minutes ago. I bundled her up and jumped in the car."

"We don't normally see birds," he said.

"Like, at all? Have you had that checked out? Considered prescription eyewear?" There was the sarcasm Brian had found so very objectionable and that Nic had become adept at keeping inside.

The Viking's bronze eyes flicked up from the computer. He didn't seem hurt but maybe a bit taken aback. "No, we *see* them, we just don't—"

"I understood what you meant. I've run into that before."

Avian and poultry veterinarians were surprisingly rare. Most vets only saw mammals and knew little to nothing about other species. A willingness to take an appointment and issue a bill wasn't expertise. That was why Nic did lots of videos on basic medicine for chickens.

"Let's cut to the chase," Nic said. "Have you treated a broken egg in the cloaca before?"

He blinked as if the question offended him. *"Yes."* It was a stew of indignation and defensiveness. "I—we can help your hen."

"Well, good."

The truth was Nic was having a terrible day. Ever since her breakup with Brian, she'd been focused on the move. On the logistics of buying the house, of packing, of trying to keep her business together. She'd kept telling herself that as awful and stressful as the process was, it would be worth it. That she'd get to Yagerstown and things would just be better. But nothing was better. Instead her to-do list kept swelling and the stresses never relented and she was almost smothered, without any end in sight.

The only thing stopping her from wailing right now was the Viking's demeanor. Something about his surly attitude made her feel like he wasn't the kind of person to lie. He wasn't trying to impress Nic. He didn't have the slightest clue who she was. But he seemed assured enough that against reason, Nic felt the panicky tightness in her chest relax.

He was going to do whatever he could to try and help Camilla, which meant the day would be better. Because as Nic had found absolutely over the last few years, every day with chickens was a good day. A better day. A day improved by the tiny sauropods who lived in your backyard, gave you eggs, and mostly just made soft noises of contentment.

She needed that. She needed to feel like she was making that more possible not only for herself but for other people in the Chickens for All community. That postage stamp of calm was Nic's, and she wasn't giving it up.

Nic answered a few more questions and then trailed the Viking down the hallway.

The exam room he ushered her into was the same as every other she'd ever been in: a stainless steel exam table half-ringed by the sterling-silver-blue cabinets that seemed standard issue for vets. A hard plastic chair stood in one corner, the perfect chair to hurt your ass while you watched a beloved friend die on the table. A sink so small no one could wash more than a single hand at a time over it. A bright portrait of a tabby cat that looked like it had been subjected to a psychedelic Insta filter.

Nic didn't set the bundle down as her neighbor washed his hands. Something about Camilla's not-purr was comforting. As long as she kept it up, Nic knew she was still alive.

"Can you set her down?" He had gathered his supplies, and for the first time, he didn't sound so harsh.

Nic didn't blame him for his animosity. He'd probably been locking up. He was her age, early thirties, and not wearing a wedding ring. A good-looking, possibly single man in a small town? He was a precious commodity and likely had plans for tonight—and she and her injured chicken had ruined them. It was a bad situation all around, and Nic had been a little bitchy.

She pulled the bundle—gods, it was so light—against her chest and once more whispered to Camilla, "I'm sorry this happened to you."

*Chickens are pets, but they're also farm animals*: She'd said it more times than she could count. On videos, in blog posts, in conference presentations and interviews. But she had no idea now what her point had been. Don't get emotionally involved? As if farmers weren't emotionally involved with their stock. As if it wasn't emotional to eat an animal's eggs. The very least humans owed chickens was emotion.

Nic lowered the towel and chicken to the countertop and finally, regretfully, stepped back.

Her arms suddenly felt empty and cold. She wrapped them around herself, trying to hold in what little heat she had.

Her Viking neighbor had put on gloves and prepared a basin of warm water, and he began gently cleaning out Camilla's vent.

For several minutes, neither he nor Nic spoke. There wasn't even a ticking clock to break the silence. It was the only time in weeks Nic had been stationary and quiet while awake. She felt a compulsion to pack something, unpack something, or scrub a surface. But instead, she watched this man, big and capable, try to heal her chicken.

"I don't think she has any major lacerations," he finally said. "But we'll start her on some antibiotics to be sure." His gaze flicked up and over Nic. "I've seen worse."

That was probably as comforting as berserkers got: *don't worry, there's more gore elsewhere.* Nic hoped that he was better at romantic gestures with whatever date she'd made him late for, not that it was any of her business. Nothing to do with romance was her business at present, and she liked it like that.

"I haven't seen a hen with an egg that's broken internally before," Nic admitted. "At least not, like, in person, but I've definitely seen more blood." Hens could certainly be jerks. When one of the girls got broody, there could be as much drama in the coop as on Sorority Row during rush week. All that pecking order stuff wasn't just talk, and Nic had cleaned some cuts in her time. "I don't usually bring them in."

"Why didn't you . . ." He left the rest unsaid, but she got the message.

If you had birds, you had to be prepared to treat birds. They weren't puppies. But this day, this month, this year, Nic couldn't.

"I could have cleaned her vent." The words were defensive, but she probably should've done that and then waited to see whether medical intervention beyond that was necessary. Almost any other time, Nic would have. That's what Brian would've pressed her to do. He would've filmed it, insisting it would be her highest-viewed video ever, and he probably would've been right.

The whole point, though, was not to handle things like that anymore. Not to turn every moment of her life into content.

"If she'd needed stitches, I wouldn't have been able to help her," Nic tried to explain. "And antibiotics—I don't have those. I figured a pro ought to see it." And maybe for once, just for once, Nic was admitting she didn't have to do everything. Couldn't he see that she was growing here?

"Got it."

Evidently not.

They went back to silence. His movements were precise. Expert. That strange mix of gentle and firm you needed to doctor an animal. She wouldn't have thought he had it in him, this giant, stern man, but even avenging Vikings had to have a soft side, she guessed. He had clearly practiced, probably on the cats and dogs and hamsters that likely came through here all the time, but his skills transferred to Camilla.

The Viking was far, far better than the last vet she'd taken a bird to because, she realized, he probably was the vet. In contrast, it had been obvious from the start that the last vet Nic had seen had no idea what he was doing. While everything she'd learned about neoplasm since Ginger's death had convinced Nic that she couldn't have saved her hen, that vet's arrogance had really burned afterward.

It was like Brian, in miniature. He'd made Nic doubt her instincts, mocked her about them, but she'd been right. It had taken Nic months to recover her confidence, to trust herself. It wasn't any wonder she'd avoided vets until today.

For her part, Camilla accepted the care with resigned equanimity. She didn't struggle, didn't cry out. Her shiny penny eyes blinked, now almost too rapidly, and her wings hung akimbo from her body. Under her feathers, she was small and fragile, and Nic shivered again at how badly wrong all this could have gone. Could still go.

When he had finished and was washing his hands again, he said over his shoulder, "Chickens have high metabolic temperatures, so there's not a huge risk of infection—"

"We really don't have to do this. I know chickens."

He turned and propped himself against the cabinet. He really was enormous. Nothing about this tiny clinical room was sized for him. Now that he'd patched up Camilla, whatever teaspoon of softness he'd poured out had evaporated again. Something about her or the situation infuriated him, and he wasn't pretending it didn't.

"Really?" he demanded. "You *know* chickens?"

"Yes." If there was anything Nic was confident about, it was that. Maybe it would help if he knew she was an ally, or at least an animal lover. They were on the same side, after all. "I'm Chick Nic."

His expression didn't change, so she added weakly, "From . . . YouTube." And TikTok, and Instagram, and her eponymous blog. She was kinda a big deal.

But then the Viking surprised her. He gave a curt nod and said, "I know."

"You . . . know?"

Normally, the rare people who recognized her couldn't wait to tell her so. They often led with it, as if they couldn't keep that knowledge to themselves for a single second longer. *I know you,* they'd exclaim, when of course they didn't. Not in the ways that mattered.

Why hadn't her neighbor said something sooner? Like maybe when they were running around her yard in the rain? Or, failing that, in the last half hour? Why had he acted like she was imposing on him?

The Viking's lips twisted into a mocking grin. "Pleased to meet you, Chick Nic. I'm Dr. Lund. This is my practice."

There was a faint buzzing in Nic's ears.

Hubris: it'll get you every time.

# CHAPTER 4

For the first time in at least two days, Will was enjoying himself. It turned out that Chick Nic had a setting other than gregarious girl next door. He'd stunned her speechless. Across the exam table, her smile had withered to a narrow grimace, and her hands had clenched the blood-and yolk-smeared towel so hard, her knuckles were pale slashes on her skin. He ought to remind her not to hurt the hen inside—but that would probably make the back of Nicole's pretty head blow clean off.

"Nice to meet you," she gritted out.

"Hmm." Even the patients who liked Will often said he was difficult. He didn't think it was difficult to expect people to take care of their own pets, even when those pets were chickens.

Right after they'd bought up all the toilet paper in a three-state radius, binged *Tiger King*, and tried (and tossed) sourdough starter, seemingly everyone in Yagerstown had gone down to Helen's feedstore and bought a box of baby chicks. At least some of the blame for those bad, bad decisions—the chicken-related ones, anyhow—belonged at the scuffed kicks of Nicole Jones.

He'd already made sure Nicole wasn't going to be bringing her birds to him, and as she was the only person in town who didn't have thirty-five years' worth of opinions about him, he didn't keep his thoughts to himself. He let her have them.

"You make those videos about how everyone should have backyard chickens."

"Not everyone."

"But everyone got on board."

"That's an exaggeration."

"Okay, not literally everyone got birds, I guess, but many, many people did. It's called hyperbole, sweetheart. But that's not my gripe. The veterinary advice you give on your channel, that comes from . . . ?"

If looks could incinerate, Will would be a pile of smoldering ashes right about now. Nicole certainly could glare; he'd give her that. Those brown eyes of hers were simmering like some witch's brew, and in some other context, with some other woman, he'd be trying to decide whether it was professional to ask out a patient's owner.

Well, he'd just made that impossible too.

"I've been around chickens my entire life," she said.

"I know how to drive. That doesn't make me a mechanic."

"Caring for a flock and rebuilding an engine aren't quite the same. The whole animal-versus-machine thing." Her eyes were nearly boiling as she tipped her head to the side. "What precisely is your problem with me? You seemed annoyed two days ago, but it's more than that now."

Will didn't unload on people very often. Even when he wasn't honing his hermit-ing skills, there wasn't much point. Most people couldn't change their behavior, because either they didn't want to or they didn't know how. Either way, yelling only made them recalcitrant. Yelling at patients—well, at patients' owners—was even more pointless. It drove them away, and it didn't help their animals.

It was also mean, and he liked to think of himself as a kind person. He'd rather present facts, gently cajole, and otherwise soft-pedal. It took less breath, and it worked better too.

He was about to make an exception. "In this very room a few months ago, I euthanized a chick who was dying due to a pasted vent."

Nicole's expression didn't soften. "That's very sad, but it isn't my fault. It wasn't my chick. And I've done a half-dozen videos on preventing and treating pasty butt—"

"A few days later," he went on, not caring how she might defend herself, "I did another one. And then another. I've had people bring in adolescent roosters they've found by the road, apparently released because people in town can't have roosters but they also don't care enough to address it when they end up with one. I've seen more chickens run over in the road than I can count, escaped from their pens or deserted by their owners. The SPCA is inundated as people get bored or tired of them." He would know. He did regular shifts there. "Your own chicken escaped two days ago."

She winced. "That's not a normal occurrence. I just moved, and—"

"Everyone whose pet escapes insists it's never happened before. And honestly? That's the tip of the iceberg. You give medical advice all the time."

"I've never claimed to be a professional—"

"But your viewers assume you know what you're talking about."

"I do!"

He scoffed. "You're an amateur. There's a chicken problem out there, a significant one, and some of it is your doing."

Nicole rolled her eyes—rolled her eyes as if his concerns were trivial. "You've never euthanized a dog? No one ever abandons or surrenders a cat?"

"Of course they do, and of course I hate that. But it isn't the same. No one made those things *trendy* in the last few years." He couldn't say the word without sneering at its bitter taste. "And now, it seems like you don't know much at all about taking care of them. You didn't bring her"—he jammed a thumb at the hen—"in as soon as you realized something was wrong. You're basically Chicken Barbie."

His pulse was going in his wrists like an overeager clock. This was why he normally tried to keep his emotions in check. Anything more than mild exasperation tended to rebound and make him feel out of control. He ought to pull this back and apologize, somehow.

Across from him, Nicole sucked on her teeth, and then her mouth widened into a faux sweet grin. "You didn't mention you were a fan."

"A *fan*? What exactly of what I just said made you think I'm a fan?"

"You're quoting Brian. The Chicken Barbie dig—that's him. Word for word. Meaning that you were following every last detail of *that* blowup. So yeah, I think that makes you a fan. Even if you're hate-watching, I still get paid."

Though her smile didn't warm her eyes and her arrogant shrug seemed feigned, he didn't care. This was exactly what he expected her to be: pure mercenary.

Honestly, her ex seemed to be even more of a phony baloney than her, and Will would admit, the vehemence with which the other man had attacked Nicole didn't sit well with Will. If Nicole was really the grasping fake that her ex said she was, why had he spent years with her?

But whatever, that wasn't Will's problem. Never mind the apology. He shouldn't have yelled at her, but he hadn't been wrong, and he wasn't going to take it back.

"I wouldn't say I followed every twist of . . . that, no, but after my patients kept mentioning you, I watched some of your videos."

He'd watched them all. She was—compelling. But there was absolutely no way he'd ever admit that to her. A team of draft horses couldn't drag it out of him.

"Well, I'll have some new content up very soon. I'll probably even talk about this. When a situation is beyond DIY and when going to the vet is a good idea. Why I should've made a different call, or at least an earlier one, than I did today."

That made . . . a certain amount of sense. In general, Will would rather his patients' owners be more cautious than less so, but it didn't change his main point. "You'd be better off telling people not to get into hobbies they aren't committed to when they involve animals' lives. Tell them to take up guitar instead."

"If I were to warn them off chickens for that reason, I'd need to include dogs!"

"That would be fine!"

Their angry words pinged around the room like hail.

Nicole set down the little bundle in which her chicken was wrapped and wiped her hands on her jeans. "Most of my viewers don't even own chickens."

"So they tune in for . . . ?"

"I guess some people find me charming."

With her long brown hair and her propensity to dress like a farm-girl pinup, they probably found her hot, but he wasn't going to say that any more than he was going to admit that he subscribed to her channel.

"You're good on camera," he allowed. "And your videos are well produced. But they make it look too easy. Make it seem like part of a—a lifestyle. It's not a game."

"It's not a game to me either," she said, her voice a low, warning growl. "But it's well after five, so I should probably let you get going, *Dr. Lund.*"

Will glanced at his watch. Heck, he was good and late for his family dinner.

In the lobby, he gave Nicole the oral antibiotics and antihistamines for her hen. He took extra time explaining how to administer them until she was nearly boiling. Then she paid, signing the charge slip with more force than was necessary. She darn near ripped through the thing with the ballpoint pen.

"I want to see the hen again on Monday," he said. "In the meantime, keep her isolated from your flock, watch for lethargy, and keep an eye on her food and water intake. Call if you have any concerns, and don't wait this time."

Nicole only gave him another nuclear-force evil glare before sashaying out.

One thing that hadn't been clear on YouTube or TikTok: Nicole Jones had a fantastic ass. He'd noticed it in the rain, and it was still true now. But that didn't change his main point: being pretty had permitted her to make something that wasn't for many people into a brand, except this wasn't like buying a ukulele or getting into canning. It wasn't a component of some—what had his sister called it?—cottagecore look. Animals' lives were at stake.

He locked the double doors after her and said "That went well" to no one before cleaning up and leaving like he'd meant to do forty-five minutes earlier. He'd let Marsha and Kim go early because he was being kind . . . but also because he was trying to save on payroll, and he felt guilty about it.

If he slammed some cabinet doors harder than was necessary and muttered under his breath, it wasn't because of his thin balance sheet. It was because of everything Nicole's visit had roused in him. The backyard-chicken movement was a debacle, and she was its figurehead. He wasn't saying no one should have chickens, only that many of the people getting into chicken keeping had no idea precisely what was involved and that was dangerous. To the chickens, to their neighbors, and to him. He didn't like mopping up the messes of others, especially not when it was done for a silly aesthetic. Most people would be better off buying their eggs at the grocery store like the twenty-first-century human beings they were.

Finally the office was back in order, and Will drove to his mother's house.

"Where the heck have you been?" Luke, his brother, greeted him at the door. He'd lost his nearly ever-present suit jacket and tie, but he was still wearing a crisp oxford shirt and dress trousers. He'd dressed that way since college, though the suits had grown more quality over time. Will had no idea how much money a lawyer in a midsize city made, but it was apparently enough to bypass Men's Wearhouse.

It didn't even bother Will anymore; it mostly seemed like it would be hot. It was June, for crying out loud. The man could put on a T-shirt.

"Last minute walk-in," Will explained.

"Oh?" Except from how Luke said it, it was clear that he didn't really care.

Luke had ditched Yagerstown the second he'd graduated from high school, first for college, then law school, before joining a firm in Richmond. Every month, he brought his wife and kids to see the family, but the visits had the air of a zoo or museum trip. *Here are the peasants, see how they live. Aren't they quaint?*

So Will didn't bother to explain, and besides, he was still seething. Nicole's arrival was going to be obnoxious. People shared every single bit of animal news with him already. *Did you know that Carolyn Smithfield adopted a greyhound?* someone might shout at him over the bananas at the grocery store. Yes, he would have.

No doubt he'd soon be asked whether he'd heard that the most adorable fake chicken expert in the country had relocated here. And he'd have to keep to himself that he'd bitten her head off. Maybe it was good he was mostly not speaking to anyone.

Compared to his office, which was quiet and hard, the house where he'd grown up overflowed with the kinds of softness that would never fly around pets: rugs and wall hangings and cushy couches and throw pillows. And when Will trailed Luke inside, it was just as bursting with noise.

"Uncl' Will! Uncl' Will!" That would be Noah, his nephew. He stood before Will with his arms raised into the air, the wordless toddler supplication to be picked up.

Will obliged and set his nephew on his hip. "Yes, kid?"

"See any doggies?"

"Three." And they had, luckily, all been in decent health. Not so much the chicken.

While he'd been incredibly pissed at Nicole, he'd felt nothing but sympathy for the hen. It truly had been an emergency, and if Nicole hadn't styled herself as some kind of expert, he would have—

"You're kinda late," his sister, Ella, said, offering him a beer, which she'd helpfully already opened.

Unlike Luke, Ella had stayed in Yagerstown, and she was the only person in the family with whom he'd commiserated about Luke's pretentions. They tended to sit across from one another at these dinners so they could exchange covert looks of scorn. He'd also coached her daughter's soccer team for two years, and, at least before COVID, he'd hung out with her voluntarily, which wasn't something he would do with most of the people in his family.

He took a swig from the bottle she'd handed him. "Don't start."

He'd already been in a mood even before Nicole had shown up. While quarantine had been a blow, his practice had already been on the rocks before anyone had known what the novel coronavirus was. It was hard out there for a vet trying to go it alone, especially when Will was struggling with massive student loans in a shriveling town where people didn't have a lot of disposable income. The practice's cash flow was slow at the best of times, and it seemed like everyone was increasingly seeking pet care out of town and buying supplies on the internet. One tech had quit, not wanting a public-facing job at that moment, and it had saved Will from having to let someone go.

He hadn't gone into veterinary medicine because of the money. Honestly, he'd been way too far along in the process before he'd ever even thought of being a vet as being a small business owner. At six years old, he'd declared that he was going to be a vet because his mother had been reading the James Herriot books aloud, and it had seemed as if there could never be anything better than a life spent taking care of animals. Sure, being an astronaut was cool, but they didn't go to the moon every day, while vets actually did medicine on animals all the time.

In the books, the money stuff had been almost comic. James Herriot had struggled at first, but it had all worked out in the end. Wasn't *that* a comforting fantasy.

Will took another deep pull from the beer.

"You wanna talk about it?" Ella asked.

*I told a woman her beloved cat had only a few weeks to live. I tried to balance my books and panicked. I spayed a puppy. I removed a shattered egg from a chicken's body and then yelled at her owner.*

There was no scenario in which Will was going to say that to Ella. There was no scenario in which he was going to say it to anyone. "How pissed is Mom?" he asked as a dodge.

"Only worried." His mother's voice came from behind him, and Will turned to give her the best hug he could manage with the kid in one arm and the beer in his other hand.

"Did I hear you say there was some kind of emergency?" she asked. "Dog, cat, ferret?"

She'd read the Herriot books to her kids because she loved animals. All of them. If she were ever made aware of the Chick Nic brand and if she could figure out how to work YouTube, she'd no doubt watch every single video immediately, finding them—what had Nicole said?—oh, right, *charming.*

His mother, who couldn't be bothered to say anything to his dad or brother about their snobbery because that would be unpleasant, would be immediately and persistently on Nicole's side. That was the problem with Nicole's pitch: it sounded good from the outside, especially when coupled with someone as fresh faced and, frankly, sexy as Nicole.

She might not be ready to confront her role in getting thousands of irresponsible people to buy chickens, but Nicole was culpable just the same.

"It's handled."

His mother regarded him again, frowning slightly, as if something was off but she couldn't put her finger on what. "You look . . . worn down."

She would normally never acknowledge something that disagreeable so he must look awful, which fit. He felt awful. His mother, however, liked for things to be comfortable, for people to be nice, and for everyone to get along. That was more important to her than anything else.

So all he said was, "Just tired." No one in his family knew the full extent of his financial worries, and he had no desire to enlighten them. It would only distress his mother and give Luke an opportunity to gloat, and Will didn't want to do either. He couldn't stand to do either. So he skirted the line between avoiding and lying to them. Everyone seemed happier that way.

"Come eat, then. We waited for you."

If someone had taken a picture of the dinner that followed, it might've looked like a Norman Rockwell: the long table, the corn on the cob, and the cute kids. But maybe those paintings were tense as all get-out too. Everyone trying to pick a topic of conversation that would be acceptable to the crowd when no such subject existed.

Will didn't care about whatever rich-person bullshit Luke did, his father couldn't hide his delight in his younger son's conspicuous consumption, and Will couldn't keep from rolling his eyes at them both. Yup, they were the all-American family.

"It comes down to zoysia versus fescue versus Saint Augustine." His father was holding court on the subject of grass because Luke and Kayleigh were about to buy sod. Not because they didn't have grass, mind you, but because they weren't happy with their current grass.

What was more expensive: a McMansion-size yard full of unnecessary sod or a new x-ray machine, as Will's was clearly on the fritz?

Will had no idea. His father had similarly never bought sod in his life, but he'd clearly studied up for this conversation, and Luke's eyes shone with the glow that could only come from thinking about something obscure, unnecessary, and bougie.

"What's on the green at Augusta National?" Luke asked. His goal for the project was for his backyard to resemble a golf course, and the man didn't even have time to play golf.

After ensuring that his mother was distracted by the green beans, Will gave Ella his first look of the evening. The "when did our brother become an asshole" look. It wasn't some secret-sibling-language thing as much as an exaggerated eye roll followed by some faux gagging. Who had time for subtlety?

Ella snorted into her iced tea.

"You 'kay?" Noah asked, all sincere concern for his aunt.

"She's fine," Will assured him. "I'll administer the Heimlich if necessary."

Noah screwed up his face as if he were scrutinizing every bit of information contained in his head but couldn't locate a match for the term. "What that?"

"It helps with choking." That wasn't too dark for a three-year-old, right?

"With puppies?" It all came back around to puppies, which was kinda depressing given that Luke and Kayleigh refused to buy a dog. A dog would no doubt get paw prints on their white couch and mess up the backyard golf course.

"Yup."

Luke shot Will a warning glare. His brother didn't want Will encouraging the kid's obsession with animals that drooled and shed and barked and dug holes.

If it wasn't a recipe for disaster and the complete opposite of everything he'd said to Nicole Jones today, Will would have already sent Noah a puppy anonymously. He'd settled for several stuffed animals and a toddler-size vet coat and every book about dogs he could find. It had only been 10 percent motivated by how mad it made Luke.

"Is everything okay?" Luke's words weren't harsh. He was even smoother and slicker than Nicole. Just like his vowels had become curiously clipped, all trace of the South gone. The angles and grit had been filed clean out of his voice. The words went down like glossy tablets, and you didn't even know you'd been reprimanded until they hit your stomach.

Will would love to know exactly when Luke had decided he was too good for this place, too good for his brother. And maybe also when Will had decided that Luke might be onto something. Because that was the real problem, wasn't it? Not just that Luke looked down his nose—across his nose, really; they were a tall family—at all of them. It was that Will trusted Luke's judgment better than his own. Deep down, Will suspected he might be more willing to settle than Luke. More willing to accept less.

It was a depressing thing to learn about himself, but the last few years had been one kick in the pants after another.

"Everything's fine," he said. "We were just talking about the canine Heimlich maneuver."

"There's no such thing."

"Yes, there is." Will had learned it during a practicum his first year in vet school. He'd let his brother shame him on many accounts, but not this particular one.

Luke gave him a warm, indulgent look. Not dead on, because Luke didn't meet Will's eyes any longer. He looked past him, to wherever it was that he was speeding. Some future beyond Yagerstown and the Lund family and Will himself. And in that place, Will wasn't worth arguing with because he was nothing but a rube.

"Boys," Mom said warningly. That doused the mood.

Luke reset his shoulders, said, "Sure," and turned back to Dad, who was, as always, pretending that his sons got along fine because that was what he always did. That was what was easier.

"Saint Augustine is out. I don't like the texture."

"Who could?"

Who could indeed.

# CHAPTER 5

"Doc! Doc!"

The shout came from halfway down the farmers' market. It was less a formal, established thing than a parking lot off Main Street that filled with white plastic tables and a motley assortment of produce two mornings a week in the summer. Despite his ongoing hermit training, Will made a point of going whenever he could. The farmers struggled even more than he did.

The person waving insistently at him was Sami Hak, a recent retiree with a seemingly endless collection of knockoff Rolexes and a pack of corgis. Only the grande dame, Mimsey, was with him today, but she was straining against the lead toward Will because she was the rare canine patient who loved the vet.

"Hey, Sami." Will stooped and gave Sami's dog, Mimsey, an appreciated rub under the chin. "How are things?"

"Her tear duct is blocked again."

"I'm sorry, girl." A trail of watery discharge tracked down Mimsey's face from one eye. She was still giving him a doggie smile and panting faintly. She didn't seem distressed in the least, but animals hid illness well. "Keep it clean. Do you have any of those eye drops left from the last—"

"I've started them already."

"Oh, good. Why don't you bring her in on Monday?"

"Sure thing. But that's not why I came over." Sami gestured behind them. "Have you heard?"

"About?"

"Our *celebrity*." He said it like as someone else might croon *bottomless mimosas*.

Before the crowd even parted, Will's head had begun to throb.

There she was in full Chick Nic drag. She'd curled the ends of her hair, and it bounced around her shoulders. Her red plaid shirt hugged her every curve, and her cutoff jean shorts showcased her thighs. She should've looked juvenile, but she only looked hot.

The *tick tick tick* of need in Will's gut was especially loud this morning, a bomb someone would be desperately trying to defuse in a movie. Why did she have to be so pretty?

"Can't be a celebrity if you're not good with an instrument or a ball," Will gritted out.

The older man wasn't listening, however. "You ever watch her videos?"

"A few." Since it was all Will could do not to pant at the sight of Nicole, there was no point in playing dumb.

"I got into them during quarantine, you know," Sami said. "I never appreciated chickens much, but—"

"The dogs would chase them, and they'd eat all of your hostas." Will had to cut this chicken thing off at the pass before it spread, and everyone in town knew Sami was fanatical about his hostas.

Sami's head jerked toward Will. "Really? She didn't mention that."

"Yeah, she sort of leaves those parts out."

A voice spoke from above him. "What parts?"

The thing about Nicole was that her voice didn't fit with the rest of her. It was low and warm. *Sincere.* Will would bet that while her audience might not be able to pin it down, it was her voice they were responding to, not her looks. That honey-whiskey drawl that promised everything warm and down home and easy. God, how he wished he could sink into the promise of that, even knowing it was empty and false.

He stood up, needing his height. Now that he was looking down on her, literally, he got back a tiny measure of control. It was a relief to not feel entirely like the rutting buck he was. "The, erm, less savory parts of poultry keeping."

She tipped her head to the side, and her lips sort of . . . shivered. Stifling a laugh, probably, but all he could think was how it would feel against his skin.

Anxiety had broken him. He'd kept his worries inside for too long, and they'd corroded his professionalism and good sense.

Nicole gave a dazzling smile. "I don't know, I did make a multipart series on chicken shit."

Across the circle of observers, Lurene Morgan's eyebrows about disappeared into her hairline, and Sami guffawed so loudly that his corgi appeared concerned.

Will could feel his mouth go hard and mulish, and Nicole's eyes twinkled—freaking twinkled. They were like perverse mirror images of each other.

"Is there that much to say about it?" Sami asked, wiping his eyes.

"Oh, yes," Nicole deadpanned. "Saying 'chickenshit' to describe fear couldn't be more wrong. Chickens have no fear of shitting anywhere."

The crowd roared, a reaction she paused to allow. Because whatever else she was, Nicole was a performer. Will needed to remember that she was always seeking to get a rise out of people. He was surprised she hadn't used her joke on one of her videos; he would have remembered it. But maybe she was trying it out here, and since it had worked, she'd debut it there later. She was always hustling, wasn't she?

"That's why chickens are difficult pets."

But Nicole wasn't put off by Will's tone. "So growly."

He literally growled, and her eyes twinkled. Again.

"They're difficult but worthwhile." She gave him a little pout, and he had to look away.

"You want to do a guest spot on my channel sometime?" she asked. "You could discuss chicken medicine."

Absolutely not. He was going to stay as far away from this woman as he could, even if they were neighbors. "You've made it clear you're expert enough."

"Dr. Lund,"—he was certain everyone else listening in missed the sarcasm Nicole heaped there—"when did I imply I didn't appreciate what you did for Camilla yesterday? Not to mention your help with Mitzi on Wednesday? I'm very grateful."

She blinked at him, guileless and mocking at the same time, and he wanted to laugh. How could no one else see what she was doing? Hell, it annoyed him, but he respected how good she was at it. She must get tired of her act sometimes, but she was also no doubt amused at how rarely people saw through it.

"How did you help her?" Sami demanded, clearly jealous that he hadn't been tapped for the as-of-yet-unnamed job. Except if Sami had been there for the chicken chasing, he probably would have had a heart attack. Soaking-wet Nicole needed a town crier to repel anyone unprepared.

"He didn't tell you?" Nicole asked before Will could respond. "So modest. The day I moved in, one of my hens escaped, and Will helped me catch her. It took half an hour in the pouring rain."

Then, Nicole turned to him with an expression everyone was going to read as *my hero* but which he understood was far more *you ass*.

There was simply no way for Will to play this. She'd skunked him, and he could only respond by doing a troll impression, which she knew and was enjoying.

In the small crowd, Lurene, who managed the Dollar General and had the biggest orange tabby Will had ever seen, gasped. "*You* catch *chickens?*" It wasn't clear which part was more surprising to her.

"He did." Then Nicole actually, literally fluttered her eyelashes at Will. He hadn't thought anyone did that outside of cartoons.

And while he knew, utterly knew, that it was an act, Will . . . was stumble tongued. She undid him. He was undone. He could stamp and rage about it, but he couldn't leash his response to her.

"Take your bow," Nicole almost purred.

He only glared.

What was she playing at? He'd been nothing but a jerk to her, so why was she teasing him like this? She had to know that he was a lost cause.

Everyone else was lapping it up, a pack of cats with a vat of cream. Which would, of course, land said cats in his office later with digestive issues.

"Well, Will is just the best," Sami enthused. "He sees all my dogs."

Lurene, clearly unwilling to miss the action, put in, "And my cat."

"Because I'm the only vet in town."

"Again, so humble." Nicole could simper with the best of them.

He grunted rather than say something like *Better than so arrogant.*

He didn't want to be an ass, as much as Nicole seemed to enjoy provoking him. All he wanted was to find his way back to level ground, rather than whatever marshy bog she'd dragged him into.

"Speaking of people who aren't humble, how's Luke?" Sami asked.

While Will's parents didn't seem aware that their younger son was more than a wee bit of a ding-a-ling, everyone else in town had definitely noticed.

It was both oddly comforting—Will wasn't imagining Luke's worst qualities—and incredibly depressing. Will might find solace in mocking his brother inside his own skull, but he never knew quite how to respond when someone else brought it up, especially as they seemed to want to offer Will a way to blow off steam, and it wasn't a route he wanted to go down.

"He's, um, fine. They were here for the night."

"Oh, they schlepped to Yagerstown, did they?"

Will closed his eyes. Was that what he sounded like when he complained about Luke to Ella? Was he that . . . bitter?

Yeah, probably.

This was his fault. Somehow Sami had picked up on Will's resentment, and he was trying to help. It was kind. Almost. Maybe it would be if it weren't in front of Nicole, who probably could make no sense of this and was going to think he took pleasure in trashing his brother to his clients.

"I don't know if they . . . I mean, is schlepped really—they drove," he finally said.

"Will's brother lives in Richmond," Sami helpfully explained to Nicole.

"He's a *lawyer.*" The way Lurene said the word was an entire encyclopedia's worth of class struggle and resentment.

"And kind of an—"

"Not around very often," Will projected over Sami, needing to end this now before it got even more mortifying than it already was.

Across the little circle, Nicole had dropped the farm-girl-pinup expression from her face. She was watching him steadily—gently. It wasn't pity, not quite. More like recognition.

What did she think she saw? A guy who clearly didn't want to talk about his brother because he was jealous, probably. Which was, inconveniently, exactly who Will was.

Will scrubbed a hand through his hair. He had to get out of here. "So now that we've covered the chicken catching and the lawyer brother—"

"And Mimsey's eyes."

"—right, and the dog's blocked tear duct, can I go buy some tomatoes?"

Lurene snorted. "Yes, Dr. Lund."

Everyone else echoed her. Everyone except Nicole, who held his gaze with those swirling brown eyes of hers.

Will had never, ever thought she wasn't intelligent. Maybe that her brains bent toward the crafty rather than the perceptive. Maybe that her talent was boosting herself. But now, his stomach roiled. Because to get what she wanted, Nicole had to be smart about people. She had to know what they wanted in order to give it to them, to know what they needed, what they craved.

And while it defied belief, he would have sworn right there in the middle of the farmers' market that of all the people in the circle, all the people who'd known him for years but from whom he was hiding so much, she alone saw through Will's bluff.

For once, he hoped he was wrong about her. He'd been hiding for so long, he wasn't certain what he'd do if someone actually found him.

# CHAPTER 6

Things kept messing her up. Nic had packed quickly, throwing her stuff into boxes without any goal or plan beyond getting the hell out of the house she and Brian had shared as quickly as possible.

Shoes in with vases? Sure, why not! Books and blankets? They both started with *B*!

But as Nic tried to put her new house into some kind of order, she kept finding bits and pieces that belonged to Brian or to his friend and their sometime roommate Jamal, a legend in the Hypebeast community. The worst was a framed fragment of paper that had been stuck in a box otherwise filled with toiletries and makeup samples.

"Oh, damn," Nic said, pulling off the hastily taped Bubble Wrap cushioning it. "Damn, damn, damn." The anniversary present she'd never delivered, and now likely never would, for Rose.

She and Brian had met when they'd both been in the wedding of Rose, Nic's childhood best friend, to Tony, Brian's childhood BFF. Everything had been peach themed: the bridesmaid's dresses, the signature cocktails, the individual cobblers the couple had opted for instead of cake. And Nic had somehow found the entire thing peachy keen once she'd met Brian, so dashing in his tuxedo and so smitten with her.

It had seemed deeply romantic: the maid of honor and the best man, walking down the aisle together, looking perfect together, getting famous together . . . and then breaking up while what seemed like a good 7.3 percent of the internet looked on.

Nic plunked down in the hallway and wiped the frame with her T-shirt. Under the glass was a passage from *Winnie-the-Pooh* that she'd read during the ceremony. She'd had it framed almost immediately, which had been Brian's idea, and she'd always intended to present it to Rose and Tony.

But on their first anniversary, Brian had whisked Nic away to Iceland, where he'd filmed tours of volcanoes and geysers for his channel, and she'd toured heritage chicken farms and marveled at skeins of chunky organic wool. She'd been gaining a following then, largely due to Brian, but she was still working as a marketer for a winery, not quite trusting that she could feel secure giving up a regular paycheck for social media clicks and fickle stans.

The next year, they'd all been in lockdown. The stress of it had been tempered, weirdly, by Chickens for All taking off. Nic's success had offset the loss of her job—not many people were visiting wineries then—and had felt like something clicking into place. And then, just as her career was taking off like a meteor, Brian had blown everything up.

He'd started by implying, always implying, that she'd been flirty with Tony. In the middle of a livestream, some silly cross-promotional thing she couldn't even remember the details of now, he'd turned to her and said, "Like you are with Tony."

"What?" Like she and Tony . . . what?

"You know."

"No, I don't." And she'd laughed. A stilted, rigid laugh, because what the heck was Brian up to? He liked to make plans and keep them to himself and surprise her, something about spontaneity that never made sense. She couldn't see what the play was here.

"But you think he's hot," Brian had persisted.

"No, but—"

"He's not?"

"He is, but—"

"See!"

And it had seemed like a joke. Like an observation. Like no big deal. Tony was a good-looking guy. She'd said as much to Rose. Why did it matter that she'd said it online?

Because Brian had made it matter.

Again on camera, again live, he'd implied—again with the implying!—that she had confessed to him that she was interested in Tony— "and this one over here with the active fantasy life. Come on, spare a man's feelings! And he's my best friend"—and her stunned, stammered denial had been taken as a flustered confirmation. Almost a confession.

"What are you doing? None of this happened," she'd screamed when it was over.

"Why are you worked up? I was just joking around."

But even though Nic hadn't known it yet, the damage had been done. No conversation she'd had with Rose after that had been the same. Nic's denials simply weren't as strong as Brian's insinuations.

"Ask him," she remembered saying to Rose.

"I did, and he said you were always so flirty, and—"

"But I'm *not*."

Except Brian had twisted every moment of niceness and warmth until even Tony had believed that Nic's friendship had been an offer of more.

When Brian had finally dumped her, finally spilled out an entirely detailed, entirely fictional story, Nic hadn't managed to say anything more than "That's not true." She hadn't parsed every detail, because how could she? How did you prove that something *didn't* happen?

The last twist of the knife was when Rose had been on Brian's channel a few weeks later, talking about Nic. About what "drama" it had all been, and how it was good it was over—or at least that was what Nic had gleaned from the one time she'd made it through the video, clomping around her hotel room, her hands slamming alternately over her ears and her eyes and pulling at her hair.

Wrong and unfair and sickening and crushing.

It had made her literally ill. Twenty years of friendship, somehow undermined by two years of Brian. What had he said not on camera? How had he convinced Rose and Tony to trust not what had happened but what he *said* had happened?

If Brian had happened to someone else, if he'd been a character in a movie, Nic would have been fascinated by him. So slick, so charming that you almost didn't notice how everything he did was for himself. How he'd suggest something to you with such sweet persuasion that you came to believe you'd thought of it yourself, and how, only later, you'd remember that it wasn't what you'd wanted at all.

You hadn't meant to get more chickens, to begin making videos at all. Certainly it hadn't been your idea to do cross-promo with that person, to put your relationship on the internet, to do another take but funnier this time, to push for that endorsement, to rent a house with other influencers, to call yourself an influencer, to get into TikTok because that was where the fans were, and you especially, especially hadn't intended to let him record that final night, that conversation that he had said would help everything, clarify everything. You hadn't meant to sit there, open mouthed, while he wrecked everything you'd thought you were building together, putting himself in the best possible light while making you look like someone you didn't recognize.

But you weren't someone you recognized, were you?

Chick Nic was like a Halloween costume. A persona. Except without it, Nic didn't know who she was anymore.

Queasiness roiled in her gut. Her memories from the last two years were bile tinged, green, unstable. The only thing she was certain of was that she'd never, not once, flirted with Tony.

And it was that certainty and that certainty alone that had Nic setting down the framed scrap of paper and dialing Rose for the first time in almost two months.

If she texted first, Rose would never answer. Heck, she still probably wouldn't answer. Nic ought to write her a letter and just mail the present, though it might seem like a sick joke if Rose honestly believed Brian's insinuations, and Nic didn't want to share her address with Rose since that would mean sharing it with Brian, but even still—

"Yeah?"

Nic clutched the phone harder. "Hey! I'm so glad you picked up, I—"

"What do you want?" Yeah, Rose still hadn't changed her mind or unbent in the least. She was still under Brian's spell. Still suspicious and hating Nic.

It was lemon juice in a paper cut but over Nic's entire body. Over her soul. But the thing about running a YouTube channel was you got really good at being faux chipper. "How have you been?"

"You're calling to ask how I've been?"

There was no way to be positive in this. No way to lie.

"I don't think we've gone six weeks without talking in twenty years."

"Yeah, well, twenty years ago you hadn't thrown yourself at Tony."

Nic was tempted to point out that twenty years ago, Rose didn't know Tony existed, but that wouldn't help.

How did you get someone to admit the truth when their self-image depended on them not admitting it? If Brian had lied—and he had—then that meant Tony had been wrong about him for decades. It meant Rose and Tony shouldn't have agreed to get swept up in Brian and Nic's online empire. It meant they'd been duped, and Nic knew in the worst way how continuing to go along with the entire charade could seem easier than facing the truth and your own complicity in it.

But she still needed to say it. "Rose, I didn't."

"Yeah, well . . ."

"This is important. I know—I know Brian can be persuasive. I don't know exactly what he said to you, or to Tony, but I would never do that, and I didn't do that." The words were an anchor, plummeting through Nic's body and riveting her to the floor, to reality. She hadn't done anything wrong. She hadn't.

Rose dodged. "Why are you really calling?"

"I have something of yours. I was wondering if I could send it to you."

"You know the address."

There wasn't the tiniest hint there of the sleepovers and the manicures and the prom-dress shopping and the *history*. How could that not leave a residue? How could Brian have snuffed that out of existence?

Nic wanted to say so many things. To tell Rose that it hurt, throbbed in her chest, in her joints, to have her best friend believe the worst about her. To pour out all the empathy and shared pain and to have it reflected back because they both knew how it felt to be manipulated by Brian. To complain about how moving on her own had *sucked*. To squeal about chasing Mitzi in the rain with Will and to speculate about his motives and his hot scowling. To admit that the events of the past few months had made Nic relive every scrap of grief from her entire life, like opening some portal to those moments of loss and pain; that it had been like losing Granny all over again.

Dammit, Nic wanted her best friend back. Of all the things Brian had taken from her, this one was the deepest cut. Rose's betrayal had hurt worse than anything Brian had done to her.

It was inadequate, but Nic settled for saying, "I miss you."

Because even if Rose would never believe her, Nic knew she had to tell the truth. The truth was the only answer to the Brians of the world because it was the one thing they couldn't fake. And no matter how many times they told you that two plus two equaled three, even at the moments when that seemed the most reasonable, you always knew the real answer, deep down.

There was a pause longer than the Postal Service had made records, and then Rose grunted. Didn't say anything, but also she didn't hang up.

Nic listened to her best friend breathing, wishing that somehow, things were different. That she'd managed to see through him at the wedding and had kept her distance. That she'd been smarter, more skeptical. *Better.*

Finally, at last, Rose said, "Okay then," and hung up.

"That could've gone worse."

Nic's pronouncement echoed down the hallway. In retrospect, the house she and Brian had shared had never been anything like quiet. They seemingly always had someone crashing in the guest room, and Brian loved to throw parties. He insisted he couldn't work without music. He blasted it at all hours, unless he was filming. Those years had been shouty and loud.

Her new house couldn't be more tomb-like. She could hear the hens singing egg songs in the backyard and the mail carrier driving down the street. Right now, someone, some kid probably, was shooting baskets. She could hear the *thump thump thump* of the ball hitting the ground as the player dribbled, and then the fuller *thunk* of the ball hitting the backboard.

The jury was still out on whether the silence was restful or creepy.

Nic picked herself up off the floor and found a spot in a closet for the frame. She wasn't going to send that until things had thawed with Rose, if they ever did.

The next item on her list was only marginally less painful: managing her social media accounts. Whatever Brian had intended with his breakup/humiliation stunt, it had led to a rush of publicity, which had probably been his goal. He'd probably spin it, in some warped way, that he'd done her a favor.

People, lots of people, were Team Nic. Whether it was because they saw through Brian or because when teams shook out, some people ended up on both sides, Nic took a certain satisfaction in her popularity. Not everyone thought she was lusting after her best friend's husband.

But Chickens for All wasn't solely about validation for Nic, and it wasn't just about making money. However it had started, she believed in her pocket media empire. She believed in empowering people to keep chickens and in bonding together over their tiny lawn dinosaurs. And that was what kept her going as she liked and responded to comments, emailed her virtual assistant, drafted a newsletter, and updated the appearances section of her website.

Then came the best part of her day, when she got outside to the chicken run. This was work, nominally, but it never felt like it. Cleaning the coop while hens pecked at her jeans and, sometimes, let her stroke their silky feathers, then refilling the water and raking the yard, before she pulled out her T-shirt and filled it with a cache of rainbow-colored eggs—blue green, several shades of brown, and creamy white.

Back inside, she slid the eggs into a mixing bowl and stuck them in the fridge . . . where she already had three other bowls of eggs. Nic appreciated the eggs, but not to the tune of a half dozen a day. At least Brian's cavalcade of visitors and friends had meant that the eggs disappeared.

Nic was going to need to make an angel food cake, or maybe two. It had been Granny's favorite, and Nic had spent many an afternoon watching her whip the egg whites to the perfect consistency. Nic's own attempts at cake had been medium-grade failures, though.

The basketball *thunked* again outside. Nic had neighbors. Neighbors with whom she'd like to be friends—because obviously she needed new friends. She'd practically moved into a small town from a '90s comedy. She was going to buy their love with delicious, delicious eggs.

She opened the fridge, grabbed the bowl that was the fullest, and set out, only to freeze in her front yard when she realized to whom the basketball belonged.

Not a kid. Not even a little bit.

Across the street, on the driveway that snaked up the side of his house, was one very sweaty, very good-looking veterinarian.

Okay, she might have to move again. No cute porch was worth this torment.

He spotted Nic and gave what seemed like a reluctant wave. He'd caught her in the tractor beam of politeness. She couldn't go inside and sulk now.

"How were the tomatoes?" She tried not to look at how his T-shirt stretched across his biceps and clung to the plane of his stomach. Did the man have anything that fit loosely? This shirt had been washed a few dozen too many times and was thinning in places, the hem fraying. Why did the wear make it *more* attractive? What laundry-based alchemy was this?

At least she'd solved the mystery of how someone who spent so much time healing sick animals maintained the body of an Olympian. Being grumpy wasn't, it turned out, his primary form of exertion.

She focused instead on the basketball hoop, which hung on the detached garage tucked behind Will's house. The net was tattered and half falling apart. It was strangely endearing.

"Tomatoes?" He was out of breath and befuddled in the best of ways.

"This morning at the market you said you were going to get some."

"Oh. They're, um, still on the counter."

She'd bought peppers and eggplants with the intention of making a stir-fry, except it was nearing seven o'clock, and she hadn't started. But it didn't seem like the time to talk about her failed dinner plans. She wasn't certain how she was going to talk about anything given that she was trying not to make eye contact with Will, and he was apparently following suit.

Without looking higher than his knees, she thrust the bowl toward him. "Do you like eggs? I probably owe you for all your help." As painful as that was to admit.

"It wasn't a big deal."

"And neither are these. I get at least three dozen a week."

"Are you thanking me or getting rid of your trash?"

On Friday, she would have thought Will's words were harsh and recoiled. But she could hear the dry wit in them now, and she wasn't offended like she would have been.

How many people in this town got that he was joking? This morning, she'd watched as Will had put a gulf between the people in town, who clearly adored him, and himself. When the man with the corgi had made some opaque reference to his brother, Will had turned the same shade of burgundy as the beets on the table behind him and basically run away. There was a story there, she was certain.

And whether out of obtuseness or something else, the guy with the corgi wouldn't have realized Will was joking. The people here didn't seem to know him at all.

"They're eggs. It doesn't have to be more complicated than that."

He must've decided to go along with her offer, because he set down his ball and took the bowl. One of his long, slightly calloused fingers skimmed hers in the process, and she trembled.

"Thanks." His breathing had evened out, and it was almost too soft in the falling light. The brush of linen over skin.

She gave herself a shake, but she wasn't an Etch A Sketch, and so it didn't erase the image of Will touching her more. Will touching her everywhere. Apparently, all the recent life upheaval had supercharged her imagination, at least where Will and bodies and clothing were concerned.

"Friends give friends eggs." Nic tried to sound certain, but certainty had departed from her life, oh, about six months before.

"Are we friends?"

"I—" Nic had no idea when she'd last made a friend face to face. Before COVID, when she'd still known how to be social, how the world worked. Before the months inside. Before her channel had taken off. Before everything had changed. In this new world, with its new rules, she had no idea what friendship meant.

Arguing over responsible pet ownership? Teasing each other at the farmers' market? Being wildly attracted to him? Sure, that was probably what friends were in the postpandemic state of things.

"Of course we're friends. I wouldn't chase a chicken with just anyone."

"I'm flattered."

"You should be. It's the lesser-known equivalent of asking someone to pick you up at the airport."

"Or helping someone move."

"Exactly. In comparison, chicken chasing is *way* more intimate." Oops. She shouldn't have said that.

Will's smile said that he would have no problem with more intimacy with her.

"So, um, do you live alone?" she asked quickly.

"Uh-huh."

"But your brother? Sorry, it's none of my business, but I—"

"You heard what Sami said. Yeah, I could tell. No, he's in Richmond. My sister and my parents are still here, across town."

"That's nice."

"What about you?"

"No, it's just me. My parents are back in Washington State. I grew up in Spokane before I moved to California, Santa Rosa for work and then Burbank"—where she'd moved to be with Brian, though she omitted that detail—"and now I'm here. All that moving . . . it makes me feel a bit rootless."

"Sometimes I think I have too many roots."

"It's nice your family is still close."

"Hmm."

Another noise that everyone else in town would probably think was equivocal, only a conversation filler, but that she knew was a rebuke. Not to her, but to his brother.

Nic tried not to feel like a lecher as she appreciated the line of his profile against the evening sky. "But it's none of my business. I'm only that annoying neighbor with the chickens."

"Never said you were annoying."

"No, you said I was . . ." She searched for the right word.

He had criticized her, been a bit unprofessional, and certainly it wasn't a good business move to get flippant with a new patient he should have been trying to charm. But his worst crime was that he'd quoted her ex-boyfriend, which he probably thought was medium-grade annoying and not like a nuclear weapon to her ego.

"Unqualified to give veterinary advice and, I don't know, inciting bad pet ownership. It wasn't a very nice way to treat a new patient."

"I have a terrible bedside manner." His Viking grin returned, and it was *a lot*. It made his face more mischievous. Roguish. Transformed the bulk of him into . . . an enticement. That expression said he might be tough on his patients but that he would be good, so very good, at other things. Bedroom things. "All my professors said so."

She shouldn't have been as susceptible to his smile as she was. They could be friends, but that was as far as this could go. She was done with men. Like, so done. The done-est.

To combat the silly, ridiculous imaginings in her head, Nic returned to the matter she'd originally been snooping about. "And brotherly relationships."

"Oh, I'm bad at those too."

"Eh, those are a two-way street." At least that was what she'd picked up from the Zeus-Poseidon-Hades rivalry and also that contemporary myth *Succession*.

Some of the heat drained from Will's eyes. "My brother and I don't get along. No, we . . . we get along as long as we don't talk about anything real. As long as it's just surface, we're fine." He grimaced as if this state of things pained him, but maybe the pain came from him *sharing* the state of things with her.

Maybe his walls had been worn down by the exercise. He'd been shooting baskets for at least an hour; that probably had depleted his willpower somewhat. That was why he'd been flirting too.

"Ah," she said, trying to keep her tone light. To a certain extent, that was how it had always been with her parents, which had been part of why she'd loved Granny so much. That relationship had always been easy. "Was it always like that?" She was helpless to resist her curiosity about him. It was his hardnesses and his sly wit and the curving tension between them. She couldn't figure him out, and she wanted to.

"Do you always pry?" That was definitely teasing, if not outright flirty. It was sort of funny she hadn't been able to hear it from the start.

"Only with my friends and neighbors." Nic managed to take a few steps back from Will and his all-too-interesting family drama. It wasn't her business, and it wasn't fair to push him like this. Besides, she was over men. "Enjoy your eggs."

"Thanks."

Nic went back to her quiet house, where all the drama was internal, and it was ten kinds of awful.

# CHAPTER 7

Will couldn't make his budget work—and he could not put this one on Nicole Jones, even if he had spent too much time reviewing their conversations. No, this was all him.

The only things Will knew about business management were to put in all the numbers and receipts in the bookkeeping software immediately and to value your employees. Unfortunately, doing the first had shown him that he couldn't do the second. There was no way to assemble this particular puzzle. He was short too many pieces, too much cash.

"This is . . . everything?" he asked Marsha again. He knew that it was, but he hoped for a miracle anyhow. His Hail Mary play was to hope he'd done a lot more business than he knew he had.

"That's the whole kit and caboodle." But however light her words, Marsha's eyes were infinitely kind. She understood exactly what Will wasn't saying.

He wasn't going to be able to make payroll at the end of the month.

That they were having this conversation in their small dispensary, the shelves of which were lined with thousands of dollars' worth of meds, was fucking ironic.

Every week, Will and Kim had to weed the shelves, looking for the compounds and injections and creams that had expired while waiting for patients who hadn't bought them. If the practice didn't have a wide range of meds on hand, then they couldn't serve their patients. But as a tiny practice in a tiny town, Will couldn't buy in bulk, so his prices were higher. They just were.

All those utilitarian cardboard boxes, the labels the ugliest colors on earth, were a money pit, sucking up the practice's margins just as surely as the fluorescent light bulbs and the rent on the building itself.

"Thanks, I . . . thanks," Will said to Marsha.

"It isn't your fault."

Marsha had been a carryover when he'd bought the practice from Dr. Sinclair. She'd answered the phones and booked appointments and handed people tissues while they wept because he'd had to put down their beloved companions. She was more of an institution in this town than Dr. Sinclair had been or Will could ever hope to be.

In a few weeks, Will wasn't going to be able to pay her.

A boulder rolled up and around the walls of his stomach, and he was tempted to let it pull him down into the center of the earth.

Never in his life had he felt worse, never had he felt like a bigger failure—and he'd grown up in the same house as Luke, a person who basically spoke in backhanded compliments, veiled insults, and demeaning questions.

When he'd set down this path, Will had seen only the science and then the animals: The reward of treating someone's dog when it was suffering from an ear infection. The challenge of identifying a cat's allergies.

What he should have been thinking about was the terms of commercial leases and the high cost of office dental plans. Or the people who couldn't afford to treat their pets' cancers. Or those who didn't wish to provide even the most basic of care to their pets. The puppy who'd died in his arms of anemia after the owner hadn't given it any flea preventive last week—and who'd then skipped out on the bill.

It was the numbers that had him up at night. The numbers were going to ruin his life, and not only his. Marsha's and Kim's too.

"It's kinda my fault," he said at last. "I could've advertised more in Floyd or Buchanan. I could have taken on a partner or something." The truth was that things had been tight even before coronavirus. That had only been the hurricane that had revealed how shaky the foundation of this structure was. Vet practices all around the country were shuttering. He wasn't going to be able to escape the flood.

Marsha clicked her tongue. "Dr. Sinclair never ran ads in Buchanan and never took on a partner, and that served him well for thirty years. It was only logical for you to assume it'd be the same for you."

Will put his elbows on the desk and rested his forehead on his hands. "It's not that I don't appreciate what you're saying." Even as he didn't believe it. "But I . . . I feel so damn guilty."

He hadn't realized it until he said it, but it wasn't only failure plaguing him. He'd screwed up so utterly—and it was about to be so public—that it was guilt.

He'd let down everyone in town who'd trusted him with their animals. Their disappointment in him would be absolute. And God, Luke was going to be the most insufferable of all. He was going to offer to help, and whether Will agreed or not, it was going to come up at every holiday, every dinner.

*It's not that I care,* Luke would say, obviously caring a tremendous amount. *It's not that I need the money back. I just want to know how you're doing. Maybe I should look at your books? Just to help. There's probably some overhead we can trim.*

Will would rather pry off his fingernails one by one with a paper clip than endure that. But the simple fact was he wasn't going to be able to avoid asking for help, or at least finally sharing the truth with everyone, for very long. The amount of grace left to him could be measured in weeks.

"You shouldn't feel guilty," Marsha was saying. "It's a waste of time. Everybody's hurting. All over the county, stuff's closing."

"Sure." He wasn't arrogant enough, stupid enough, to think this was all about him. But he had made some dumb choices, and even if this was national—hell, global—he was still going to be the one pulling the trigger. Firing people—shit. He'd never thought he'd have to do that. That had never factored into his vet dreams. "But you're not going to talk me out of it. It's a pretty entrenched belief of mine at this point."

"Because you're kind."

"It's not—no. Anyone would feel this way."

"Anyone would not. Dr. Sinclair wouldn't have given a tinker's damn about anyone else."

"Well, he hired you to be his conscience." It was a story Will had heard from many people. The old vet had certainly had a cold, formal manner. Will had never really managed it, though he had done a pretty good imitation of the old man with Nicole Jones when she'd come in on Friday.

God, he felt guilty about that, too, but it was a tiny shadow compared to how he was going to feel when the axe fell and he lost everything he'd worked for.

Marsha cackled at his joke and patted his hand in a way that would have made him grit his teeth from anyone else. "You know what you need to do. No, you know what? Let me do it for you. I was going to retire soon anyway. I need to spend more time with the grandkid. I missed almost an entire year of his babyhood during that quarantine. I need to make up for lost time! So let's call this my two weeks, and you try to keep Kim on a little longer."

His jaw clicked shut so fast, Will almost bit his tongue.

Kim was the only tech he had left. Between Will and Kim, they could cover Marsha's job, maybe, but if Marsha left, the clock would be more than ticking, it would be booming.

"No," he got out. "You don't need to do that. The writing's on the wall here. I appreciate it, but you can't delay the inevitable."

The inevitable being his failure, Day-Glo and likely visible from space. At least if the practice folded, Marsha would be able to apply for unemployment. It wasn't much, but it was all the severance he could offer her.

Marsha just shook her head. "Don't argue with me. It's not gentlemanly. I'm done! It's been a terrific forty years, and it's over."

Will sat back in his chair. She'd managed that, and him, effectively; he had to give her that. "Well, if you insist on leaving, can I at least ask for your advice?"

Unlike anyone in his family, Marsha was able to give her opinion without a hint of pity or judgment. It was one of the many things he loved about her and one of the reasons he was willing to ask what she thought.

"Shoot."

"Other than payroll, the biggest expense is rent." Technically, it wasn't rent but a deed of trust, and the bank was Will's trustee. They were the ones who might be able to help him or who would swoop in and evict him if he fell behind.

Another was the litany of bills for services he simply hadn't been able to deny but also couldn't collect the payment for. Will had long since given up hope of making a dent in *that*, though. "I was thinking about calling the bank, see if they'll give us a break." After all, who else would take this space? Nobody else would be clamoring to move in or buy if the trustee evicted Will.

No, if the bank wouldn't cut him a break, he was going to have to close or sell the practice to some corporate megachain, which Will had specifically structured his career to avoid.

Will didn't want to think about the vacancies that were popping up all over town. Each one of those shops had been full. Each one was somebody's dream and lots of people's livelihoods. It almost defied comprehension. Every story was individual, but they were all echoes of the same sad song.

There were so many folks who, like him, had been only barely on the right side of the balance sheet before coronavirus and who had never had enough to save for a rainy day, let alone for a flood; who'd kept it together through brazenness and luck and then watched the tiny bits they'd cobbled together cave in.

The businesses that were doing okay were the big conglomerates—but Will hadn't wanted to go down that route. One of his closest friends from vet school, Owen, didn't even practice anymore. He worked for the megachain Peticine, buying up the little cogs and welding them onto the big machine. He'd even offered to buy Dr. Sinclair's practice for Will, but Will had said no. Will hated that way of doing business. He had always thought he was smart enough, hardworking enough to avoid this turn of fate. Now Will had to accept that he wasn't special.

Yup, he'd mucked up but good.

"Call 'em." Marsha gave him a grandmotherly pat. "I can't believe you haven't reached out to the bank already. And hey, there's still a box of those T-shirts in the storage room. Maybe we should hock the rest."

That would net a whole hundred bucks—if they could move them all. "The x-ray machine is on the fritz again. If we sell those and hold a bake sale . . ." It wouldn't make any sense. Will's problems were so much larger than that.

She pointed with an excited finger. "There's that genius vet I know! What about a car wash? There's lots of folks in town who'd pay to watch you getting sudsy."

Will gave a dry laugh. "I doubt that."

"Then you're not as smart as I thought you were. You could charge extra for taking off your shirt, which I can say now that I don't work for you." She winked.

Thinking about getting shirtless and wet only made him think of Nicole Jones. For the rest of his life, contemplating water would probably only make him think of Nicole. God, it was such a waste that the woman was so . . .

So *what?* Reckless in getting people to buy chickens? Maybe. Maybe that was still true.

But every conversation they had forced him to give up another one of his assumptions about her. If he kept it up, he was going to have to admit that he liked her.

That was the only possible explanation for his telling Nicole about Luke last night. It had been a sort of begrudging liking, a lot of lust, and a distinct helping of weakness on his part. But as soon as she found out he was a failure, she'd stop flirting with him, and that would be the end of that. He'd mentioned Nicole to the head of the local chicken advocacy group this morning, so she'd connect with more people in Yagerstown. Then he could ignore her, confident that she wasn't alone in town.

Will needed to put it, and Nicole, out of his mind and concentrate on his own problems. Get back to his hermit training regime.

"We're going to have to disagree about shirtlessness," he told Marsha. He would have to come back around to the bake sale and car wash ideas, though. "Are you serious about resigning?"

"*Retiring.* I am retiring, and it's long overdue."

"That's true. I'd like to . . . throw you a party? Buy you a watch? Isn't that what people do for retirees?"

She cackled. "I don't need a party, and who wears a watch? That's why I have a phone. I'll take some flowers, though. I'm partial to gerbera daisies. Mostly, I need you to get up off the mat. To see this isn't your fault. You've gotta let go of all that stuff, Will. It'll eat you alive."

"Sure." But he didn't convince either of them.

Marsha swished out of his office, and once she got settled behind the desk, she called back to him, "Your next appointment is here, Doc."

"Who is it?" He closed the offensive spreadsheet and rolled his shoulders. He hadn't realized he had an appointment. He'd been planning to sit here and scowl for a bit. Maybe stomp around and groan. He wasn't going to have an office to be melodramatic in for much longer.

"It's that chicken girl. The pretty one."

Will closed his eyes. Took a deep breath. And almost slammed his head on the desk. He couldn't face Nicole right now. That night in his driveway, she'd seemed . . . soft. Curious. Close. God, so close. And things had seemed possible.

He hadn't been thinking straight then.

Today, he was sober.

This would be a quick visit. He wouldn't think about her hair. He wouldn't confess anything. Under no circumstances would he flirt.

"Be right there," he said through clenched teeth.

It took a minute to get his head clear; then he walked down the hall to the only exam room that had light under the door.

Inside, in worn jeans and Chuck Taylors, stood Nicole. She had her back to him, and her hair fell loose around her shoulders, long and shiny with the slightest curl to it.

Right, he'd already failed to ignore her hair. This was going to be disastrous.

He shifted his attention to the exam room table, where, in a cage, was the hen he'd treated three days prior. The chicken was clearly feeling better, and she was pecking at the wires. Her claws couldn't find purchase on the barred floor, and she kept slipping around and righting herself.

Will didn't get the attraction of chickens at all.

"Here?" he called down the hallway, as if there were another patient waiting.

If the gruffness of his voice bothered her, Nicole didn't show it. No, when she turned, she sent a thousand-watt grin over her shoulder at him.

It shorted out Will's heart.

Before, when he hadn't yet worried about where he'd get his next case of toilet paper, when his practice had been limping, if not running, he would've smiled back. He would've dropped whatever bias he had against Nicole. He would've tried to figure out why she loved chickens so much. He would've wanted to see who she really was under the facade.

Now, when he'd been confirmed as a failure, he just couldn't. He wouldn't. He was going to keep her at arm's length, right where he'd shoved everyone else.

"Morning, neighbor," Nicole said.

Here was where a normal person would have returned her greeting. Been *friendly*. Shaken hands—hugged, maybe. Neighbors did that. People were freaking reveling in that stuff after not being able to do it for so long.

But, Neanderthal that he was, he only managed to grunt and busy himself with washing his hands.

Behind him, Nicole was still keeping up the sunshine act. "How are you? How were your eggs?"

His eggs had been great, the yolks as bright as the yellow brick road. Much as he wanted to do a speedy exam on the avian patient and then get the hell out of here, he did have to acknowledge the gift.

"Good." Maybe he could limit the entire visit to single-syllable statements.

He opened the cage and extracted the chicken. She regarded him through beady, blinking, but bright eyes. She looked much better than she had on Friday, when frankly, he'd been wondering whether she'd make it.

"How is she?"

"*Very* good. She's active, eating well." Nicole's smile was blissful. She really did love her birds.

"Any bleeding?" he asked.

"Nope."

He inspected the hen's vent and asked about how administering the meds was going. Nicole's answers were so *warm*. Despite how he'd been during her last visit, she was so present. It was yet another knock against him.

"Do you think she's getting better?" Nicole asked.

"Uh-huh."

"I feel so guilty about not noticing it sooner."

*Join the club.* He didn't say a word, though.

"If I . . . when I was defensive on Friday, that was why."

The noise he made wasn't even speech. It came from the deepest, most empathetic part of him but somehow still sounded like rock drawn over rock.

"The last time I took a chicken to the vet, he was dismissive, unhelpful, and incompetent. He told me that my bird was fine, and she . . . she died a few days later. A neoplasm, I think."

Christ, Will hadn't known any of that. He only managed to nod.

"I don't think there's anything anyone could have done for her, but he told me I was overreacting. It just *stung.* So I haven't been back to a vet since, and I've tried to, I dunno, empower people. But I'm not a pro, you're completely right about that. I'm sorry. I'm going to try to make it better."

Oh hell. How was he supposed to give a one-syllable response to that?

"That would be good." Because it would be. Nicole had hundreds of thousands of fans; it would, in fact, be good if she acknowledged that veterinarians played a role in animal care.

"I'm terrified about what will happen when Camilla tries to lay." Nicole's voice was low. She stepped closer to him, and he could feel the heat from her body across the cold of the stainless steel and linoleum of the exam room.

He restored the space she'd eliminated between them. Tried to snap back into vet mode. Tried not to feel so much for her. "We'll do a hormone implant to suppress ovulation. Give her time to heal." They probably had one of those in the dispensary, if it hadn't expired.

"I didn't realize that was an option." Nicole tipped her head to the side and gave the hen a long, assessing look. "Maybe she should retire."

"You can decide that later."

When he was back with the meds, the break from Nicole hadn't helped. He was still bonkers attracted to her. Equally vulnerable to her smiles, her compliments about how he was with the hen.

Which was probably why, when she was leaving, ten minutes later, he said, "She'll be fine. You didn't screw up too badly."

He knew, *knew*, he was talking to himself. But when he saw Nicole's face fall, when he realized what the words would mean to her, he didn't apologize or explain, though he knew he should. Because he was quite simply past the point when he could do so. He couldn't fix this. He couldn't fix anything. He couldn't let her get close to him.

So when she slid the Chick Nic mask back into place, when she glared and stowed her hen back into its cage and went to deal with Marsha, he let her go. Because it was better that way. Better for them both.

# CHAPTER 8

Hours later, Nic was still mad. She glared at Will's ridiculously cute house. So ridiculous. So cute. So visible out of seemingly every window of her own house. She'd finished unpacking, checked off all her administrative tasks, chatted on Twitter with some fans, and then she'd turned to fuming about Will's pronouncement that she hadn't caused too big a disaster.

Okay, well, she had screwed up. She knew she had. She should've been more vigilant. More proactive. The moment she'd taken Camilla in to see Will, she'd known she'd messed up. But he wasn't supposed to say that! He wasn't supposed to rub her face in it! Not after she'd forced confessions from him with eggs!

Whatever curiosity she'd felt about Will, whatever attraction to him, whatever small measure of friendship they'd had was as done and finished as *Friends* after the reunion special.

"He's judgmental," she said to no one. She'd taken her iced tea outside to the porch because you couldn't feel alone when you were outside. There were always crickets chirping and cicadas buzzing, always the jeweled spill of sky, at least what she could make out between everyone's floodlights.

Down the street, as far as she could see, porch after porch stood empty. Unoccupied shadowy cages, leaving her and the bugs alone. What was the point of all this yardage if no one used it?

Nic took another sip, if only to hear the ice cubes clink. In the silence, there was no one to say you weren't good enough, she supposed. No one to suggest another way to do your hair or another way of handling that promo or another A/B test to run on Facebook advertising.

No one had some perks, and Brian's voice had to disappear from her head one of these days.

Nic's phone chimed, and because she had nothing better to do, she picked it up.

Please join us!

Well, wasn't that cult-y?
The first few lines of the email were visible too.

Dear Nicole,

We're the co-presidents of BROODY (or BackyaRd Organization Of (Gallus) Domesticus (Keepers)—Yagerstown), and, while we know this sounds cliché, we're your biggest fans. I (Carolyn) was talking to Will Lund this morning, and he said—

That had probably been a short conversation. Will had likely insulted Nic and then stormed off. Hotly.

Out of perverse curiosity, Nic clicked through and kept reading. The writers, Carolyn and Emily, explained that BROODY had started several years ago as an informal chick swap, but it had grown during quarantine. They met monthly at the Knights of Columbus Hall: but we'll reschedule around you if you're amenable. And Will said you're new to town and lovely, and we'd just like to welcome you too.

Will had sent Nic . . . friends. He'd been short and difficult, but he'd sent her friends. He'd tried to give her what she hadn't even realized she'd been so openly hurting for.

Across the street, a door swung open, and Will emerged onto his porch.

Nic sank back into her chair, suddenly wishing she hadn't turned on the strand of twinkle lights. Will was clearly brighter—well, darker—than she was.

On Friday, maybe, it would even have been comforting if Will had told her that she hadn't killed her bird. After their conversations, though, it had felt like a blow.

Except something had been off with him, right from the start, today. He'd been too tight. Too unwilling to meet her eye. Too . . . drawn.

But somewhere in there, he'd sent her friends.

After a few seconds, Will sighed. The bugs must have gone on strike because Nic could hear it echo across the street. A deep, long, endless sigh of frustration and exhaustion that Nic knew all too well.

His sigh was a pin into the balloon of her anger. What was he frustrated about?

She watched for him to take out a phone or a tablet. She'd be able to see his expression then and judge his mood, at least as much as you could judge the mood of a man you'd met five times. Not that she was counting.

He was outlined by the light coming from the Johnsons' porch. Bare feet crossed at the ankles. Long, long legs stretched out in front of him. Tattered jeans that pulled taut across his thighs. With his head tipped back, she could see a bit of stubble running along his jaw.

It was a damn shame that he was as stern as the lifeguard at the pool and twice as likely to whistle at you for running—and that that was her personal sexual kryptonite.

But no phone appeared. No e-reader. No light.

It was just as well; it wasn't any of her business, and—

Will sighed again.

Dammit.

Nic knew a thing or two about distress. While she didn't want to feel kinship with him or his pain, she did. After the last few years, she knew the bunions on the feet of distress.

"You should probably get a dog," she said to herself. If she had a dog, she wouldn't feel the need to meddle in the lives of her neighbors.

Except if she had a dog, she'd have to take it to Will. Because something about this, about them, was inevitable.

She set down her tea, opened the screen door, and, against her better judgment, proceeded through her inky yard, across the street, and to the door of Will's porch.

"Hello." The sadness was there, too, in Will's voice, and while she was still annoyed with him, so annoyed, the obvious brokenness of him woke its twin in her. "Saw you coming."

"And to think I was worried about your eyesight."

"You aren't running around, so I assume the hens are locked up for the night."

"Yup."

"No one's egg bound?"

"That was egg yolk peritonitis. It said so on your bill."

"My *bill*."

Oh, this was about his practice.

"The very same," she replied, trying to guess what might have him rattled.

"If you're not having a veterinary emergency, is this a social call?"

She couldn't say, *I'm here because I think you're sad, and it turns out I'm sad too.* He'd deny it and snap at her again, and she'd end up back on her porch, alone, which was precisely where she didn't want to be.

"We're friends, remember? And I heard you were talking about me today."

"From?"

"Carolyn something or other. She keeps chickens."

"Oh. Yeah. Well, you gotta meet more people sometime." He said it as if there were no worse fate, not as if he'd given her something valuable.

"But I wouldn't have met them." At least not so soon. "It was . . . nice."

He snorted. Yeah, he wasn't nice.

"I wanted to say thanks."

A beat passed. Two.

"Are you going to ask me in?" Because while Nic might stroll over here wanting to . . . chat—pry, both—she wasn't going to open the man's porch door unless he wanted her to.

"I'm not good company right now."

Which wasn't no. It was not an invitation, sure, but he wasn't sending her away, maybe because he was every bit as lonely as she was.

They both needed dogs.

She opened the door and took the faded white wicker chair across from him. It creaked under her. "Me neither."

Will dropped his chin and looked at her. As far as she could tell, there were bags under his eyes and a grim tiredness around his mouth. He was still unfairly good looking.

"Do you want a beer?" He held up a bottle she hadn't noticed on the floor next to him.

"No, thanks." She only intended to stay long enough to annoy them both and chase away some of the chill from her heart.

Silence settled between them. Not an aggressive silence or a moody one. The bugs took up their song again, but taking its cue from Will's mood, it was almost dirgelike.

"I was rude today," he said.

This surprised the hell out of her. "You were. I didn't dig that. But you seem . . . off."

"Me being off doesn't make it okay."

"Agreed."

"I'm sorry."

He'd sent her friends, and he'd *apologized*. Who the hell was this man? "Accepted." She waited. "Why are you off?"

After all, it wasn't enough for him to try to patch things up, if that was what he was trying to do. He needed to fix whatever had been wrong in the first place.

He took a long sip of his beer, and, like the previous night, she wasn't certain whether he would answer.

Then, "COVID destroyed my practice."

"Oh." Quarantine had raised her boat while sinking so many others, and she'd watched it happen through the smallest spaces between her fingers. She hadn't wanted it, her success. Not that way. Not in any way that hurt someone.

Something—tears, frustration—built in her eyes, and she rubbed at it quickly. "God, Will." She considered reaching across the porch to touch him. But knowing that he'd probably bristle, thinking she was pitying him, Nic stayed where she was.

Besides, she wasn't certain whether it was an impulse to comfort or raw lust plus rationalization.

"I'd probably be in trouble no matter what, but I don't think I can bounce back."

Nic honestly couldn't believe he was telling her this, but perhaps the night had opened up chinks in his walls. She couldn't be blamed if she wanted to peer in them.

"I'm so sorry."

"It's not your fault."

"I'm still sorry." She exhaled and sank further into the chair. The cushion on it was mostly broken down, but in the best way.

It wasn't right that he'd been a jerk, but now she knew why. And he'd acknowledged and apologized for it without prompting. He'd tried to introduce her to more people in town so that she wouldn't be so lonely.

If he kept this up, it was going to be difficult to remember she was off men.

"So . . . what does a YouTube star do on her night off?" he asked, taking another long sip of his beer.

"Pries into her neighbors' lives. Come on, you already know this about me." She'd done it with him the night before.

"I'm tired of talking about me, I'm boring. All . . . broody and shit." It was clear he thought there could be nothing worse.

"You're a veterinarian. I'm certain you have strange cases and observations about animals and people for days. Like a new James Herriot." A much better looking one. "Have you ever thought about wearing some tweed?"

He'd look incredible in tweed: a Ralph Lauren catalog come to life but twice as hot.

"Tweed? Are you kidding me? In the South?" For a moment, something like *pleased* settled onto his features, but he stifled it almost as soon as it appeared. "That's not me."

"Come on, I used to work in marketing. Marketing." She stretched the word out to five syllables. "You in some tweed with a cow would be a great ad. How's your northern English accent?"

He gave her a dirty look, and she had the feeling, if they'd known each other better, he would've coupled it with an obscene gesture.

She laughed, deep and full. "I'm serious. I could put this together for you." It would be good to use her skills to help someone.

"I won't be your pity project."

"I'm way good at this stuff. You should be so lucky." She'd often been told that she could charge a top-market rate for doing social media consultations, not that she was going to tell Will that in his current state.

His expression was hard and joyless again.

She'd messed up, mentioning advertising. "Is it that dire?" she asked gently.

"My administrative assistant—Marsha, you met her today—offered to resign to give me another few weeks of solvency."

"Shit."

"Yup. I have no idea why I'm telling you this."

But she loved that he was. "I'm irresistible."

He chuckled. "Maybe."

Which wasn't no.

As much as Nic would like to believe Will was attracted to her, she suspected he was spilling this out for an even more dangerous reason. *Recognition.*

It was what had her crossing the street and snooping in his life, and it shook something deep inside her. She clearly couldn't trust herself to make good decisions where men were concerned. The risk to her own heart and self-worth were just too great.

Except then Will said, "I've just . . . failed."

It wasn't just what he'd said: it was how he'd said it. As if all the fight, all the exasperated sternness that had animated him when they'd met had gone clear out of him. Leaning back in the crappy plastic Adirondack chair, his feet bare, his beer drained, Will was an empty husk.

Nic had been a husk those first few days after her relationship with Brian imploded. Not, she knew now, because she would miss anything inherent about the relationship. But because she'd given away so many parts of herself in those years. Not only to him but to random people on the internet too. And she hadn't known why, or even really been aware she was doing it, until it was too late.

She'd been mourning for herself.

The look on Will's face, she knew it. Had been there. Had been him.

Their paired emotions mixed with the attraction that had been simmering between them from the start, ignited, and became a Molotov cocktail of bad ideas.

He hadn't failed. And neither had she.

Nic stood, her pulse suddenly thumping in her fingers, in her wrist.

"Yeah, I wouldn't blame you for leaving. This is all more real than a YouTube star wants in her time off." Will gestured to the screen door with his bottle. "Thanks for . . . listening."

"I'm not leaving." Nic strolled across the porch until she stood with her shins almost brushing Will's.

His eyes caught the light, and his expression was—hopeful. He was glad she was staying. Glad she was within arm's reach.

The physical draw between them wasn't a mistake or a misfire. She might not trust it, but she could use it here to distract him. To distract them both.

"Oh . . . kay." The word was taffy. Stretchy, uncertain. With maybe the smallest hint of arousal. "What are you doing, then?"

Ever so subtly, his tone had shifted, become rough in a way that had nothing to do with grumpiness and everything to do with sexiness.

Which was all the encouragement she needed to set her hands on the arms of his chair, bringing her face to within inches of his. The air between them and around them almost hummed. There were so many reasons not to take this any further . . . but on the other hand, there was the shape of Will's mouth.

It was a crooked finger and a green light and a get-out-of-jail-free card, and for the moment, that was enough.

She brushed her lips over his. It was less a kiss than a glancing touch, and like a meteor, it left fire in its wake. Nic rocked back on her heels. She wanted to touch her mouth, to test whether he'd singed her, but she didn't trust herself to move her hands—because she'd end up touching him next. Her grip kept her anchored on the right side of her resolution to give herself more time to heal after Brian.

But there was a lot of land on this side of the road. The side where she and Will could distract each other.

So she kissed him again, properly this time. Prolonging the contact for more than two seconds. Letting herself experience him.

And it was—wonderful. Somehow, his mouth forgot to be grumpy, and it was soft instead. When her lips parted slightly, really took hold of his and staked a claim, he tasted like beer and velvety night air.

Nic hadn't wanted to know Will ached like she did. She hadn't wanted to know what his skin smelled like. She hadn't wanted any of this knowledge. But she had it now, and it was multiplying inside her, pushing roots into her heart.

She could water them and give them sun to see whether they could bloom. Or she could take this one little thing, for her and for him, and hope that it would be enough.

Will cupped her jaw, changing the angle of his head so that he could really kiss her, and the slide of his tongue against hers sent Nic's pulse into a frenzy. His other hand settled on her waist, urging her forward. She was certain that if she let him herd her into his lap, whatever happened next would be warm and amazing.

But this wasn't about that. It certainly wasn't about whatever yearning was sparking in her heart. She was in a no-yearning zone.

She put a few inches between them and tried to find the coy, playful space again. It was safer. "So?"

"Well, I'm not thinking about my terrible day." He flexed his fingers into her hip, and it was all Nic could do not to whimper.

She had to get on firmer footing here and corral whatever pesky feelings she was having. Feelings were what messed everything up. They needed to just . . . not feel . . . together.

"But you're still thinking?" she asked.

"Not sure how to stop that."

Time was so funny. The two hours in which Nic had made dinner, eaten it, cleaned the kitchen, folded laundry, poured herself another iced tea, and sat on her porch—those hours had passed in a flash. Nic couldn't remember a thing about them except that they had passed, must have passed, because she was here.

The moment when she stood, inches from Will, contemplating the halo of light on his hair and lips? Well, that was never ending.

He raised his chin, almost in slow motion, until his mouth could reach her. *"Nic."*

Will had never called her that before. Every other time had been *Nicole,* as if he were giving her a diploma. That *Nic* was more intimate than his tongue on her neck. Than the heat pouring off him, enticing her to curl up in his lap. Than the way she moaned—actually *moaned*— as he did beautiful things to her throat and the underside of her chin and her collarbone.

It was the shards of her heart, rasping even now against her sternum, that kept her hands on the arms of the chair and her feet on the ground.

She had made such bad and destructive choices. Like . . . the most bad. The most destructive. Nic had spent years dating a sociopath. Her best friend wasn't even speaking to her. She had proven that she couldn't be trusted, not even by herself. Especially not by herself.

No, she had to get out of this, this erotic fever dream, somehow and go back across the street to her house. Her house forty feet from his. Her house where she'd have to see him every day.

What on earth had she done? She was supposed to be avoiding arrogant men, avoiding men altogether, not making out with them.

Gently, she pulled away. Every bit of her body resented it, but, well, it wasn't in charge.

She took a few shaky steps backward.

Will's posture now was somehow both boneless and authoritarian. Zeus reclining on his throne would look like this. He set a hand over his mouth. Those long fingers of his drummed on his face absently while he watched her.

"Yeah, that worked." And there it was: amusement. Awe. Everything she'd wanted to give him.

That gave her the confidence to turn without a backward glance and to say, "Well, good night then."

She walked home feeling foolish but much less alone.

# CHAPTER 9

It was harder than Will would've thought to avoid his neighbor. Since that night, a melody of her name had been playing in his head: *Nic, Nic, Nic, Nic.*

If he lived to be a hundred, he'd never forget her strolling across his porch. The scent of her skin. The warmth of her mouth. The sounds she'd made as he'd kissed her.

Holy shit. Just . . . holy shit.

Will stopped his car at the corner near their block and stayed there for much longer than normal while he surveyed her yard, her windows. When he didn't see any movement or light, he inched down the street warily. What the hell was he going to say to her when his attempts to hide failed?

All he could do—beyond this ridiculous camouflaged-spy routine—was wait to see how she wanted to play it so he could take her lead. She was a lightning strike, and he was the old oak she'd singed. Days later, he was afraid that he might actually incinerate when they made eye contact again. *Poof,* from a single glance.

He'd never been the kind of man to need a "don't fool around with your neighbors" rule. He'd never really fooled around with anyone.

He'd always thought he would marry his high school girlfriend, Cecily, but she'd left him in college for greener pastures, and, based on the Christmas cards he still got every year, she was happier for it.

Then there had been Sarah, the chemistry teacher at the high school, but the fact that he couldn't take off for long vacations in the summer had grated and eventually broken them. The last few years, as the demands of his practice had grown, he'd just stopped dating.

He clearly needed to reconsider his position on dating because kissing Nic had been an entirely other thing—BASE jumping off a skyscraper, maybe—from what he remembered.

No, that was silly. It had been only a kiss, but it had seemed like . . . everything.

And since he wasn't certain how to navigate things with her without begging her for what she clearly didn't want—she'd been the one to leave him panting for more—he parked in the garage rather than the driveway and practically ran inside with his groceries because he didn't know how to do this. How to navigate this next step without making himself look ridiculous.

Instead of knocking on Nic's door, he picked up his phone and made the hard calls. He accepted Marsha's resignation, and then he phoned Kim and told her that he'd have to reduce her hours. Marsha had asked why he was calling, had said that she already considered the matter done and dusted. Kim was understanding, but he could hear the tightness in her voice, could almost hear her calculating her monthly expenses and how much this would cost her. He hoped he'd be able to make it up to her someday.

Then, he called his trustee at the bank and begged for mercy.

Will had never thought of himself as a proud man. Or at least not as a man with undue pride. He scoffed at those kinds of men, at the Lukes of the world, and even at the men like his dad who deferred to those guys. Who assumed that nice cars and fancy suits and the stuck-up attitude that sometimes came with them actually made someone better than their more modest, threadbare, lower-paid counterparts. The Wills.

But saying to the person at the bank that he didn't have the money to cover next month's mortgage payment was goddamn humbling. It made him want to vacate his body. Or, barring that, move to Casablanca, open a bar, and say cynical, cutting things to Nazis.

Instead, when he called the bank, he had to discuss the details of his cash flow problem with someone named Frank who was so kind, it made Will's eyes sting while he dug through a bunch of paperwork and flayed his soul via spreadsheets.

Afterward, Will set down the phone and stared at it.

He had another call to deal with. And it was going to be even harder.

The idea had started when he scheduled an early visit to the dentist. He knew he ought to get some of that stuff done while he still had insurance. Like maybe also taking advantage of his phone-counseling options while he could.

If he didn't want to talk to his family—and he didn't—and he didn't want to talk to his friends from vet school—and he didn't—and he didn't feel as if he could let Nic in any more than he already had, was he going to stay coiled and wary his whole damn life?

A few weeks before, he would have said yes. But now, he was tired. So tired his joints ached with it. He didn't even have to talk to anyone at first, just fill out a form.

His cursor hovered over the radio button next to the word *depression* for a bit, though. He clicked it and then submitted the form in a rush, before his pride could swell up and stop him.

He was depressed. He was. As a scientist, there were truths he couldn't deny, and this was one of them.

So then Will sat in his living room, staring at his phone and trying not to hurl. He answered midway through the first ring, which made him feel clumsy and too anxious, except you didn't have to try to impress your therapist, did you?

When the session ended and Will stumbled to the window with a glass of water—who knew that a conversation could feel as exhausting as a half marathon—across the street was Nic, right there in the front of her house, watering her flowers. She wore a cutoff jean skirt and an orange T-shirt sporting a prominent bleach stain.

She was the most beautiful thing he'd ever seen. And the kiss, it was going to haunt them. Or haunt him, at least.

Just . . . how?

And also . . . why?

Will almost kept hiding. It would have been easy to go into the kitchen and heat up something in a box and then slink back to his room.

But later on, he knew that he'd been simply too tired to resist the pull of her. For whatever reason, they'd shared something. And he didn't want to avoid her any longer. If he could call the bank, if he could talk to a therapist, he could talk to Nic.

Will steeled himself, opened the door, jogged across the street, and said, "Hey."

Brilliant, absolutely freaking brilliant.

She gave him a casual smile over her shoulder. "Haven't seen you lately."

"Um, I . . . yeah."

"Been busy?"

How was it possible for her to be so cool? She wasn't even looking at him, just spraying the pansies she'd planted at some point, flashes of yellow and purple in between the bushes and decorative grasses, like they hadn't made out like horny teenagers a few days prior.

"Sort of." He didn't want to get into how he'd spent the last several days. For everything that he'd revealed to her, and he'd been far more direct with her than he had been with, say, his parents, he hadn't gotten into the truly humiliating details, and he didn't want to.

Those were between himself and Frank. You know, the really key relationships in his life.

"Save lots of dogs and cats?" she asked.

"A few."

"No chickens?"

"Not a one."

Then she giggled and beckoned him closer. This had not been how he'd imagined this going.

What was she thinking? He hadn't a clue. Between everything that had happened, he felt like he'd spent all day in the sun without a sip of water.

He stopped about six feet from her. "How . . . are you?" he asked quizzically.

She turned off the sprayer and brushed her hair back from her face with an elegant sweep of one hand. "Stop being weird," she instructed.

"I'm not—" He was. "Okay. I'll work on that."

"It happened." Something hot crept into her expression, and he recognized that flesh memory in the deepest part of himself. She'd pulled away from him much, much too soon. Nic gave herself a little shake, but he had no intention of dismissing the sensation. It was keeping him going through everything else.

"It happened," she repeated before giving a little shrug.

She was obviously saying it had been a one-time deal—and he knew that he was lucky to have gotten a one-time deal.

He tried not to feel disappointed. He had so many other things to be disappointed about.

"Thanks," he said. "For clearing the air like this. I had been feeling weird." That was the mildest way to put it.

"I could tell, and you're welcome. But we're better off as friends, like we said before." She beamed, and it was as shiny and fake as a used-car ad.

He could take comfort from the fact that she didn't seem any more convinced by this explanation than he did, but all the same, he attempted to change the subject. "How's your hen?"

"The egg-bound one or the escape artist?"

"Both, I guess."

"Good." When she smiled now, he could tell it was real. While he didn't get it, would never share it, she really did love her chickens. Whatever else was or wasn't true about her career, she did legitimately like chickens. "All the girls are good."

"The girls?"

"The ladies. The team. Charlie's Angels. They have different names, identities."

"Hashtag squad goals?"

"Oh, totally."

"I should get back." He had a lot of things to accomplish—so much stressing to do. "But I saw you and wanted to—"

"Stop avoiding me?"

"Something like that."

Then he made himself scarce before he could do anything stupid. Such as touching her.

# CHAPTER 10

Nic tapped her fingernails on the steering wheel of her car, pondering the Knights of Columbus Hall across the parking lot. Inside, BROODY was expecting her.

On the one hand, she loved chicken people.

But on the other, she'd grown accustomed to loving them virtually.

Behind her monitor or phone, she could choose her words carefully, editing and rewriting until they were perfect. There, if someone mentioned Brian, she could at least cringe privately before tossing her hair and pretending that it hadn't bothered her at all. *Brian who?* was one of those things she wasn't going to be able to pull off in person. She wasn't nearly a good enough actress, and her skills were rusty.

For half an instant, she almost stayed in the car. She almost drove home. She had a chicken community safe on the web. She didn't need to add to it.

The problem, of course, was Will. He'd sent BROODY to Nic. He'd sensed that she needed people, and so he'd found a way to get her some.

Stiffly, almost grudgingly, Nic climbed out of the car and crossed to the door. The bulletin board in the vestibule was covered with sherbet-toned fliers. Obviously the place was a de facto community center, with bingo and spaghetti dinners and scouting meetings scheduled almost every night.

Through the second set of doors, someone laughed. Real, in-person, honest-to-gosh belly laughter. The years with Brian had been loud and they had been long, but they hadn't been funny. Meanly amusing, maybe, but there hadn't been much in the way of sincere joy in her life in so long.

Nic followed the joy.

A group of about half a dozen people sat in a loose ring of plastic folding chairs. The person laughing was a middle-aged woman whose curly blonde-gray hair danced down her back, curls springing up this way and that. When she glanced toward Nic, her expression was warm but still distracted, still wrapped up in whatever had been funny. But then she truly got a look at Nic. She started, and a different kind of smile, less familiar and more welcoming, broke over her face.

"It's you!"

"It's me." Nic waved to the group. "Hi, I'm—"

Everyone shouted her name, and—it was a lot. Good yet numbing, like jumping into a pool right as dawn was breaking. Refreshing, but also a bit of a shock.

They invited Nic to sit, and they offered her iced tea and cookies, and someone complimented her shoes. Richard, Gwen, Nevaeh, Arnold, and Emily introduced themselves. While some of the BROODY members were laconic, reserved, Arnold was almost bouncing out of his chair.

*Why? Why me?* Nic wanted to ask.

But even worse was, once the introductions were done, Nic could only look back at the group, wide eyed and expectant, and wish she'd never come in. She had no idea what they wanted from her. The last time she'd done this, she'd had a topic. She'd had a PowerPoint, for crying out loud. Also, she'd driven across three counties for that meeting, and there hadn't been any potential for ongoing friendships or relationships. This made her want to vacate her body.

"Um, is this all of you?" she asked. "The entire . . . brood?"

"It's fallen off a bit in the last few months as people have gotten the hang of it," Carolyn said. "After they hatched."

Arnold nodded. "We had a big group for our virtual beginners' classes, during the pandemic. Have you met Helen yet? At the feedstore?"

"No, but I'll have to go soon."

"Well, Helen is the best. She got 'em all outfitted, and then we taught them what to do. I've been keeping chickens for thirty years."

That ought to show Will. Arnold wasn't jumping on some bandwagon because Nic had made chickens so irresistible.

But even still, Will's words echoed in her ears. "And how did the newbies get on?"

"Better than you might expect. Everyone gets a little tetchy once the chicks start chafing at the brooder but before they're ready for the coop, of course."

One of the first videos of Nic's that went viral had featured one chick after another leaping up to the edge of the box she'd been using as a brooder, then hopping down and wrecking the bathroom where she'd been keeping them. She'd marveled at the view count slowly clicking up while she'd used an old toothbrush to scrub the desiccated poop out from between the bathroom tiles. Her phone, a tripod, a little editing, and some cute animals, and millions of people were eating out of the palm of her hand.

"Chicks play the long game." To put it mildly. The chicks themselves were adorable, until the novelty wore off for you and for them and they tired of the brooder and made a mess of wherever you had them. Then there could be a six-month-long drought after they'd moved outside before the magical first egg appeared and made all the months of raising them and feeding them worth it.

But speaking of worth it: "Dr. Lund—" Nic didn't want to use his first name with strangers somehow. It seemed too intimate. It wasn't as if anyone in town needed to know what had happened on his dark porch. "He said that there were some problems."

"You can't let him bother you." Nevaeh shook her head. "He'd find a storm cloud in the desert."

If Will was pessimistic—okay, so he *was*, there was no use denying that—it was with good reason. Besides, his clouds seemed to be clearing, or at least getting less stormy.

So rather than laugh at him, Nic just said, "He always puts the well-being of the animals first."

"And we love him for it, but the man doesn't appreciate chickens."

Nic certainly couldn't argue with that. "So, beyond your beginners' class, what does BROODY do?"

Chicken groups had varying levels of formality. The truth was that chickens weren't that hard. The people Nic knew who had dogs spent much more time taking care of them than any established flock took up, at least if you weren't constantly trying to generate content. It was the social media side of Chickens for All that ate up so much of Nic's time, not the flock itself.

Carolyn and the others explained how BROODY had started in order to lobby the city council to allow poultry licenses within the city limits.

"We were birthed in the crucible of politics." Except Richard didn't seem to be joking, not even a little bit, and Nic wasn't certain whether that meant that Yagerstown's city hall was unusually cutthroat or whether Richard described everything in such terms.

But since they'd achieved that first goal, things had lightened up. They told Nic how the folks in the country—a line that seemed porous to her since the town's development was sparse at best—who could have roosters and hence could hatch their own chicks would sell or trade them to the rest.

"Heritage breeds, you know," Arnold said, growing animated. "Hedemoras! Tolbunt Polish hens!"

"Hey, I'll take a Tolbunt chick next year." Nic had always coveted a hen with the distinctive dramatic crest and feathers speckled cream, gold, and black. They resembled nothing so much as fashionable Muppets: beautiful but somehow also ridiculous.

"Done!"

She suspected that whatever she might ask Arnold for, he'd find a way to get it for her. It made her heart stumble in her chest to know there were people who'd never met her before but who, for whatever reason, *liked* her.

"We just can't believe you're here," Carolyn said in a fake whisper. "A real celebrity. A real chicken celebrity." As if that were the realest kind of celebrity.

Nic tried to demur. "I'm not really famous. I just make videos."

"But they're terrific videos! You give out such great information. You're the best advocate for our movement on the internet."

"I—thank you. I want to say, though, that I've been . . . reevaluating. And some of the folks I knew in the past, who helped me, promoted me, some of them dabble in a—a language that, now that I have some distance, I can see is wrong. I always knew it, I know—I'm babbling. I just—I'm not sure that I've always been a good face for chickens."

Right behind her eyes, a bubble of pressure kept expanding, filling with her regrets and her feelings and her inadequacies. It kept growing while she talked, and it felt as if Nic's head was about to burst from it—or it might push all her unshed tears out in a great rush.

Across the circle of chairs, Carolyn looked alarmed, Arnold mad, and everyone else uncomfortable.

"Do you mean that Brian person?"

"Yes. He . . . he was not a good face for the backyard-chicken movement. For any movement." Chickens were bound up for Nic with the memories of her granny, with romantic notions about knowing where your food came from and trying to find balance in modern life, and with fun—because chickens were ridiculously persistent prehistoric beasts under the feathers and the mealworm addiction. Nic should never have let Brian anywhere near them.

"He was a mealymouthed snake oil salesman." It was clear from Richard's tone that *mealymouthed snake oil salesman* was the strongest phrase in his vocabulary. "We couldn't believe he did that to you. To *you*."

Oh gosh, they'd talked about it. Nic wanted a trapdoor in the floor to open and deposit her deep beneath the crust of the earth. "I appreciate that, but I'm still sorry for my misjudgment."

Carolyn's expression was flabbergasted. "You don't need to apologize. You wanted to believe the best of him, and he let you down. He ought to apologize."

There was a better chance of a McDonald's opening on the moon. "That's nice of you to say."

"Anytime." Carolyn gave an airy wave of her hand. "And isn't it nice to cut the deadweight loose? Like a long overdue haircut. More tea?"

That was when Nic decided that she really might be able to love BROODY. Might be able to love Yagerstown. She'd come here to hide, in some ways. She'd been so focused on the moment of flight that she hadn't thought about the life that came afterward.

Now, she had the space to do just that. To believe that maybe, maybe she was free of Brian, and she could think for the first time about normal life. And the person who was giving that to her was, bizarrely, the neighbor who couldn't stand chickens: Will Lund.

How, in just a few weeks, had he become the person she could share her deepest fears with? How had he seen that she needed a wider circle of people and then connected her to them?

She didn't want to let the spark of it, the promise of it, make her heart light.

But it did.

As Nic walked to her car half an hour later, a woman about Nic's age jogged across the parking lot toward her. She had a long red braid and a sweetheart-shaped face that immediately reminded Nic of Anne of Green Gables.

"Hey, so I'm Emily Babbit," she said, which of course she'd mentioned forty-five minutes earlier. "And we . . . know each other."

Nic was stumped. "We do?"

"Yeah, I'm a forum moderator at Chickens for All. I'm BabInTheWoods."

If a tremor had jolted the ground, Nic wouldn't have been surprised. That was the name of one of the oldest, most involved members of Nic's community. *This* was BabInTheWoods?

But other than knowing that Bab lived in rural Virginia and used she/her pronouns, what did Nic know about BabInTheWoods?

Well, Nic knew that she loved homesteading and heritage breeds. That she thought show chickens were ridiculous. That she preferred oystershell grit to flint grit, and she mixed oats in with her grain pellets.

Okay, Nic knew her pretty well.

"Oh my gosh, it's so nice to meet you." Nic shook Emily's hand again as if she hadn't already done that and then felt doubly foolish.

"There's no reason you would've known," Emily said quickly, apologetically. "I never post selfies. And I should have said something when you came in, but I didn't want to because I didn't want to come across as a fan—not that I'm not a fan, but I didn't want you to think I was, like, a stalker. You know, as if you had walked into some *Misery* reboot? Anyhow, I didn't want you to think I was going to *Misery* you. Wait, does that make sense as a verb?"

In the silence following her question, Emily blinked, processing what she'd just said. She slapped herself on the forehead. "Oh God. This is why I didn't want to say anything. I am sorry for my deep and abiding awkwardness. I just don't know how to be cool meeting one of my . . . idols. Which I also should have kept to myself. Right. Awesome verbal diarrhea, Emily. Which you're totally fixing by comparing it to intestinal distress."

Nic wanted to laugh, and she wanted to commiserate. "You know," she said conspiratorially, "I think pretty much every Stephen King title can be used as a verb. To *Shining*."

Emily stopped hiding her face. A beat passed, then she picked up Nic's joke. "To . . . *Carrie*."

"To *Pet Sematary*."

"Oh no, not that one. It's too scary to contemplate." Emily bit her lip. "Can we start over?"

"One hundred percent."

"I'm Emily Babbit."

"Nic Jones."

They shook for the third time, and it took everything Nic had not to spit out, *I think we're going to be really good friends.*

"Will you think *I'm* creepy," Nic said instead, "if I ask if you'd like to have coffee?"

"I would *love* that."

Nic suspected they both would.

# CHAPTER 11

When the email appeared, it was the least surprising thing in the world. Just as you might expect to get boatloads of candy on Halloween or spill coffee down your shirt first thing Monday morning, of course Brian was going to crawl back into her life. Of course he was going to try to rope Nic into some ridiculous and humiliating public scheme in the process. Of freaking course he was going to make it all about him.

The subject line read, Comment on Brian's quotes? (READ BEFORE YOU DELETE).

It came from Nic's virtual assistant, Lylia. And it was only out of respect for all the hard work that Lylia had done for her that Nic didn't immediately trash it.

> I know you're going to hate this, but really, it's an opportunity. Are you thinking that now? Are you focusing on the word OPPORTUNITY?
>
> Okay, here we go: do you want to comment on a story about Brian talking about you in his latest episode? I totally get why you didn't want to six weeks ago, but you have to discuss it at some

point, and the reporter is reasonable and not on Brian's side.

Get back to me ASAP.

"Arggg." And, when that didn't seem like enough, Nic shouted at the computer, "He stinks worse than rotting asparagus. There's my comment."

But she was going to need something stronger. And not *he's a fucking asshole* either. The truth was that Lylia was right. There was no way she could maintain any sort of public persona and refuse to talk about Brian forever.

She'd tried. After she'd left, after she moved across the country and said not a single word about him. She'd hoped he'd grown bored, but it sounded as if he'd merely switched tactics.

"This is low even for you," she muttered as she opened an incognito browser window and pressed play.

Brian didn't look good. That was her first, admittedly bitchy, thought. He was sallow, his eyes shadowed and his cheeks hollowed. He did his normal opening, his patter for likes and subscribes, but the real subject of the video was ostensibly testing kitchen hacks. Except he was using each as an excuse to subtly or not-so-subtly shade the people whose content he was mocking.

Nic's stomach curdled, and she felt green. How had she ever convinced herself that she loved this man? How had her best friend chosen to believe this—this *jerk* over her?

Then he arrived at the only thing she wanted to hear: what precisely he was going to say about her.

"Finally, some of you have been asking about Nic Jones." This was probably a lie. His fans, all fans, tended to bring up only whatever was most recent, and at this point, she was ancient news.

"The truth is, I'm worried about Nic," Brian said. "I've tried to reach out, but she won't talk to me." That was a horrid lie. He'd never once attempted to call or email.

"Despite everything she did, I still really care about Nic. Always will. Which is why I need your help. If you know her, reach out. Let her know that you're concerned about her and you want her to get the help she needs. She hides it well, but she's hurting."

That bulging pustule of a man.

Nic was shaking now, her fingernails actually clattering on her laptop. She couldn't decide whether she was more livid or angry. Maybe with shades of rage, furiousness, and fear.

He was concern trolling her. Aggressively. She wouldn't put it past his fans to find out where she lived and sic social services on her. Or even a SWAT team. The risk here was real to her, but also to everyone at Chickens for All and everyone Nic cared about online and in real life.

The adrenaline tasted metallic in her mouth, but she told herself not to be scared. That was what Brian wanted. He wanted to terrify her. It was working.

She snapped her computer shut and picked up her phone. Her palms had gone so sweaty, she almost dropped it while calling Lylia.

"Can you believe this?" she demanded.

"Sadly, I've seen your inbox, so I can. This is why I even passed the request along. Nic, you don't pay me for strategy, but you need to say something. Brian is carving you up like a Thanksgiving turkey here and feeding you to the wolves."

Nic might even need to consider having a security system put in. Brian had handled all that stuff before, which suddenly seemed incredibly menacing. He hadn't taught her how to protect herself in the world he'd dragged her into.

But something else nagged. "He's carving up a lot of other people too." And when she'd been with him, she'd done that, too—or at least had let him do it.

Had she been a . . . mean girl?

But Lylia didn't let her get the question in. "And those people can't hit back like you can because right now, everyone will talk to you. You can play some defense here and really make a difference, not just in how he talks about you but with his place in the ecosystem."

"Everyone's lodged interview requests? Like who?"

"Like the legacy press."

"Newspapers care?" It was always curious what stayed within the community and what spilled out into the wider world.

"Yes! Sometimes I think you don't get how big you are."

Nic had never felt less big.

But one problem at a time. First, she had to try to thwart the mob.

"So this reporter you like, tell me about him." Not that the details mattered. Brian had succeeded in forcing the issue.

After Lylia finished, Nic sighed. "Okay. I'll talk to him. Briefly. Not about the breakup. Just about the move, and I'll give him . . . I dunno, something. Something small." She could try to include something about how Brian was being weird with some patter about her hens. That ought to work.

"Good. Good. You're making the right call."

She certainly hoped so. And if she were, it would be the first time in a long time that that was true.

So Nic grabbed another bowl of eggs out of the fridge and went to get a second opinion.

# CHAPTER 12

Will had been trying to nap on the couch, a skill that seemed crucial to all the men in his life. His grandfathers, his uncles, his father: weekend afternoons, they watched some kind of sports and napped in the living room.

But just as Will was apparently bad at running his business, he was apparently bad at napping, because he couldn't fall asleep. The things he ought to do, the things he probably shouldn't have done, his mistakes and miscalculations galloped through his brain and made him twitchy.

Right when he'd given up on finding the peace required to sleep, a knock sounded on his door. There, looking distraught, her bun half falling down and a mixing bowl filled with eggs in her hands, was Nic. She was trying to smile, but her eyes were as unsettled as Will felt.

"I thought you could use some more." She thrust the bowl at him.

"Thanks . . . neighbor."

Beyond that, Will was at a loss. What did you say to the woman with whom you'd shared the most intense kiss of your life, who you still thought was a menace, but who was also kind of your friend? Especially when she was palpably in need of . . . something? How did you find and provide it?

"I'm bringing you these eggs in the spirit of our close friendship. This is an exchange. I'm going to give you these, and you're going to tell me the truth."

None of this made any sense. "Okay."

"Am I a bad person?"

Will literally rocked back on his heels. "Are you a *what*?"

"I'm buying your honesty with eggs, remember. So give it to me straight."

"Why are you asking me this? What happened?"

She watched him, seemingly trying to decide something. "You know my ex, Brian?"

"Uh-huh." Will knew that her ex was always doing all those ridiculous internet challenges. He'd crop up on Nic's videos sometimes, and she tended to treat him like a visiting dignitary.

It didn't make any sense to Will. Even though Will had been a jerk about Nic's knowledge about chickens, she had expertise. She offered something of value to her viewers. In contrast, her ex just made jokes. How that was entertaining, Will would never know.

"You've seen his videos?"

"A couple." Not nearly as many as Will had of hers.

"Well, then you know Brian can be . . . cruel."

"Yes." The guy had seemed smarmy and glib and sneering and mean, and that wasn't just Will's jealousy.

"I was with him for years. Years. So what's the difference between him and me?"

Will wasn't going to pretend that he didn't know what Nic meant, because at least some of why he'd assumed she would be awful was because of her ex. He couldn't pat her on the shoulder and tell her it didn't matter when it had mattered a lot to him.

Nic watched him levelly with those mesmerizing brown eyes of hers, and when he didn't answer, she asked, "What's the verdict?"

"I've watched—and I can't believe I'm admitting this—almost all of your stuff. And you weren't that way."

For a second, it looked as if she wanted to laugh. "We will circle back around to this revelation at some point. I'm going to demand you make several top-ten lists of all your favorite moments. Maybe a mood board of the best Chick Nic looks." She went serious again. "But Brian's latest video tries to get his fans riled up about me, saying I need an 'intervention.' It's such a jerk move, but it's typical for him. So even if I wasn't actively being an asshole, in those years I could've been one through osmosis."

"But you weren't. You left—"

"I was dumped."

"—and I respect the hell out of you for it."

"You respect me?" This seemed to amuse her.

Without any humor or irony, he said, "Yes, I do."

"Hmm."

He hadn't convinced her, but she didn't look as if one of her chickens had run away anymore.

For about the millionth time, he wished he could touch her. But Nic had made it clear that while she'd wanted to distract him that one night, it wasn't something she wanted to repeat. Except she'd come to him when she was upset, and that was enough to make him a little light headed. If she wouldn't let him distract her in the fun way, he could at least be her friend.

"Do you want a beer? An iced tea? We could sit on the porch." He wasn't certain what she was going to say. He wasn't certain what he wanted her to say. If she didn't want him, he'd probably be better off keeping her at arm's length—but he'd prefer if she could just want him.

She flashed a seductive smile. "I don't think I can be trusted on your porch."

"I'm pretty confident I can fight you off."

"Okay, then. I'll take a beer."

He ushered her through the house, suddenly self-conscious about his furniture—too much lingering IKEA?—and when he'd vacuumed last. "The porch is through there."

When he joined her outside, she'd chosen the swing. Not wanting to think about why he took the cushion next to her and not his typical chair, Will handed her a bottle.

"So what are you up to?" she asked.

"Trying to nap."

"Trying to nap? How do you *try* to nap? Don't you lie down and fall asleep?"

"Got some things on my mind."

"Such as?"

He could make something up, but he didn't want to be dishonest with her about this any more than he wanted to lie to her about her culpability for her ex's behavior.

"Well, my new friend Frank at the bank hasn't decided whether to save my ass yet."

Nic took a sip from her beer, and he was curious how she'd answer. As always, stuff just seemed to slip out of his mouth around her.

"I'd guess there's paperwork involved," she said at last. "Red tape and all that. What did you expect? Magic?"

He could've kissed her for trying to make a joke. "That kind of makes it even more depressing. My entire career comes down to a few sheets of paper."

"If it helps, it's probably a fuck-ton of paper."

He had to laugh then. Because it was funny. Because it shouldn't make him feel better, but it did. Because she was trying as hard as he had to . . . comfort. It was like trying to break in a new pair of jeans: awkward but worth it.

"So," she said, entirely too nonchalantly and clearly trying to change the subject, "what was your favorite Chick Nic episode?"

"We can't let this go?"

"We cannot. Spill it, Lund."

"Damn." His honest answer was—all of them. She was gorgeous and funny and compelling. There was a reason he hadn't been able to stop watching even when he thought he couldn't stand her. "I like the funny ones. The chickens running away from the soccer ball with the *Raiders of the Lost Ark* soundtrack playing, that was a good one." He'd actually sent it to Marsha.

"You have good taste. That went viral and was on some late-night television shows."

"I like all the breed-background ones too." He'd had no idea how many different kinds of chickens there were.

"But you don't like chickens. So why did you keep watching?"

"You know why." He kept his eyes on her face so that she wouldn't doubt what he meant.

A slight blush painted over her cheeks. "Okay. Except I'm not that pretty."

"Sure you are. But also you have so much passion for chickens. It's . . . infectious."

"That sounds like a bad thing. 'Sorry, ma'am, you've come down with a bad case of backyard-chicken pox.'"

She did a pretty good impression of him, and he almost pinched her . . . but it wouldn't stop with pinching her, so he kept his hands to himself.

"It feels like you're giving something back to people," he said. "You know a lot, and it shows."

"Hidden knowledge. Secret knowledge. That's what chickens have always felt like to me."

"How did you get into chickens anyhow?"

The smile she gave him in response to this question felt so fucking *real*, as if he'd said a magical phrase and unlocked something. She slipped off her flip-flops, pulled her knees up to her chest, and rotated so that she could face him. "Well, that's easy. From my granny, Ida Mae Reston. She grew up here."

Will had to tear his attention from her toenails—which were painted the same shade of pink as ballet slippers—to process what Nic was saying. "From Yagerstown?"

"Yeah. It would've been eighty or ninety years ago. They moved away when she was a teenager, but it was the background to all her good childhood stories. It sounded like this . . . I don't know, *paradise* is too strong a word, but it seemed like a place where I would be, could be, happy."

He wanted that for her. If this was the place where he was striking out, maybe it could be the place where she could shine.

But then again, Will sort of suspected she could shine anywhere.

"I hope it will be."

"Me too. But yes, the chickens are from her. She kept them her whole life. Even when it wasn't trendy." She gave him a rueful look, and he rolled his eyes. "Fair enough, chickens are hip, and I'm just a fake. For some people, though, this isn't about the perfect shot or a brand or whatever. And my granny was one of those people."

That was as much as Will could take. He set his free hand on her ankle. Even when they'd kissed, he'd barely touched her. Her skin was soft and warm, and he was acutely aware of the structure beneath. He'd never found a lateral malleolus sexy before, but because this one belonged to Nic, he did.

She'd tied one of those old-fashioned friendship bracelets around her ankle. It had probably been vivid green and blue at some point, but it had faded from being washed in the shower. He'd never been jealous of some colored thread in his life.

Holding her gaze, making sure she was okay with him touching her, he ran his thumb under the bracelet. If the contact had been up her shirt or under her shorts, it couldn't have been more intimate. Nic's breath caught in her mouth, and he could see her pulse elevate in her neck. He did it again, and he would've sworn they breathed in unison.

It wasn't 1895. An ankle wasn't supposed to have him panting. Nic could pretend all she wanted, and he would take his cues from her, but they weren't friends. Friends didn't go wild at a casual touch. Friends didn't want to casually touch each other into next week.

"Nic," he managed, though his voice sounded as if it were being dragged out of his solar plexus, "you're one of those people."

"Am I?"

"Yup. You're amazing. That's why I couldn't stop watching."

"That's the nicest thing you've said to me."

If she'd let him, he'd get better at saying nice things. He'd turn into a goddamn poet for her.

But for now—well, he stroked her ankle one more time, and then he took his hand back. She was going to have to ask for more if that was what she wanted.

He took a long pull from his beer and tried to think cold, calm thoughts. Fjords. Polar ice caps. Nic's elevated breathing didn't help a thing.

But when he'd relocated his brain, he told her, "You don't have to keep bringing me eggs, you know. You can just come over."

"But I have all these eggs."

"You're enough by yourself."

And that seemed to stun them both, so they left it there.

# CHAPTER 13

Lylia's reporter's story had appeared, painting Nic as reasonable and Brian as the vaguely creepy guy shouting at the sky, but Nic didn't feel better. It was walking on eggshells, waiting for the other shoe to drop, or some other cliché about fear and anticipation. Brian hadn't responded yet, but she knew that he would and that when it came, his reaction would be catastrophic.

All she could do was film new content and take care of her chickens. She couldn't hide in the corner waiting for the inevitable awfulness she'd conjured by daring to hit back. At least she had one thing to distract her: trying not to think about Will.

Not thinking about how his biceps filled out his worn gray T-shirts, for example. Not thinking about how he tried to cheer her up without babying her or telling her not to feel the way she did. Not thinking about how cute he was when he attempted to downplay his own issues. Not thinking about how she'd left his porch feeling tingly and aroused, charged and frustrated, all at once because he'd briefly touched her ankle. Her fucking *ankle*.

But there was no point in lingering on those things. For reasons she still couldn't quite explain, she'd run here to Yagerstown. She couldn't make a big ole mess by having a fling with a neighbor before she'd even finished unpacking.

So she planted a garden instead: spread gravel over the coffee filters in the beds, then added the peat and the potting soil. Made little hollows and gingerly inserted the seedlings, their roots minuscule and fragile and so gosh-darn hopeful, it almost hurt to look at them.

The chickens watched these proceedings with naked interest.

"These aren't for you," she told them.

Mitzi pecked the ground as if to say *That's what you think*.

The garden might be located on the roof of the coop, outside the fence line, where the chickens couldn't easily reach them unless they broke out again . . . but that was a logistic problem.

Chickens were the best creatures in the world when you had unwanted insects. Nic had already seen them make quick work of several cockroaches—God, she hadn't considered the roaches when she'd decided to move south of the Mason-Dixon Line—but they were absolute murder on plants, especially newly sprouted ones. Forget a plague of locusts; a plague of chickens could make quick work of a green field.

Nic wasn't a serious gardener, and this project, which she'd been recording all the way along, was mostly for show. Some of her fans would be delighted if it got destroyed, actually. That would mean more content, different content.

It was an odd relationship to have with people.

Nic repositioned the tripod. The one sucky part of living alone was having to learn how to film by herself, but she took the last bit of footage she needed. Her hands were still dirty, she was certain her hair was a disaster, but that would add to the naturalism of it. Now she had to cobble it together, add graphics, schedule it to drop, make the social media teasers . . . and fifty other things.

She stowed her phone, gathered up the now empty soil bags and seedling trays, and carried the trash out to the bin, but on the street, apparently walking home after his run, was one very sweaty veterinarian.

"Dr. Lund." She focused on wiping the dirt from her hands and not on the way his shorts clung to his hips. "How are you?"

"Fine." That was more than accurate. "Planting things?"

"Just some herbs, which the girls will eat as soon as they can figure out how to get out of the coop. And they will, the cheeky buggers. So I've been wasting my time for the sake of content." In other words, Tuesday.

"At least you'd know where they went if they got out."

For a while, they stood there looking at each other. This was the place where real neighbors, ones who weren't caught in a web of lust and maybe liking, would say *All right then, have a nice day* and go their separate ways. But they were stuck in Hephaestus's net, and she had no idea how to get them out of it. How to get them to somewhere safe.

It was her own fault, she'd made this happen, but she was at a loss here. Why did he have to be so good looking? Why did he have to try to make her feel better?

In her yard, one of the girls gave a long, loud cry.

Will's attention snapped to the fence. "She okay?"

"That's an egg song. It means she laid an egg. Probably. There's always some guesswork involved. I don't see any hawks, though." Red-tailed hawks were the bane of chicken keepers everywhere. "You should come meet them. The girls."

It suddenly seemed vitally important that Will see this part of her life, and not just when it was going terribly because one of them had escaped or was almost dying. But when things were normal, with their best feet, or, um, hocks, forward.

But Will didn't budge when she started toward the gate. "Thank you, but I've already met two. Is that enough?"

Silly Will. Nic held out her hand. "That doesn't count. You were wet and mad in the first instance and in professional mode in the second. Come on."

He looked at her hand, which was still filthy, and then he said, "After you," and the words brushed down Nic's spine, setting her alight.

Without pondering the fire he tended to stoke in her, she swung the gate open and waved him into the yard. "Here they are. You know Mitzi."

The chicken in question, a gorgeous buff Orpington, was scratching at the ground, digging herself a dust bath. She looked up for a minute, comb flapping, and then went back to work as if Nic and Will bored her. Pretty much everything bored her that wasn't freeze-dried mealworms.

"The escape artist," Will noted dryly.

"And Camilla's still on her own." She marched back and forth in the isolation cage, seeming curious and annoyed and as if she expected the cage to disappear momentarily. In other words, precisely as she had done for the entire time she'd been in there.

"And then we have Dorcas." Nic pointed. "And that one is Hermes. There's Mal, short for Maleficent. Athena's next to her, and last but not least is Margaret Bourke-White."

They were a brick-hued Rhode Island Red, a variegated gold Ameraucana, a black-and-white-barred Plymouth Rock, a dazzling California White, and a fluffy Silkie, respectively. A kaleidoscope of colors and sizes. Nic was biased, sure, but they were incredibly lovely chickens. Almost objectively lovely chickens. Their beauty had been certified by the internet, and, of course, the internet was never wrong.

"It's different in person, I guess." He pointed to Margaret Bourke-White. "Like, you don't call her that normally, right?"

"I abso-freaking-lutely do."

MBW strutted right over to them, her plumage bouncing majestically. She was the only member of the flock who would voluntarily seek out humans who weren't holding food. Basically, she was a dog in poultry form.

"You ever petted a Silkie?" Nic asked.

"Nope."

"Well, you should." Nic crouched down. "Who's my pretty girl?"

MBW preened as if to say *I am!*

Will sank to his knees, and Nic tried to ignore how warm he was. How near he was. He stuck a finger through the fencing skeptically, and MBW cocked her head and edged closer, before deigning to allow him to stroke her. Then she leaned into the contact, and Nic tried not to be jealous.

"Holy cow." Will's smile was nova bright. It wasn't a smile that touched only his mouth or his eyes but something he did with his entire body, and Nic felt it in every cell of hers.

He ought to smile like that, sunshiny and unchecked, all the time, but it was probably good he didn't. Because if he kept looking at her like that, Nic would absolutely do something stupid, such as throwing her arms around him and kissing him and thus summoning the apocalypse in the process because she broke stuff. That was who she was.

"She's so soft." Nic had stopped staring at him, but the smile was in his voice. "But I still think you're lying about the names thing. When the cameras are off and I'm not here, you probably call them Bird One, Bird Two, and so on."

She snorted. "It's not as if they answer to their names. They're mostly for me."

"And the internet."

"Let me get some treats. They'll like you more if you feed them."

"I don't want them to like me."

"Of course you do."

She went inside and washed her hands quickly, returning with a few big handfuls of mealworms. "Get the gate for me."

He opened it, and they went in, where they were quickly surrounded.

"Here." Nic shoved her cupped hands at Will, who took a few pinches. "They'll peck harder than you're expecting, but—"

"I know chickens." He offered this with a wink, parroting her own line back at her. Then he squatted down, which did *amazing* things to his thighs, and the girls went to town.

"Hey now," he chided, moving his hands away from Mal, who could be very greedy. "Let your friend get some before you—I'm all out."

She laughed. "I'm not surprised. Here you go." Nic poured the rest into his hands.

As the flock continued to eat, he asked, "What's happening with your ex?"

That helped. It reminded her of why she ought to stay away from normal people. "Oh, I did an interview, trying to head off his attacks, but of course my inbox is flooded." She didn't think about what her mentions must look like.

"His fans, they bother you?"

"Only of course."

"Is that dangerous? Should you . . . get security?"

"I'm thinking of having a security system put in."

Will dusted his now empty hands together. He radiated anger. "Do people ever show up at your house?"

"Obviously, I've taken a lot of precautions over the years to avoid being doxed, but the truth is that when you put as much of your life online as I have, there are always risks."

She didn't want to think about them. Mostly, she succeeded in locking those worries away, but sometimes they flitted out, as if escaping from Pandora's box or something.

"Do you want to stay at my place?"

The idea was absurd—and so sweet it almost made her teeth hurt. "That is very kind, but no." She couldn't share a house with him. It would make bad decisions inevitable.

"You need my number. Please, it will make me feel better."

"Sure."

Right as she finished entering it into her phone, though, Will jumped up with a hissed "Son of a bitch." He turned and glared at Mal, who quirked her head at him inquiringly. "She bit my . . . rear. I'd like to file a complaint with the manager."

Nic couldn't help it. She threw her head back and laughed. "Sorry, that's the one downside of chickens."

"The one downside?"

"Yup. Your ass is just irresistible."

Will's eyes heated. "Is it?"

If Nic took a single step toward him, she knew that he would kiss her senseless, even here in this chicken yard filled with lawn dinosaurs with a taste for sweaty Spandex. His eyes promised that all she had to do was signal that she wanted to be more than friends, and he would be on board.

One of those **Danger!** signs flashed in her brain, right next to one reading **Yes!**

This felt so new, so scary, so impossible, and thus Nic did what she always did. She filled up the space with chickens.

"Here,"—she turned and scooped up MBW, who'd been nuzzling Nic's calf—"take her for a bit."

Will regarded the ball of floof in Nic's hands skeptically. "I'm—"

"In more desperate need of a cuddle chicken than anyone I've ever known."

He took the Silkie carefully, adjusting her until he had her nestled along one arm like a football. The hen instantly laid her head against his chest. "Aw, that's . . . that's not fair."

It struck Nic that it wasn't just her own chickens: every time Will saw animals, they were in distress. He didn't get the fun side at all.

He ran a finger down MBW's feathers. "I really can't believe she's so soft."

"The joy of Silkies. How's your butt?"

"Recovering." He sent Nic a burning look. "I'm going to get you back for that."

"One, I was not responsible. But two, I'd like to see you try."

*Don't make bets you don't want to pay out,* Granny had liked to say. But the problem was that Nic wanted, desperately, to pay out.

Which Will must have known, because he took a step toward her, and for all that his arms were filled with a chicken, he had naughty intent in his eyes. *"Nic."*

But before he could do anything, before he had touched Nic, Maleficent saved the day by nipping at his shoelaces, followed by the hair on his legs.

"This one," he said of MBW, "is okay. The rest remain nuisances."

The memory of his scowl—and the grin he'd broken into afterward—kept Nic smiling all day.

# CHAPTER 14

When his sister pulled into his driveway and hopped out of her car with a wave and a "Hiya," Will immediately panicked.

"Did I forget a dinner?" He gave Ella a half hug, careful to keep his distance since he was sticky from shooting baskets. These days, though, all it took to get clammy was stepping out of the AC. Sometimes he imagined what a humidity-free life might be like, on the coast or in a desert somewhere, but he probably wouldn't know what to do with himself if he didn't need two showers a day for half the year.

"Nah, Luke begged off this week. I wanted to grab your edger."

Will was relatively certain Ella had her very own edger, as their father seemed to think power and yard tools were the perfect solution to all holiday gift needs. But that meant this visit had an ulterior motive.

"I could've dropped it off," he said.

"But that's all you would have done." Meaning that he wouldn't have stayed to chat.

Ella's expression wasn't open to any bullshit, but he tried it anyhow.

"How's Hannah's soccer team doing?"

"You'd know if you were coaching."

He'd ducked out because he knew coaching meant lots of chatting, so he would have inevitably faced a lot of well-meaning questions about how things were going. He felt bad, and he missed the girls, but he'd put in his time. He had coached for two years when he didn't even have a kid; he deserved a break—which was pure rationalization.

"I'm certain the Rumbling Puffins are doing fine without me." He hadn't been that good at running drills and calling plays, and honestly, he was utterly terrible at pep talks and too pessimistic by at least half.

"They are, but that's not the point."

Somehow, she knew.

Well, she couldn't *know* know. Will was certain Marsha had kept the details to herself because she was discreet and kind and Ella had never met Nic, but Ella suspected, and that was almost worse. Like a puppy with a chew toy, she was going to keep pestering him until she ripped his squeaker out, so to speak.

He made one more attempt at deflection. "What are you talking about?"

"I already have one brother I don't like, I don't need another one. What is happening with you?"

After the last few weeks and, if he were being honest, after sharing some of his worries with Nic and starting therapy, Will no longer thought it would be impossible to articulate how he felt. He knew that he could open his mouth and let the words out, but somehow, while he could risk that with Nic, he couldn't with his sister.

"I've been busy."

"You're always busy. Try again."

"Would you believe I've been distracted by sod?"

"Nope." She'd normally say that with warmth, but now it was firm. He'd really pissed her off.

"I don't want to bother you." Which was the honest-to-gosh truth. Ella had enough going on without him dumping his screwups in her lap.

"Jeez, what do you think family is for?"

"Tense dinners. Photos for your *live laugh love* frames."

Nope, no reaction there either.

"What's going on?" she demanded. "Because it's obviously something."

Cold. The prospect of telling her, of admitting the magnitude of the mess in which he found himself, made him cold like Alaska. At least he wasn't sweating any longer.

"At work, there's some stuff, some money stuff," he allowed, "but it's . . . I would feel lesser if I told you."

At the word *lesser*, she rolled her eyes, and Will had a flash of sympathy for Luke. While Will found nearly everything about his brother intolerable, he understood that part of what motivated him was pride. Will's pride was hollering like a stubbed pinky toe at the moment.

Will had worked hard in school and at his job, and some part of him had always believed that his hard work was buying something. What he was losing wasn't only a business; it was an entire way of being in the world. And since his family was going to keep on being that way, he was also losing his place with them.

Maybe that was why he could talk to Nic about it, because when he'd been watching those videos and he had seen her ex-boyfriend betray her like that, he'd seen that same look on her face. He'd seen the moment when she realized it was real, it was happening, and nothing would ever be the same.

Ella didn't know that moment, but Nic did. Will did.

"Are you in trouble?" Ella asked.

"Like with the law? No. With my health? No."

"With anything?"

"Yes. I don't want to dissect it with you, though. It's too . . . fresh." You waited to have a corpse to do an autopsy.

"Jesus, I want to help."

Which was what he'd expected she would say when he'd imagined telling her. Okay, it was what he'd *hoped* she'd say when he wasn't in a terrible mood and had been picturing this.

Most of the time, he'd imagined her aghast and disappointed and only barely able to hide it.

But Ella was a second-grade teacher; her husband taught English to high schoolers and coached volleyball. They didn't have any extra cash, and Will wouldn't have taken money from them even if they'd had bathtubs of it. There came a point when you could plug the holes in the boat, but if you were headed for Niagara Falls, it wasn't going to make much difference.

He appreciated that, at least without knowing the exact nature of his problem, she wasn't judging him, but he also couldn't accept any help from her. "There isn't anything you can do."

"Are you talking to someone about it? Mom and Dad?"

"Please don't tell them."

"What would I tell them? You haven't said anything."

"I can't—they won't—"

"I get it."

And she did. If there were things that Nic could understand because she'd had her illusions shattered, too, then there were things that only Ella could get because she'd grown up in the same house, where softness and comfort were not to be confused with each other. Where niceness and kindness were opposites. The exact environment meant to produce someone like Luke, but where Ella and Will had somehow emerged from the mold as well, maybe with their corners knocked off, not quite fitting.

No, he'd tell Mom and Dad last, and he'd have to wear some kind of armor to do it, something to protect whatever soft parts he had left by then. Because while Ella might be handling this better than Will had thought she would, his parents were going to be brutal and unforgiving.

"So who knows? If it's a work thing, you've talked to Owen about it?"

Owen had been Will's closest friend at vet school. For a while, Will had thought his sister had a crush on him, but nothing had ever come of it. But Owen had taken some corporate job with a big vet chain on the West Coast. They exchanged the occasional text on New Year's Eve, but Will had flat-out ignored Owen's latest. Will didn't have anything to say that Owen would want to hear.

"He wouldn't . . . no."

"You're carrying this—whatever it is—all alone, aren't you?"

Nic knew, and Marsha knew, and Frank at the bank knew: that was enough for a bridge game. What did Ella expect, that he was going to hire a skywriter? "I have shared the details with two professional and one personal contact." Not to mention his therapist.

"You sound so much like Luke."

That was true and intensely mean, but Will loved Ella for it because he had earned it. He was being an absolute ass, but he hurt so badly, he simply didn't know how to be different.

He hadn't realized how stunted he was as a person until this thing had crashed over him, stripping away his defenses and making him face himself as he was. He'd been reduced to his most elemental parts, and some of his elemental parts were kind of embarrassing. He didn't want to show them to anyone else.

"I should give you a noogie for that."

"Well, if I were still taller than you, I'd put you in a headlock. You're being absurd."

"You were taller than me for, like, one year."

"I didn't take full advantage. I would like a do-over." She gave a queenly shake of her head, which she could do because she had that tall and elegant look. "I love you."

And she meant it. To Ella, it was that easy. You loved someone, and then it all worked out. The details didn't matter. They weren't important.

Will had always been a little more skeptical, had always felt as if people were hand-waving over the most important bits. After the last few years, he knew that he'd been right all along. Love was good, love was necessary, but it wasn't enough.

"I love you too," he said anyhow. Because he did.

"You don't have to shove people away. You can let us in, you know."

"Sure." But that didn't mean that he had to. "Do you really want my edger or what?"

"Yeah, mine won't turn over."

"Come on, then." He'd take tools over his feelings any day.

# CHAPTER 15

Nic fumbled with her menu, which rammed her water glass and almost flung it across the table. It was official: Making new friends was like dating. Maybe even worse than dating. God, she was going to have to learn how to date again, wasn't she?

Making friends when you were kids was easy. Friendships sprang into being like Johnny-jump-ups when you were under twelve. How had Nic and Rose become friends? Nic couldn't even remember. It had just always been that way. There had never been an awkward getting-to-know-you phase, no stumbling hesitancy because you weren't certain whether they liked you as much as you liked them. Kids were so wonderfully unselfaware. Nic would give anything not to be cognizant of herself in her skin for just ten minutes. What a relief it would be.

But just as Nic was beginning to worry that she had the wrong day or the wrong time or the wrong tiny diner in the wrong tiny town, Emily swung the door open—sending the bells hanging from the handle jingling—and gave Nic a quick wave. She hugged the hostess—of course she knew her—before taking the other side of the booth.

"I have had a day," she said, taking a swig of water.

"Oh no, do you need to reschedule?" Nic winced at how needy and crestfallen she sounded.

"No, no! I'm so glad to see you. But there was a hawk."

"Oh—crap." It was scary to curse in front of someone for the first time, figuring out whether you both had the same definition of profanity. But hawks? Nic hated those things in the strongest terms.

"I'd let my flock out to free range while I weeded the garden, and luckily, I heard the commotion. They'd just scattered." She demonstrated with her hands.

"Is everyone okay?"

"When I came around the corner, the hawk took off. It took me a while to round the flock up and get them back into the chicken yard, but I finally found them all. They may never leave the coop again, but no one's hurt. No thanks to those soulless bastards of the sky." Her eyes flicked up. "Sorry?"

"No need for sorry. Red-tailed hawks are fucking terrifying."

Emily beamed, as if Nic had passed a test. "Agreed. So have you been to Lulu's?"

"Nope."

"I'm amazed Will Lund didn't mention it to you." Emily had opened her menu, but she shot Nic a look over the top of it.

A beat passed where Nic could've picked up that ball, but while she and Emily might be on cursing terms, they weren't quite on dishing-about-men terms—which was fine. Nic wasn't ready to dish about Will with anyone.

Whatever it was that she and Will were doing or not doing, that was. She needed to figure that part out before she dished about it with anyone.

"My grandma grew up here, like, a century ago, and he said that this place might have been here then."

"That's so cool! Yeah, it's an institution."

"I'm trying to find all of those."

"I'll make you a list."

"Tell me what's good." Thinking about Granny calmed Nic's nerves enough that she could actually read the menu.

"Everything, but especially the chicken and waffles."

"I have to say, I love fried chicken and I love waffles, but I don't think they go together."

"You have clearly not spent enough time in the South."

"Not yet."

"Why did you move here, if you don't mind me asking?"

Nic didn't mind at all. She told a short version of the story after they ordered, in which she tried to make the Brian stuff sound comic. But Emily's grimaces and constant commentary—"What an ass, no—asses have redeeming qualities! What a mosquito"—reminded Nic how badly she'd needed that and how long she hadn't had it. Even before Rose betrayed her, anything that Nic might have said about Brian would have inevitably made it back to him through Rose and Tony . . . which had seemed cute at first but had mainly been isolating.

In the end, losing Brian had been bearable because he was awful. But losing Rose? That was the harder cut to heal.

When she'd decided to move to Yagerstown, she'd been thinking about space and a fresh beginning. She hadn't let herself imagine new friendships, maybe because the need for them still smarted so badly.

"So is the farm a full-time job, or—" Nic asked.

"God, no. What I make at the farmers' market barely covers chicken food. I work at the SPCA."

"Cool! Will said—that is, Dr. Lund said you all received some surrendered chickens."

Emily's eyes were twinkling again, but she kept in whatever saucy comment had prompted it. "A few, but not as many as dogs and cats. Look, I know Will has quite a lot to say about chickens, but you can't let him bother you. He's like that about all the animals."

"What happens to the homeless chickens?"

"We can't keep them at the shelter, we're just not equipped for birds, but BROODY fosters and rehouses where we can."

"I'd love to help out. I can donate feed and equipment." And money, but she left that part off. It might sound crass or braggy. Nic felt deeply weird about her success.

"Sweet. I'll add you to the list."

Nic gave Emily her number and then asked, "So you've always lived here?"

"Pretty much. I tried to leave a few times, but nowhere else felt like home, you know?"

"I don't, but it sounds nice." And it did. "How's the dating scene? What, I'm single."

"Uh-huh." Emily wasn't going to keep that commentary inside much longer. "Well, it's abysmal. Setting aside a certain veterinarian— and no, don't even ask, that never happened, he's not my type—there are, like, three single guys our age. I was seeing a volunteer firefighter from Boones Mill for a while."

"That sounds . . . hot." Firefighters weren't Nic's particular daydream, but she knew they did it for a lot of folks.

"It should be. And you think you'll give the fantasy thing a go, right? Play out some scene in the bedroom. But I'm telling you that the boots, they squeak."

"Squeak?"

"Yup. A total mood killer."

A beat passed. Two. And then Nic roared with laughter. "That wasn't where I thought that story was going."

"Believe me, me neither."

And as Emily told hilarious stories about her job at the SPCA and about the origins of BROODY, about the eggs she was hoping to hatch—she kept roosters, something Nic had never done—some break in Nic's chest set. It wasn't healed. It wasn't erased. It couldn't be. But it stopped throbbing.

Which was why Nic didn't hesitate to ask Emily, as they were saying goodbye on the sidewalk, if she wanted to come over sometime for wine and chicken watching.

At the top of an unsteady ladder, Nic had a horrible realization: you couldn't learn everything from YouTube. With a new, hastily purchased, net in one hand and her phone in the other, she contemplated Will's now naked basketball hoop.

"This shouldn't be hard," she said to it. "It's literally child's play."

But the rusted metal of the hoop and the stiff nylon of the net didn't want to play together.

She'd watched the video twice. She'd switched to a different video. So she searched for and watched a third video; she'd simply given too much of her life to YouTube for it to desert her now. In this one, a too-chipper kid in Utah demonstrated how to install a basketball net.

"And that's all there is to it!" he chimed. "Don't forget to like and subscribe!"

"Not happening." Nic dutifully made a loop, dragged it through the metal fastener, and pulled . . . until it fell out. "You're a liar," she said to the kid's paused face. "Liarliarliar."

No wonder Will had never bothered to replace the ragged old net. Maybe backboards were disposable, single-use items. She should've bought an entirely new backboard. She was at least competent with power tools.

Maybe she could come at it from the other side?

As she tried, the ladder wobbled beneath her. "You're not allowed to collapse." She gave it a commanding jab with her finger, and it swayed again.

But then, something even more appalling than ladder disintegration occurred. Will pulled into his driveway with a first-class frown on his face. There was the angry Viking she knew so well. He climbed out of his too-manly-by-half Jeep without ever once breaking his eye contact with her.

Mother of Persephone, why did that have to be so sexy?

"What are you doing?" he demanded.

"Breaking and entering." She could at least try for coy, but given that she was clinging to splintering wood, the effect was flimsy.

"On a ladder made of . . . matchsticks? Seriously, what the hell is that?"

"It was in my shed. The previous owners left it behind." Which had probably been a solid choice, unlike the ladder.

"What are you doing in my yard?"

She hadn't meant to ever have to explain this to him. Her plan had been to be finished with this project before he returned. He'd given her BROODY and Emily, and he was hurting. She wanted to do something for him in return. Something secret, something small. But she'd wanted to just . . . mark what he'd done. Make it even between them.

Trying not to reveal any of that, she said carelessly, "Replacing your basketball net."

"What?"

"Don't make it a big deal. I'd noticed yours was kind of shabby, I was at the Target in Roanoke picking some things up, and I walked by the sports section. So I bought you one. I didn't want you to know it was from me."

And that was the only thing it represented.

"So I'd just think it was a random new net? Like from the fairies?"

"Everyone knows fairies are bunk. It could be a gift from Britomartis."

"Who?"

"The goddess of nets."

"Oh, of course. That's what I would've thought."

The problem was that when he glared at her like that, she wanted to make him keep glaring. She wanted to see whether he could shoot lightning out of his eyes. She wanted to know when his control would break.

"You wouldn't have thought that because you are clearly not whimsical enough." He wasn't whimsical at all. "But isn't this what people do for each other in small towns? Small gifts? Thoughtful caretaking?"

"No."

"Ah. This is what I get for mainlining *Gilmore Girls*." Not to mention Granny's stories, but she couldn't assume Yagerstown today was the same place it had been ninety years prior, even if Emily and everyone at BROODY was lovely.

For a long minute, she gazed down at him from the top of the ladder, and if it hadn't been groaning—literally groaning—under her, she would have enjoyed it. It was nice to tower over him for once. Was this what it was like for him all the time? No wonder he was so domineering.

Will took several deep breaths. "Get down."

"If you insist. But only because you asked so nicely." Honestly, the ladder seemed to have only seconds left. He was probably saving her life.

Once she'd returned to terra firma—home sweet home!—Nic skipped a few steps down the driveway and watched Will clamber up the death trap. He managed to install the net in about two minutes flat, which was decidedly aggravating.

Then he descended and continued his program of glaring at her.

If this were the Olympics, she'd give him a 9.2. You always had to leave some room for improvement.

"I would've been very upset to find your body in my driveway," he said, sounding deliciously growly. "Imagine how difficult it would've been to convince the cops I had nothing to do with it."

"But now you'll miss all that fun! Should I apologize or . . ."

Will's chest worked like a bellows. If he threw in some stomping, he could play the indignant bull.

"That can't be good for your blood pressure," she chided.

"My blood pressure is *fine*. What were you thinking?"

She hadn't been. She'd just wanted to do something for him, which she couldn't say because it would sound . . . ridiculous. Exposed.

The look went on too long. There was some normal length for a look, three seconds or ten seconds or something, and they passed it and kept on looking.

She wasn't supposed to want this, not now, and she wasn't supposed to want this with him. But she did.

She ought to say something. Why wasn't she saying something? Had he asked a question?

Oh, yes, what had she been thinking?

"Just being neighborly." Her tongue stumbled over the words in her mouth.

Will's gaze left her face, but it went to her body, and that didn't help. For all that she'd kissed him, he hadn't touched her. But with his eyes sweeping over her legs, up her torso, she wanted him to. Gods, did she want him to.

"Hidey ho, neighbor." And he crossed the three feet that had been between them and slid his hands around her waist. His expression had been hard, his nose almost cleaving the air, but once they were inches apart, that irritation melted into something else. Surprise.

He shifted closer, the hard plane of him filling her vision until there was no sky, no outside, and nowhere to place her hands except his shoulders.

That seemed to be what he'd been waiting for, because once she touched him, his mouth descended on hers.

For one heart-stopping moment, it was simply the touch of lip to lip. Just that one minute point of contact, and Nic couldn't catch her breath. The jolting thud of it happening turned to softness. A kiss that felt like gold. A kiss so sweet, so sincere, it was almost melancholy.

He'd wetted his mouth, or she had, and it amplified everything. The subtle texture of his lips. Their warmth. Everything else in the world had frozen, and the only movement anywhere was Will's body against hers.

When she grazed him with her teeth, the kiss went molten. It was flicking on a lighter but getting a blowtorch instead. His hands on her hips constricted, released, and tightened again. As if he wanted to be tender but had forgotten how.

The kiss felt as if it had been building for an age, even though Nic knew it had only been weeks since their last kiss. But her grip on logic loosened the more he kept licking into her. Making her tremble. Making her moan. Turning her in a few short minutes—seconds, eons—into goo.

This wasn't a tentative, gentle kiss; it was a taking. Based on the hungry noises she was making, Nic was ready to be plundered. Will's arms came fully around her, dragging her up to him. Hard on soft, and hot everywhere. Everywhere.

After what felt like too long, they separated a few inches, and air poured in between them. Her lips, abraded by his kiss, were suddenly so cold. For a minute, they swayed toward each other; then they pulled away. One of them laughed softly. They were ridiculous. But . . . then they had another near kiss. She bit her lip. Nope, they had to end this. What were they doing?

Nic dropped back onto her heels and raised her hands from his shoulders, curling her fingers into her palms to stop herself from reaching for him again. She didn't know whether it was a gesture of defiance or surrender, wisdom or foolishness.

But if she didn't know, she shouldn't kiss him.

Slowly, slowly, Will let go of her and stepped back.

"Glad that ladder didn't kill us?" He said it lightly, and it took her a second to realize it was a question.

He was offering her an out. She could play it off as a *thank god we're alive* kiss if she wanted to—if she were still trying to maintain that they were friends.

He was still trying to give her all the power and to follow her lead.

Some part of her wanted to scale him like a castle wall and kiss the coldness right off his face just to show him what she thought about that.

But she knew that she was still a mess, still holding the ragged edges of her chest together, basically. She wanted Will, that much was clear. Holy Pan pipes did she want him. But she wasn't ready to have him. She might not ever be ready.

She ought to take his chivalry—even if it was just for now.

"Yeah. We have so much to live for." Like potentially more stolen driveway kisses.

"Right." Will gave his head a firm shake. "So, can I get that for you?" He pointed to the death trap ladder. The surprisingly erotic death trap ladder. "Maybe carry it straight to the trash?"

"Nope, I can handle it."

"Thanks for the net."

But not for the kiss?

Oh, well, it was probably better not to acknowledge it. Just like their nuclear-grade chemistry. "You're welcome. Have a nice evening."

After a few seconds of struggle, she managed to force the rusting hinge up so she could close the ladder. Then she hauled it onto her shoulder and proceeded across the street—her burden creaking with every step—without once looking back. But she didn't need to because she could feel Will's eyes on her every step of the way.

If Orpheus had been leading Will out of Hades, doubt would never have entered the equation. Will's scowl wouldn't have permitted it.

Setting the kiss aside—shoving it aside, really—she didn't want to give any more thought to why there was that kind of awareness between Will and her.

# CHAPTER 16

*Could you provide the following documents to support your request to defer payment on your deed of trust?*

The question mark was amusing, as if Will had any choice in the matter. As if he could say no. As if he were going to pass up a chance for clemency by refusing to do a bit more paperwork.

Or, as Nicole would have said, a fuck-ton more paperwork.

As he gathered, scanned, and batched more evidence that proved that no, he really *was* a complete idiot where money was concerned, Will tried not to think of Nicole's ass at the top of that ladder. Her jeans pulled tight against her curves . . . and every bit of her braced as the ladder swayed in a circle because it had been about to come crashing down, depositing her nose first on his driveway. He especially tried not to think about how she'd tasted, and about the hot-as-hell noises that she'd made as he'd kissed her.

All because she'd noticed he needed a new basketball net.

He had no other word for it. It had been sweet.

He'd thought sweetness had gone out of the world. This was like finding a dandelion under the once-a-year January snow. But as into their making out as she'd been—and she had been into it—she was still maintaining that they were friends.

It had taken a *long* cold shower for him to get over kissing her in his driveway. He probably still wasn't over it. He was starting to take it a mite personally.

Kim stuck her head into his office. She'd dyed her pixie cut fuchsia over the weekend, and it kept startling him. He was going to miss the turquoise ombré.

"Boss, there's no one on the books for the rest of the day. And I've walked and fed—where necessary—every pet we're boarding." All two of them. "I've swept and wiped down all the exam rooms too."

"Are you asking for something to do?" She knew him well enough to know that she didn't need to try to impress him; Will already thought she was the best tech he'd ever had.

"I'm saying you should tell me to go home."

Argg. It was humiliating having his staff—okay, just Kim at this point—attempting to save him money rather than getting everything he owed them.

"I'm trying to pay you for the full eight hours!" It certainly wasn't Kim's fault that they didn't have enough business.

"Or you could tell me to go home so I could do this job interview early."

Oh. She was trying to be kind to Will, but she was also looking out for herself, which was exactly what he wanted her to be doing. This was the Titanic before doom had fully set in. She didn't need to go down with it.

"Of course you should go." She had to jump in that lifeboat before people started fighting for the last seat.

"I'm not going to take it if—"

"You should take it." On that point, he was going to insist. He'd accepted Marsha's resignation reluctantly, but he certainly wasn't going to screw Kim over.

"You know this is what I'm supposed to do."

What he knew was Kim wasn't satisfied with her associate's degree and she was saving for college with the hope of going to vet school herself someday. She had a real gift with animals, and he fervently wanted all her dreams of having her own vet practice to come true. But he also had to wish the numbers were different, the industry was different. It was probably too late for him, but maybe things could be better for Kim.

"Yep, but today, what you want to do is to pay your student loans, your rent. To eat."

She gave a shrug, one that said she would take care of herself but she hadn't quite surrendered her hope. She wasn't as beaten down as he was. "I still think you'll work it out."

"If I don't,"—when he didn't—"you take care of you."

What had Nic said the other day? *Isn't this what people in small towns do?* He certainly wanted it to be, minus the rickety-ladder bit, but he'd been pushed under by the big wave, and he couldn't help anyone else when he was still pinned to the bottom of the sea.

"You take care of you too," Kim said.

For the rest of the day, Will tried to decide what that would look like.

Will turned his car toward the Lions Club park. He was only going in order to hug his niece and to see whether the kids' ball-handling skills had improved. It was this or go over to Nic's to see whether she was trying another death-defying stunt so that he could swoop in and kiss her again.

In comparison, crashing a youth soccer practice was way super cool, though the thought of Nic in his arms again had a certain—appeal, Will thought as he climbed out of his car.

"Will!" Ella almost bounced on her toes. She had one of those fancy insulated wineglasses in her hand, but he knew it held only ice water.

The only real way to get through these things was with booze, but alas, the park had strict prohibitions on alcohol.

The situation on the field resembled a bar fight with fewer broken chairs and bloody noses—so basically it was a totally normal practice. A kindergarten-through-second-grade soccer team was many things, but it wasn't disciplined.

Kent, the head coach, was currently working with three kids in yellow jerseys near the goal box. He'd clearly tried to set the rest up in some kind of passing drill, but instead, one girl was sitting down, her lap filling with plucked clover blooms. Three other kids were playing keep-away in the traditional way, with the ball in their hands. Hannah, Will's niece, was resolutely focused on passing the ball with her partner, but stress at the other kids' lack of focus radiated off her like heat off the pavement in August. It was probably going to start disrupting the gravity around her soon.

"Coach Doctor Will! It's Coach Doctor Will!" That would be Travis, Will's biggest fan. He'd tried to talk his parents into getting a pet just so that they could come visit the clinic. He'd been crushed to learn that the only option his parents were amenable to—a goldfish—was not a creature that Will was able to care for.

"What are you doing here?" Hannah deigned to take a break from passing to give him a half hug. She wasn't quite willing to take *that* much time off during practice. She had bigger dreams for her soccer career than that.

"Got off early. Wanted to check in on my favorite team."

"Thank God you're back." Kent had come to see what the melee was about, and he was grinning ear to ear like a frat boy at the sight of a keg.

"I'm not back." Will raised a warning finger, not wanting Kent or anyone else to get the wrong idea. "I just came to watch."

"Well, even so, can you help out?" Ella gave him the same slightly desperate smile that she'd used to coax Will into coaching in the first place.

Well, what else did Will have going on? He could keep the kids on task for a bit.

Truth be told, that was all Will's "coaching" had ever amounted to. Kent got things started, and then Will stood there and glared to minimize the dillydallying. So that they didn't dillydally too much, anyhow. No youth soccer game was complete without some kid wandering around the field aimlessly and occasionally shooting on their own goal.

Will ought to say no. He certainly had no intention of coming back full time. But, just this once . . .

"Okay, but I gotta tell you, Puffins, you look pretty undisciplined."

He sounded stern. He sounded pissed. But the thing about kids is that they were as immune to Will's attempts to be firm as Nicole Jones had proved to be. None of them so much as wilted at his tone.

"Yes, Coach Doctor Will. We'll be very disciplined." Travis saluted Will as if he were some kind of general. "But can I tell you something?"

Will knew from experience there wasn't going to be any way to stop him. "One quick thing."

"I have a tooth coming in *in front of* another tooth."

"That's great, kid. Let's work on your passing. Nora, who is your partner?"

The girl with the clover stood up, and it rained to the ground. "Don't have one."

"You're with me, then. Line up." Will found himself reaching for his whistle and then covering the gesture by scratching his chest. You didn't get a whistle when you'd resigned as coach. "Pass!"

There was a dutiful chorus of thunks as half the kids kicked their balls to their partners. Most, of course, went wide. One shot backward into the watching parents. Nora regarded the ball Will had passed to her as if it were a large but not terribly frightening spider.

"Let's go again, but with small, controlled kicks. Everyone know what that means?"

Hannah had the good sense to roll her eyes. She really had nothing but disdain for the yahoos on her team.

"Coach Doctor Will?"

"Yes, Travis."

"I have a wart. It's on my finger." He held it up, and all the kids oohed.

Will scratched the bridge of his nose. "Your parents should put some wart stick on that. Okay, Puffins, pass!"

The balls again shot in every direction. After all the others had gone off, Nora gingerly approached hers and then . . . nudged it with her toe. It rolled about six inches.

"A little harder than that," Will said.

She shot Will a dirty look, but then she really connected with the ball. He reached his right foot out to stop it.

"Good. Really good. Let's see you do it again." He passed the ball back to her. She watched it roll past her. "You've got to get those."

She was too young to sass him by pointing out that he hadn't mentioned that part and, besides, he'd overshot her in the first place, but he'd bet that if her parents were still forcing her to play in three years or so, she'd have a mouthful to say then.

For the next five minutes, Will ran the drill, switching in and out with the various partners, offering tips and encouragement. By the end, at least 10 percent more of the shots were finding their targets. It wasn't much, but it was something.

Kent came over. "I think we're going to scrimmage now."

"I should—"

"Stay and coach the blues. It's only fifteen minutes more."

"Please!" That was Travis, of course, of the goldfish and the concerning tooth-growth situation and the wart.

And how, really, could Will tell Kent no? Wasn't Will here because even hermits needed to be needed sometimes?

"All right, blues," Will said, "let's do this."

If *this* was to commit a dozen offside offenses, pass badly, and be reminded four times not to sit down on the field—ever—then the blues did exactly what Will wanted.

But this was what he wanted, wasn't it? Because despite his frustrations, Will had fun. The kids' frustrations weren't his, and they weren't life or death. It was a pleasure to gently cajole them to play better, and there was nothing better than a big old grin on a kid's face when she was missing half her front teeth and couldn't control the ball for crap but loved being in the twilight sun.

Eventually, Hannah broke away from the pack and made a serious run on goal. Will kept pace with her up the field.

"Run where the ball isn't!" he shouted to the other kids, who, left to their own devices, tended to clump around the ball like kitty litter. Some of them managed to scatter in the penalty area.

And Hannah, because she was a consummate team player, nudged the ball toward a shocked Travis. Wonder of freaking wonders, the kid received it and dribbled for a few paces before passing the ball back to Hannah. The little move bypassed the only defender in that part of the field, who'd stood statute still watching his teammates actually play some soccer.

Then Hannah drew her foot back and, in almost movie-perfect slow motion, shot. The ball flew past the stunned goalie and snagged in the back of the net.

His niece, because she was cooler than Will could ever hope to be, gave a pleased shrug while the rest of the blues cheered. The poor goalie collapsed to the ground with a howl—God, Will hated that part—and Kent went over to comfort the kid.

"Good job." Will offered his hand to high five.

"Uncle Will, nobody does that anymore."

"Oh, sorry."

But under her bravado, Will could tell that she had enjoyed the moment.

Having patched up the goalie's feelings, Kent blew his whistle, the show-off, and reminded everyone about the game on Saturday, and Will was almost sorry it was over.

"You're certain I can't convince you to come back?" Kent said once he'd crossed to Will. "I'll buy you all the beer you can drink."

"I'll buy you both beers if Will stays," Ella said.

"I don't know. I've . . . got a lot on my mind."

"And the Rumbling Puffins aren't the best distraction?" Kent gestured at the field. "It looked like you were having fun."

"I don't think I smiled once."

"If we all needed to see you smile to know you were enjoying yourself, well, we'd be waiting a long time."

"Nah," Ella said. "I don't buy that. I for one saw Will smiling as soon as you got out of your car. That might have been pre-Puffin, in fact."

If Will had been smiling, it had been because he was thinking about Nic.

Nic would tell him to do this. She would think it was wonderful.

Which was probably why he asked, "Saturday at ten?" before he could talk himself out of it.

"Yup, right here."

Ella let out a little squeal.

"Don't," he warned. "No squealing. I'm not saying I'll finish out the season. Let's just see how it goes."

"It'll be great," Kent assured him. "I think I have an extra shirt. I'll drop it off."

"No need. I have one from last season."

"It's a new color. Let's just say you'll be safe during hunting season."

"It matches a puffin's beak." From Hannah's tone, Will assumed the flaming orange had been her idea.

Ella snorted. "You've always looked great in neon tones."

"I'm not going to get in the middle of this sibling situation," Kent said.

Which sounded like something Nic would say, but Will bit the words back before they popped out of his mouth. After all, neither Ella nor Kent had met Nic, and if Will brought her up, there would be questions.

If he returned to the Puffins, there would be questions when the truth about his business came out. He didn't want to add questions about Nic onto the pile.

"There's no sibling situation. I'll see you on Saturday."

He and Ella started toward the parking lot with Hannah trailing them.

"So you're back?" his niece asked.

"For now."

"Why'd you leave in the first place?"

"Have you considered a career as an interrogator?" Will asked his niece. "And why are you laughing?" He directed the latter at his sister.

"Because if I'd have known one conversation could've made such a difference, I would've borrowed your edger months ago."

"Oh no, you can't ever go back to that well. I'm on to you now."

"Nah, you'll never see me coming. I can always ask for your drill and your hammer, and then, at last, I'll show up in need of a cup of sugar."

But Ella was right: for whatever reason, Will was feeling almost cheerful, so he only ruffled her hair good naturedly.

# CHAPTER 17

Nic heaved the box up onto the Formica countertop of the SPCA. "So I think I got most of the things on your list."

Emily huffed out a laugh. "Yeah, I'd say so."

Someone had brought a hen into the SPCA a few hours earlier. Whether it was feral, lost, or abandoned, no one knew. But Nic had put together a box for the friend of a BROODY member who was going to take care of her: grain pellets, scratch, a bag of Nic's own special chicken-treat blend, a waterer, a dust bath mix, wood shavings for the egg box, and an old beginner's guide to chickens.

"You said there was just an old coop in the guy's yard, but he didn't have any gear."

"Yours is not the first offering."

Nic popped up on her toes and craned over the counter. There were two other cardboard boxes—each filled to the brim with chicken stuff. "Oops."

"What can I say? Chicken people like to try to recruit other chicken people."

"Everyone deserves the joy of chickens. How have you been?"

Over the weekend, Emily had swung by to meet Nic's flock. They'd drunk iced tea and devoured a truly Instagram-worthy cheese board—which Nic hadn't bothered to post on Instagram. It was the most normal she'd felt in years.

"Excellent, though continuing to dream about that fig jam."

"If you can get me a lead for local figs, I'll make more and give you some jars." It was another holdover from Granny, who'd always believed that the best jams and jellies had to be made at home, even if it turned out a little runny, as Nic's often did. Nothing made her feel accomplished quite like opening the pantry door and seeing a row of jars with handwritten labels.

"You are the best." Emily tipped her head to the side. "And speaking of the best, you know who's here making rounds?"

It did not take a rocket scientist to make a guess about that; a backyard-chicken influencer did just fine.

Nic hadn't seen Will since the kiss. It had been hard to think about anything else. She'd caught a scent like his skin yesterday, and she'd pinkened from scalp to toes. That they had chemistry, that the second kiss was as good as the first had been—that wasn't a surprise. It was a relief.

But it was also like being handed a knife, blade first. It could still cut her, destroy everything she might be building here. Except he made her feel gorgeous. Powerful. Alive again.

Nic was going to have to make a choice about him, and fast.

"Dr. Lund?" she managed.

"Yup. And I'm not buying this coy act—I was at that farmers' market." When Nic didn't say anything, Emily rolled her eyes and pointed. "He's in the cat room. It's that way."

"I thought we were friends!"

"Friends shove friends at the folks they're clearly lusting after."

"I'm not lusting." She was so lusting. "Fine, but I'm just going to say hi."

"Which is good because there are windows."

Ignoring the implication of that, Nic walked down the hall and around the corner. Then her heart seized in her chest because Will was sitting in an old glider, absolutely covered in cats.

Sprawled across his lap was a large gray one with white socks. It was sleeping or pretending to sleep. A brown tabby reclined on one arm of the chair with Will scratching under its chin. And a small tortoise kitten was perched on his chest. He was cradling it in place, as it looked around the room triumphantly.

*I have claimed him,* the kitten's expression said. *He is mine.*

Well, the kitten might have to fight Nic.

Will's attention was on the cats, but after a few seconds, he looked up and locked eyes with Nic. For a second, heat flared between them. Even through the cinder block of the walls and the thick glass of the cat room windows, she could feel it. He started to get up, then seemed to remember the cats and fell back into the chair. His cheeks were coloring slightly as he grimaced and then shrugged.

Every beat of it, she felt. Nic ran a hand through her hair, gave her heart a quick talking-to, and went in.

"See," she greeted him lightly. "I would have thought you were a dog person."

"Because I'm male?"

"No, it's not a gender thing. It's your energy." His entirely too potent energy. "You jog, for crying out loud."

"It's not a good idea to take a dog jogging in the South for a lot of the year."

"You could drive a person up the wall, you know."

"Is it working?" His eyes said he wanted it.

Her eyes probably said she was a goner.

"So who are your friends?"

"That's Moby in my lap, and Matilda on the arm." Neither had so much as acknowledged Nic. "And this one doesn't have a name." He tried to hold the kitten up, but it had sunk its claws into his shirt.

"No name yet?" Nic knelt and ran a finger down the kitten's head. It pushed into the contact and purred, making its entire small body rumble.

"The kittens never last very long. It's coming out of isolation today, and it'll probably be adopted by the end of the week."

Nic continued to pet the kitten, trying to focus on the softness of its fur and not the heat of the man holding it. "Why don't you adopt it?"

"I'm not home much."

"Which is why a cat would be such a good choice." She turned her attention to the kitten. "You like him, don't you?"

The kitten blinked several times. Its eyes were the color of pale jade, and its gold-and-brown-mottled fur stuck out of its too-big ears in tufts. Its expression was sassy and comical, and Nic had never been so certain that Will needed anything like he needed that kitten.

"It says yes."

"This is why you can't let animals make important decisions."

"It's adopting a pet, not diplomacy in eastern Europe." She shifted her weight onto her knees and looked up at Will. It was a suggestive position. She wanted that with him, the heat, the sex: she could admit it. But she wanted him to take care of his heart too.

"You always," she whispered, "see animals when they're hurting. I bet there's trauma to that, over time. My flock . . . they aren't affectionate, really."

"Don't insult my girl Margaret like that."

Nic smiled. "I wouldn't dare. But as bad as things have been for me over the last few months, I can always go out into the yard, and they run to meet me. Okay, so they want apple cores and mealworms, but . . . they make me happy. Caring for them, meeting their needs, sharing that with people, I don't know, it's just—nice. I think you could use that."

Will shifted his hand under the kitten, and his fingers came to rest on Nic's wrist. He could probably feel that her pulse was racing, that her skin was heated. Being close to him, touched by him, did that to her. She couldn't hide it, and she didn't want to.

"I'll think about it," he said.

"You should."

Slowly, regretfully, Nic got up. If she didn't move, she was going to end up dislodging those cats and crawling into his lap, and as Emily had pointed out, there were windows. Someone could come by at any minute.

"I'll see you around, Will Lund."

"You can count on it, Nic Jones."

And she could feel his attention on her, hot and heavy, all the way down the hall.

As soon as he'd gotten the kitten home, it had promptly attacked and destroyed a roll of toilet paper and had a fight with Sunday's newspaper, which had been folded on the floor by the coffee table, before disappearing. It had taken him an hour to find it under the guest bed, with only its skinny, slightly crooked, tail visible when he'd stuck his head and a flashlight under there.

"Nic said if I adopted you, I'd always have companionship." But the kitten hadn't responded to his guilt trip.

Will had finally given up waiting for it to come out and so he had gone to his own bed, and now it was exploring the upstairs. He'd closed as many doors as he could, but he could hear it throw its weight against the bathroom one, its soft paws slipping over the wood it desperately wanted out of the way. It was determined but powerless—which felt like one of those metaphors Ella's husband would point out to his students.

Then . . . silence. Who knew where she was going now. Will wouldn't be surprised if she found a way to get into the attic crawl space.

A soft weight landed on his comforter.

"Now you want to talk."

The kitten stalked up to him. She placed one front paw, then the other, on his chest before lowering more of her weight onto him. Her whiskers brushed over his face, so lightly he almost thought he was mistaken.

"Hey." His voice sounded rough, and he felt foolish.

But then the damn cat began to purr, and some bolt or screw that he'd tightened to the point of pain loosened in his chest. What was it that Nic had said, that having your own animal was nice? He could see that.

He rubbed a finger over the kitten's shoulder, which felt as fragile as a sparrow's. "How does the house seem? You going to be okay here?"

The purring continued. She bumped her head against his chest, and he rubbed that spot between her ears where you could feel the jut of her sagittal crest. She liked that, and she rotated her head back and forth, getting him to put pressure where she wanted it.

"You think you're in charge now."

She purred in affirmation.

"I guess you're going to need a name." He ought to ask Nic how she'd named all those chickens of hers. "Nic seems to like mythology and old movie-showgirl names. Maybe . . . Gilda? But you seem kinda like a badass in the making. So Amelia?" He couldn't think of any other daredevils other than Evel Knievel, and he knew Nic would have a fit if he named the cat after a motorcycle-riding stuntman.

The kitten settled next to him, propped up against his side, and began vigorously cleaning her belly, purring loudly the entire time. Grooming behavior: that was a sign of real trust.

"You're going to have to leave the toilet paper alone."

Her entire body shook as she cleaned herself. She was too small to do anything with only part of herself. She was half eyes and ears, which he knew didn't make anatomical sense, but it was how he felt when he looked at her.

"You probably shouldn't sleep with me. I could roll over on you."
But he also knew most cats slept with their owners. As he drifted off,
he thought he was probably going to have to stop lecturing his patients
about that.

The next morning, he woke to find the kitten gone. But in the living
room, he discovered that she had located, and shredded, an athletic
sock of his.

"You're going to be a hoot."

The kitten tipped her head to the side.

"That's your name, isn't it? Hoot."

The kitten blinked, accepting this. She was so damn cute, he could
only bring himself to be mildly annoyed, both at the cat and at Nic for
saddling him with it.

Nicole. She was somehow always in color, and not the regular
Crayola shades but those saturated, intense hues that didn't come from
nature and were the sole province of computer animation. In the cat
room at the shelter, in her yard, in his, she shimmered.

It was just a crush. He knew it, but that didn't seem to blunt it at
all. He liked her. Cared about her. Dreamed about her. He was almost
ravenous to kiss her again, and only a little bit because she'd talked him
into adopting a bomb disguised as a ball of fur.

# CHAPTER 18

The feedstore was about a quarter mile down the road from Will's practice. It was a low wood-clad building that resembled a refugee from another century—perhaps the nineteenth. That siding didn't know the meaning of *stain* or *polyurethane*. The door was a modern metal-and-glass thing that didn't fit with the rest, but when Nic pushed it open, it set off an actual bell, and then the scents of hay and molasses hit her with a double-barreled shot of nostalgia.

Nic could feel her tension ease with each breath. This was why she liked chickens. They brought you into places like this.

"Be right there! Son of a gun." The woman's voice seemed to come from the office behind the register. From the sound of keys clacking and curses muttered, she was having a fight with a computer.

Nic had been there a time or twelve. She and technology had called a hostile truce, which mostly involved Nic recognizing its power and mystery and tech not undermining her quite as often.

"No rush," Nic called back.

She wandered through the stacks of bunny bedding and small-animal feed, past a wall covered with bright birdhouses, and up to a rack of brooder equipment. The tubs and heat lamps were marked down since the season for baby chicks and ducks had ended for the year. There was far, far more of it than Nic had ever seen in a feedstore in midsummer before, so either the feedstore had overordered, which seemed unlikely for a place that appeared to have been here since before the war—the Civil War, that was—or the chicken trend was cooling down compared to the previous year.

Maybe Will had a point about chickens becoming too trendy.

For Nic, chickens were tickets to places like this, places that time had forgotten. They were Granny's stories, and they were knowledge from before the internet or electricity. They were connecting you to what you ate and teaching you that it had a personality. Distinct Jurassic personalities.

Was it bad if someone's chickens were there to spice up—poultry up?—their Insta feed? If it was part of some homesteading thing that they'd grow out of as soon as chinoiserie or the '70s revival or whatever displaced it as the next big Thing?

Nic shifted her weight, feeling small and perhaps a bit chagrined.

"Lookin' to stock up for next year?"

Nic startled and found a woman standing beside her. She was in her fifties perhaps, with salt-and-pepper hair pulled back into a tight bun, though her ocher skin was almost unlined. Her T-shirt declared "Cow Whisperer" and featured a large bovine silhouette. Faded Wranglers and Carhartt work boots completed the ensemble, and something about her outfit and demeanor was so very much like Granny, Nic had to smile.

"Hey, I know you," the woman said.

"I'm sorry," Nic offered preemptively. The woman had none of Will's prickliness, but Nic wanted to be prepared. Maybe she could have apology cards printed and just hand them out.

"Don't be, your videos saved our bacon. Helen Washington."

"Nicole Jones." They shook hands warmly. "Emily Babbit told me about your place. But did things fall off?" Nic gestured at the discounted merchandise.

"Not too bad. It seemed like most folks stuck with it."

"Well, it gives them an excuse to visit your store. What a great place."

"Thank you." Helen looked around with an expression of genuine fondness on her face. "It was my daddy's and my granddaddy's before that. I love every floorboard and nail. Except for that damn—sorry, darn—computer. It can go straight to hell. Spreadsheets my butt."

Nic's heart squeezed, hard. Her own family might have shopped here. A baker's dozen questions leaped into her mouth, but she let them drop. Helen hadn't been here ninety years ago. So "It's wonderful" was all she said.

"You're not here for my decor. What can I do you for?"

"Two bags of feed and some grit."

"Crumbles or pellets?" Helen asked, flipping into business mode.

"Pellets."

"The extra protein stuff for layers?"

"Yes, please."

"Excellent. I'll see you up at the front when you're ready, then I can carry it around to your car."

After Nic completed her circuit of the store, trying to soak up some small connection to Granny, she went up to the register to pay. "I don't want to put any pressure on you, but I'd love to film here at some point."

Helen's brows shot up, framing her brown eyes. "Really? You'd do that?"

"I used to do 'Know Your Local Feedstore' pieces a lot." Quarantine had put an end to that, and she'd never really gotten back to it. It was one of the many ways her channel had changed as she'd gotten bigger. But she could return to doing things her way now that Brian was out of the picture.

"You'd be perfect," Nic said.

Helen looked away, her face suddenly tense. "They opened a Farm Depot over in Hollins, and we've held on okay so far, but, well, a little publicity never hurt anyone."

See, the business climate wasn't only about Will.

Nic had turned down brand sponsorship from Farm Depot, a megachain that, among other things, sold chicks and poultry supplies, though she wasn't going to say that to Helen. She knew that a lot of her viewers bought their feed at Walmart and their chicks at other big chains. It wasn't her job to tell people what to do, and for the love of Penelope, she knew she'd bought truckloads of stuff from Amazon. But she could highlight Helen's store, emphasize the magic of it. That was one way to use her power for good.

"Absolutely. I've been wanting to do a miniseries about food options, and it would be great to get the seller's perspective."

"And what about a certain vet?" Helen pushed the charge slip across the counter toward Nic to sign, her expression too neutral. "I saw you chatting with him at the farmers' market a few weeks ago."

So this was the other part of small-town life, wasn't it? The part that Will found stifling. Everyone knew what everyone else was up to.

Nic could only hope no one had seen her kissing him in his front yard, not to mention in the dark on his porch a few weeks ago . . .

"He's not a huge fan of my work," Nic offered, knowing that it wasn't so simple but assuming that would be enough to satisfy Helen.

"Dr. Lund is a puzzle," the feedstore owner agreed. "I worry about him."

Nic didn't want to say that she did, too, so she made a noncommittal noise.

"Did you hear that Marsha retired?" Helen asked.

"Yes, I met her, and Will mentioned something about that. We're neighbors."

Helen gave her a look as if to say, *Yes, I knew that. Everyone does.* "If Marsha were just leaving because she was ready, that would be fine.

She's earned it. But I . . . well, Will's in trouble. Maybe he could use some of that publicity."

"I . . . I'll ask him." And really, Nic ought to. She'd mentioned it once jokingly, but she hadn't asked again because she'd assumed he'd turn her down flat, and maybe he'd be right to do so. If he went on her channel, he'd become a target for Brian, and he didn't need any of that mess—which was precisely why she was leaving him alone. That and her no-men pledge.

"He called to put some liniment on hold. Would you mind taking it to him? Since you're his neighbor and all?"

"Sure." Nic couldn't decline that small favor. It would seem petty and not at all in keeping with the love-thy-neighbor nice thing.

After Helen and Nic loaded her car—there was no way Nic was going to let the older woman get the forty-pound bags of feed—Nic pulled onto Route 74 and started for home. Will's clinic was on the way, and it would be the easiest thing in the world to stop. She wouldn't even have to see him. The receptionist had retired, but there was probably still a tech. Nic could drop the liniment and go.

But she just . . . kept on driving, speeding by his practice with a resolute eye on the road, until she got home. Then she unloaded the feed and the grit, setting them next to that death trap of a ladder, and took the liniment into the kitchen.

All afternoon, the bottle winked at her, physical evidence of her bad decision-making.

She wasn't doing men right now. She especially wasn't doing her neighbors. It would be better, for herself and for Will, if she left him alone.

But she didn't want to. The simple truth was she hadn't seen him in a few days, and she wanted to flirt with him. To feel the attraction and interest between them, to know that Brian hadn't stamped those out of her.

Selfish. She was being purely selfish.

Once she'd gone a few more rounds in the debate, she sent Will a text. It was after dinner but not yet all the way dark. She was going to deliver this medicine and then retreat behind her walls. Good fences made good neighbors and all that—good neighbors who weren't recklessly indulging their destructive crushes.

**You around?**

And I mean that in the absolutely least booty call way imaginable, she added a moment later. But of course feeling the need to add that disclaimer, assuming that it would be possible for him to misread her first text in that way, contradicted her denial. It made it seem like she was most definitely proposing a booty call, which, honestly, she sort of was, or else she would have been fine with dropping the liniment off at his office.

She thunked herself in the forehead with her phone several times. It didn't help.

Yeah. What's up? he replied, thankfully fast enough that she didn't have to move to Australia.

I have something for you, she texted back. From Helen Washington.

**I'm around.**

Was everything he did clipped and direct? What would a flirty text from Will even look like?

Right, she'd never know.

She grabbed the liniment and marched across the street. He was sitting on his porch again—the infamous porch—sipping a beer.

"Here you go!" Her tone was loud and cheerful, almost daring their neighbors to look because this time, this time there was going to be nothing to see. Unfortunately. "I was buying some chicken feed today, and she said you reserved it."

"I did. Why were you talking about me, though?"

Oh crap. Nic had no answer for that. "I'm beginning to see what you mean about how everyone knows everyone here."

He chuckled. "The real estate agent should've warned you."

"He was so happy to sell the house, he wasn't about to bring up the downsides." She should go now; it would be rational, reasonable, neighborly. She'd done her good deed.

"You want a beer?" Will was apparently not on board with this keeping-your-neighbors-at-arm's-length plan . . . and Nic had no self-control.

"Sure."

"You can meet my cat."

"You adopted the kitten?" This was going to be so good for him— and she told herself that was why she was happy. Not because he'd done what she'd suggested.

He opened the door, and she trailed him inside.

The kitten trotted up to greet him and then slid to a halt when it saw Nic.

She stooped and held out a hand. "What's he calling you, precious?"

"Not precious, that's for damn sure. She's already destroyed a sock, two rolls of toilet paper, and the contents of my bathroom trash."

"Well, they probably deserved it. What's her name?"

He grimaced. "Hoot."

"Oh my gosh, it's perfect. Hoot." The kitten had inched forward and was sniffing Nic's fingers.

Nic stretched one finger up and over the kitten's head, and after a second, Hoot arched into it. "What a good girl you are."

"Don't romanticize her. She's a menace."

"I think you could use some . . . well, not menace." But joy, he needed some joy.

He came back and handed her a beer. He held up his, and they clinked.

"To Silenus," she offered.

"Who's he?"

"The Greek god of brewing and drunkenness." Not that they were going to get drunk. She waved goodbye to Hoot and followed Will out to the porch. "Jolly guy riding on a donkey. He's in *Fantasia*."

"Isn't that Bacchus?"

She scoffed. "Puh-leeze. You're always doubting my knowledge. Don't mess with me where myths or chickens are concerned."

"Interesting. Where does that come from?"

Nic was grateful the night hid her blush. "It's also Granny's fault. She used to read books about mythology to me. She loved them, so I did too. We always talked about going to Athens."

"Did you?"

"No." Nic said it matter-of-factly, but the sting was just under the surface, somewhere in the vicinity of the upper left-hand side of her chest. They'd never made it; she hadn't been able to give Granny that. "We never had money when I was younger, and once I got out of college and might've saved enough, she was sick. Later, I didn't want . . . I didn't want to go without her."

When Nic was a kid, having a passport, let alone leaving the country, would've seemed impossible. Something people did on TV and not in real life, or at least not in her life. That she had actually traveled abroad was incredible, but somehow she didn't, she couldn't, go to Greece. Greece was reserved for the one person she'd never be able to see it with.

"I'm sorry," Will said.

They'd spent so much time apologizing to one another, but it felt thoughtful. Considerate. Like they both knew they'd been bruised, and they were trying to take care with one another. It had been so long since anyone had tried to cushion any blow for her or had acknowledged any hurt.

That felt more weighty than she wanted, so she tried to play his sympathy off. "It's not your fault."

"I can still be sorry."

Which shouldn't mean anything and yet did. "Brian, he wanted to go. Said I needed to rip the bandage off. I told him no."

"How did he take that?" Will's voice implied that he could guess.

"Not well. It was a few weeks before he dumped me." It had been quite a fight. She should've seen what was coming. Hers had been sheer obstinate blindness.

"I don't want to be that ass who's always dunking on your ex, but he totally sucks."

"Yes, he does."

"Why?"

"Why am I telling you this? I think because I can't see you." And because she liked him. More than she should. Far more than was a good idea. Emotions were such assholes, and she was going to get hers in check soon. "It's kinda anonymous, talking in the dark like this."

And yet not at all anonymous. It was Will. Out of seven billion people on the planet, she was talking to *him*.

"I didn't mean why are you telling me this, though I know what you mean." The air between them crackled, hissed. "What I wanted to ask was why you stayed with him. Why you started going out with him in the first place."

"Well, he's charming." That was the simplest true explanation, the one that indicted her the least. "Really charming, when he wants to be. Brian can make you feel like you're the only interesting person in the world. And he . . . projects it somehow. I think that's what viewers like about him. But he can turn it off like—" She snapped loudly.

"And so you . . . ?"

"Didn't know at first, obviously. And when I first saw him do it, it was jarring, but I thought it was about persona, exhaustion. That sort of thing. And then later, I thought I was special. I thought I was an exception. That he cared enough not to do that to me. And honestly, he still made me feel good sometimes."

She wasn't the helpless victim she knew Will wanted her to be.

"Take my videos," she said. "When I made my first one, I thought it was terrible. And even as Brian was telling me it was great, I didn't—I knew he was exaggerating. But I was so low in that moment, I seized onto it, even knowing that it was a lie. Even knowing that I was only with him because breaking up with him would have been exhausting. I wasn't happy with my job. It just wasn't really my thing. But I was sort of . . . existing. Until he convinced me to try doing something I loved on the internet, and so I got some chicks. And it worked. It *worked*. I'd spent so long trying to be what I thought other people wanted me to be, and then somehow I did this ridiculous thing and was rewarded. I was still riding the high of that, right up until the moment he dumped me."

She'd never said it all out loud before, and of everything she and Will had shared, it felt the most revealing. It was important that he know what she really was, flaws and all.

Silence filled up between them like one of those woodland ponds in the spring, after the snow thawed. Nic wanted to fidget, to run, to apologize, but she forced herself to sit there with what she'd admitted. To see what he thought about it, about her.

Finally, gently, Will said, "I can understand that."

"So while I blame him, I also blame myself. I know that I was using him, I guess."

"That is *ridiculous*." The quietness had evaporated. He really could turn it off abruptly, and it was disturbing how much it reminded her of Brian. "It isn't using someone when the person you're with makes you feel better. That's just . . . love."

"What if I didn't love him?" Nic still wasn't sure whether she had or hadn't, or whether she wanted to convince herself that she hadn't because then it meant her judgment wasn't that bad, that she had seen through Brian. It would be easier in some ways if she hadn't loved him. She didn't deserve easy, though.

"Are you trying to get me to scold you?"

"Maybe. Maybe I feel guilty."

"Well, you'll have to find someone else to do it."

"You'll do. Remember the Chicken Barbie quip?"

"Gah, I regret everything about those first days."

As they both did, apparently. At least now, the conversation felt playful again. "But you were so cute when you were chiding me."

"Damn it, I . . . okay, well, that was it. Your one free chiding from me. The rest will cost you."

She laughed. "So stingy."

"But I'm serious." His voice went into another, more sincere register. "Nic, you didn't do anything wrong. He's the ass."

"I appreciate that you'd defend me."

"Because you aren't defending yourself!"

"I could say the same. I could say that you're an amazing vet. And that you got pulled under by circumstances entirely beyond your control, and now you're flagellating yourself about it, and you should stop."

"Sure, but—"

"And that even when you were being sort of a jerk to a new patient, it was because you care about animals. I mean, I won't put up with the rudeness, but I get where you're coming from." She had been miffed, but now that she knew him, it seemed like the most obvious thing in the world. Maybe even a little admirable.

If he was going to try to get her to admit she'd been snowed, Will could admit that he wasn't solely to blame for his own pain.

"You should probably be a little mad about it," Will said. "You should probably be more mad about stuff. You have anti-anger issues."

"I'll just outsource all my anger to you."

"I can handle that. Who was the god who made the thunderbolts for Zeus?"

"Hephaestus. And they were lightning."

"That, then."

She laughed. "That is a very weird vow, and I like it. But will you listen to what I'm trying to say to you?"

"Probably not."

"You stubborn, stubborn man."

"You woman who can't hold on to anger."

She was a woman who should go home if she was going to stick to her plan here. If she stayed any longer, she was going to do far more than kiss him again, and she shouldn't want that—which was almost enough to convince herself that she didn't want that. Almost.

"Ah, well, I guess it's time to call it a night."

Oh, that hung there. Not a statement, entirely. Not a question, really. The promise of it, in it, under it, charging the air like before a thunderstorm. Lightning bolts indeed. When this tension broke, when the storm came, *if* it came, it was going to curl her toes, her hair. It might level the house. Level the two of them.

But she'd been through this, and given the comments she'd spent all afternoon deleting from her blog and the folks she'd been blocking on Twitter and Insta, she was still paying for it. Will wasn't Brian, and maybe it wasn't fair to make him pay for someone else's crimes. Except love wasn't fair. It wasn't easy. And she needed to be more whole, more healthy, before she could take another risk.

"I'm glad you adopted Hoot," she said, standing.

"I think I will be too."

"I know you will be. Thanks for the beer."

"Thanks for the confessions."

"Anytime."

But only as friends, and only when they kept the lightning banked.

# CHAPTER 19

There was still no answer about pressing pause on his real estate payments to the bank. *Yes* was what Will needed, what he was literally begging for. It would mean saving Kim's job, his job, and good veterinary medicine for all the animals in town. But it simply seemed impossible.

And so while *no* would be devastating, then at least it would be over. He'd face the failure, the shame, and the public scorn that would inevitably follow, but at least he could stop pretending. He could be the person out in the world that he knew himself to be, no more hiding.

Kim could see the writing on the wall. She'd taken over where Marsha had left off as his cheerleader, but he'd told her he would understand if she wanted to quit or take that other job.

"Oh, I think I'm in it until the end," she'd said, way too kindly.

So they'd tried to pretend everything was normal, keeping the 75 percent schedule that wasn't enough to cover their expenses, all while slowly bleeding out.

And every morning and every evening since she'd brought him the liniment, Nicole would text him.

> How is Hoot? I've started using her name as an exclamation. It's very satisfying if you get a papercut.
> (Hoot!!!)

There are still no rabid Brian fans at my house.

The girls discovered a nest of caterpillars today. I apologize for the ensuing lack of butterflies.

(That's a big word for a TikTok star. Tomorrow, I'll break out sartorial.)

((What does sartorial mean anyhow, doctor?))

I bet you're regretting giving me your number now.

But he wasn't. At all. His only regret was his single-syllable responses. He didn't want to ignore her, because then she'd stop. Equally, he didn't want it to seem as if he was responding to her maybe flirtation with flirtation of his own. At least now he knew that she wanted that from him.

He'd been out of it for so long, he didn't even know where the flirting/not flirting boundary was these days. This made the roundabout thank-you he'd arranged a foolish idea. It was foolish for reasons that Will didn't even want to begin to contemplate, such as the public-ness of it and because it was going to shift things with Nicole.

But shift them from what to what?

They'd been on this Tilt-A-Whirl for weeks now, hooking up, flirting, then pulling back, and he didn't know where the ground was anymore.

Still disoriented but trapped by what he'd set in motion a week ago, he texted Nic around lunch one Saturday.

Do you have a few hours today?

To?

Take a little trip downtown with me.

Yup. Just give me 10 minutes.

It was almost a relief that he had to see it through, that he was stuck now. He pulled out of his driveway and parked in front of Nicole's house. He drummed on the steering wheel, trying to look like a man who knew what he was doing, which wasn't who he'd been for years.

But exactly ten minutes after her text, Nicole bounced out of the door looking, if not fresh as a daisy, then sexy as one.

"You weren't busy?" he asked as he started down the street. He was trying to ignore the way he could smell her laundry detergent mixed with something that was probably her skin: clean, floral, and intoxicating.

"You're saving me, actually, from a million administrative tasks."

"We shouldn't be too long."

"I'm trying to express appreciation. Seriously, *thank you*."

All Will managed in response was to clear his throat gruffly. He didn't want her appreciation; he wanted something more sweaty and primal, and he was going to have to learn to deal with disappointment.

For a few minutes, they drove in silence, the town he'd known all his life flashing by the windows. He couldn't imagine how it must look to her. Run down. Rusted. He just hoped what he had to show her would make it worth it.

"How is Hoot?"

"Now that all shoes with laces go immediately into the closet? Bored."

"Oh, you're so mean. You ought to get her some toys."

"I bought her an entire box of toys yesterday! She doesn't want any of them." Or she did, but only for as long as it took to lose them under the couch.

Nic was smiling softly, smugly. He wanted to tweak her nose.

"Where are we going anyhow?"

"It's funny you haven't asked until now."

"I've known you for, what, almost a month? I'm fairly sure you're safe."

Nothing about what he was beginning to feel about her was safe, but he said, half joking, "How long does it take to make up your mind about that?"

Her answer was careful. "I'm not sure. With Brian . . ."

Oh crap. He hadn't meant to invoke that jerk-wad. "It seems like you were right about him."

"*Now*. It took me a while, though. But with you"—she was trying to brighten her tone, and it was almost working—"you were so tart from the beginning, I knew what I saw was what I was going to get."

*Tart* was one word for him. "We're going to the Yagerstown Library."

"Oh, I love libraries. I haven't been there yet."

"Figured as much."

When they parked, she stood outside his car for a minute and stared rapt at the building. It was one of the fancier ones in town.

"Is it a Carnegie library?" Her voice was filled with wonder.

"A what?"

"Andrew Carnegie. You know, the industrialist." Will hadn't known. "Or was he a banker? I'm not sure, but he was one of those robber baron types. Anyhow, he felt guilty later in life, and tried to make up for his greedy ways by building libraries all over the country in the late eighteen hundreds."

"No idea, but the person we're going to see will know." He gestured for Nicole to go down the walkway in front of him.

"Oh, who is that?"

"Ichabod's owner. The most cantankerous cat in town." At least he hoped Hoot wouldn't turn out to be that difficult. Will held the library door open for Nicole. "He won't be here, though."

You couldn't not love Nanette. It was simply impossible. The librarian just radiated warmth and competence, like the love child of chocolate chip cookies and the Dewey decimal system.

"Hey there! I was hoping you'd make it," she called as she came out from behind the circulation desk.

"Sorry we're late. But I was trying to maintain the secrecy."

"Oh." Nanette's eyes sparkled. Obviously, she thought this was some sort of courtship gift. She'd probably called Marsha and Leonie to share the news, and within weeks, everyone in town would have decided that Will and Nicole were going to end up married. Likely, Will would never live this down, but at least the coming failure of his practice would overshadow this little bit of gossip. No one would remember about his not quite girlfriend when they found out he was bankrupt.

Nanette turned her attention to Nicole, that *going to the chapel* gleam still in her eye. "So Will tells me that your family used to live here."

Nicole had been taking in the wood-paneled lobby and had missed the subtext. "That's right, but it was forever ago. I liked the idea of . . . coming home? Not quite, but something like that."

"Coming home. No, that's it. Anyhow, Will said you wanted to find out more about them, and we have all the county historical society papers in our archives. I started with the men's clubs, looking for the last name Reston. And it worked. Once I had a first name and some firm dates, it was pretty easy to find some more stuff. I pulled it for you."

Nicole's mouth dropped open. "Granny's family? You've her family?"

"Would you like to see?"

"I—yes. *Yes.*" But when they started toward the archive room, she sank her nails into Will's forearm, and he stopped.

"Is this okay? It's not like . . . too much?" He knew that it was. Whenever Nicole got over her surprise, she was going to ask him why he'd done it, and he wasn't going to have any good answers, or at least not any answers he wanted to share with her while she was still insisting they were friends.

"Too much? It's the nicest thing anyone has ever done for me." She held his gaze for a long minute, and the space around them compressed, snug and private. "I'm overwhelmed."

He should've given Nanette's name to Nicole and omitted himself from all this. He felt like a Peeping Tom, but as a few seconds passed and the shock melted from Nicole's face, leaving pure joy behind, he knew why he hadn't. He'd wanted the credit, had wanted this moment with her.

"It's just some old papers," he deflected.

"Shut up."

And so he did.

They followed Nanette into the historical society, which was merely a brass plaque outside a small conference room in the corner of the library. Nanette had arranged some books and newspapers on the table, however, and Nicole was beaming at them. He had the sense that if they had been jewels and gold bars, her happiness wouldn't have been more complete.

"This was the first one I found." Nanette pointed. "It's the register of Elks Club members from nineteen thirty, but he's listed for several years."

"This is my great-grandfather's signature? Like, his actual signature?"

"Yup."

Nicole leaned close to the page, hovering above, not touching, only blinking in wonder. "Wow."

"That's only the beginning. I'm certain this isn't even all of it, but it's enough to get you started. I liked this one the best." She pointed to a newspaper. "He apparently liked to write letters to the editor. He had strong feelings about potholes. You should give me your number, and we can set up an appointment to dig even deeper."

"Yes, please."

After she jotted her number down for Nanette, Nicole read her great-grandfather's irate words to herself, her lips moving as she did. It was very, very hard for Will to keep his thoughts pure, even in the presence of a kindly librarian, with Nicole's mouth doing that.

"Oh my gosh, 320 Sycamore. That's . . . that was their address."

"Oh, yes." Nanette laughed. "They used to publish the addresses with the letters for some reason, probably so everyone would know they were real."

"Will, is that street still there?" Hope vibrated under Nic's question.

"It is. And, well, Nanette told me about this one, and it turns out I know the people who own 320 Sycamore. They're around and said we could stop by."

"I can go to Granny's *house*? I can see her house?"

"Yes."

"I . . . can I look at all this stuff first?"

He laughed. "Yeah, there's no rush."

Rush, no; risk, yes. Risk to his heart, because he was absolutely sinking into it, but there was no time limit. He could spend all day with her, and it wasn't going to matter at all. He'd still be wildly in like with her, and she'd still be insisting they were only friends.

# CHAPTER 20

As they pulled up to 320 Sycamore, Nic was almost vibrating. Beyond a few hurried thank-yous to Nanette and Will, she hadn't managed to say much, because what would be enough? She was going to take the librarian some eggs, a card, and flowers, but Will—how was she going to explain what this gesture meant to her?

Since Granny's death, Nic had felt unmoored. Of all the people on earth, Granny had been her main tether. The person she'd trusted the most, the one who made her feel like herself. She'd tried to transfer that to Brian, but that had blown up in her face like a grenade, and she was still reeling from it.

Being here, at her house, was like getting Granny back, or at least seeing a shade of her. Will had done magic with this.

*Why*: that was what Nic wanted to know the most. Why precisely had he gone to all this trouble for her?

"This is it," he said.

The house could have wandered off a farm, not unlike Nic's bungalow. It was painted pale yellow with french blue trim. Huge, shaggy azalea bushes framed the brick front steps, decorative grass lined the flower beds, and a swing hung on the porch. Add a box for the milkman and a Buick Roadster and it would be exactly as Nic had imagined.

"It probably wasn't this color." Of course that didn't matter. "But it's Granny's house."

"It's funny you keep mentioning your grandma and not your great-grandparents."

Nic could feel Will's attention on her, but she couldn't drag her eyes from the structure itself, from the windows and the line of the roof and the *houseness* of it.

"I know! I'm so weird. I just . . . I never met them. They're less real to me. That's ridiculous."

She finally turned to Will. She could feel his attention straining toward her. He wanted so badly for her to be pleased. What she felt would probably be enough to flatten his car, but it was a tumble of emotions she couldn't yet differentiate or explain. She couldn't share them with him. Not yet and maybe not ever.

After a second, Will's determination went soft. "Of course it isn't." He got out and came around and opened her door.

"I'm dawdling. Sorry."

There wasn't any judgment in his expression, just understanding, which felt somehow scarier. She hadn't felt wordlessly understood by anyone since Rose had stopped speaking to her, and, before that, since Granny had died. She'd never had that with Brian and would never have expected to. But, suddenly, the lack of recognition, of support, seemed too much to bear.

"Come on, let's see this house."

The Wallaces were, of course, lovely. Their dogs were patients of Will's, and Nic was realizing that while she might be more famous, his celebrity was fathoms deep in Yagerstown.

"We were so excited to find out who had lived here," Gail Wallace gushed as they stood awkwardly in the front room, Nic barely containing the urge to skitter all over the house and look in every closet.

Nic tried to flip into Chick Nic mode, to be poised and professional and contained, but she couldn't manage it. "I should write down all the stories Granny told me about this house. Parties they had, that kind of thing. I wish I had pictures to share with you, but Granny had a flood when I was a kid, and she lost everything. All that was left were the—the words. The memories."

And Will was making them real again by helping her find this place.

"Oh, I am sorry. I don't want to disappoint you, but I'm sure a lot of it has changed. We almost had to gut it when we bought it. It had been the victim of some horrible eighties remodel. But we think that banister is original"—Gail pointed to the stairwell, which curled around the first floor—"and the paneling in the dining room."

Her husband snapped his fingers. "And that live oak, in the back, that's definitely as old as the house."

"Granny told me about that tree! Perfect for climbing, she said."

Actually, what she'd said was that she'd climbed the tree and watched the boy next door undress, which had prompted Nic to lecture her and then Granny to reveal that he was in on the ritual, that it had been a mutual sorta thing, and that had been an entirely other side of Granny—one which should probably stay in the past.

Nic decided to keep the tree's erotic history to herself.

For the next twenty minutes, Nic followed them around, trying to soak it all in, to listen politely to their description of their remodeling efforts, all while the voices in her head kept shouting that this was where Granny had grown up. Where she'd learned her good sense. Where she'd laughed and screwed up and stirred endless pots of drama.

Seeing the house, recognizing the swinging door between the kitchen and the dining room and the glazed tiles around the fireplace and the little window at the turn of the stairs from Granny's tales proved those stories and also somehow made them seem more like stories. Pushed them further into the past. Nic had never felt closer to her grandmother, but she'd never felt the veil between them more, at least since Granny's death. It was finding and losing her again in the same heartbeat. Her heart pinwheeled in her chest, flashing two different colors over and over again.

It made Nic clam up, trying to figure that out. If she'd been on her own, her wide-eyed, ebullient-grief two-step would have been intensely antisocial, bordering on rude. But she wasn't alone.

Will stepped in and smoothly made conversation with Gail while Nic found her footing. He asked about the dogs, about the kids. As the choking feeling eased in her throat, Nic could see how he was good at his job. He might sometimes still be the grumpy lecturer bent on animal welfare at the cost of everything else, but he liked his patients and their owners, liked the people of this town.

And then he'd done this. She was just full, so full, of the kindness of it. The . . . consideration. It was a hundred things she couldn't stick labels on.

After they'd seen the entire house, she thanked the Wallaces as best she could, but she mostly stayed quiet until Will pulled into his drive-way and turned off his car. So many emotions still fizzed in Nic's veins, the bubbles in a can of ginger ale.

She waited until he'd turned the car off before she set her hand lightly on his forearm. She kept touching him, and she couldn't seem to help herself. The "corded" thing made much more sense now—which wasn't the point. This wasn't about the attraction between them. She had to find some way to express to him what this had meant to her.

"Thank you."

Will brushed off her words and her hand. He shrugged and slid out of his Jeep. "It wasn't a big deal."

She clambered out after him. "It involved librarians. It involved phone calls. Do you know how much I hate the phone?"

"Everyone hates the phone." He was trying not to smile.

His obvious struggle to keep his feelings in, and knowing how dazzling his grin would be when it finally broke out, made her want to keep pushing him.

"This is my point. That was some above-and-beyond-the-call-of-duty friend stuff there. It deserves a serious thank-you."

They were friendly in the same way that Harry and Sally from that movie that was always on cable were—and she knew how that one ended.

"You mentioned your grandmother, said you'd moved here because of her. I thought you'd want to see where she grew up."

"But this is my point! Of course I wanted to. It didn't occur to me that I could. Or if it did, I wouldn't have known how to do it. It would have been some flash in my head, and I would have had to let it go because how would I make that happen? But you, you were able to. That's amazing."

"Not amazing," he deferred.

"I haven't felt this close to her since she died." Nic hadn't felt this much herself since long before she'd broken up with Brian. Will truly didn't know what he'd given her.

"It was nothing."

The thing she was coming to understand was that Will got gruff when he was embarrassed. Or angry. Or experiencing any emotion stronger than hunger. Feelings clogged him.

She had experienced that in front of Granny's house. She'd reached her saturation point and had needed a minute for all that stuff, good and bad, to filter through her. She was still feeling a little numb, to be honest, but she knew one thing for sure: she wasn't interested in being only Will's neighbor.

She'd been holding back until she knew she wouldn't muck him up, until she felt healed, but it was waiting for a bus that was never going to come. Risks were risks precisely because there was no guarantee. She had to weigh what she stood to lose if she didn't act against the potential consequences. That was the only calculation that mattered, and somewhere this afternoon, the balance had shifted and crashed into the ground.

It would hurt if Will weren't the man she was beginning to suspect he was. It would be awkward if they were to give this a try and have it not work out. But she didn't want to keep hiding anymore. She didn't want to make more decisions out of fear, not when joy was right there, heavy on the branch and ready for her to grab with both hands.

Nic strode around the front of his Jeep until she was standing less than an arm's length away from him. "I won't argue with you. But while *thank you* doesn't seem like enough . . . thank you."

Will's jaw worked. "I didn't—I mean—"

"Accept it. When you do nice things, people will thank you. If you don't want them to, then you shouldn't do nice things. Don't help them catch their chickens. Don't help them find their long-lost family homes. Don't do anything at all."

That cleared his throat. "Do fewer nice things. That's the Nic Jones way?"

She laughed. Tried to laugh. But the thing was that being this close to him, having him be nice to her, it didn't make her gruff. It seared her. Brought back memories of his mouth fused to hers.

Will Lund was many things, sweet not among them. No, he was salted caramel, where the sugar was just turning bitter. What he was was more precious than mere sweetness.

Which was why she closed the distance between them. It was different from when she had come to him on his porch. Different from their desperate kiss after near ladder death. It was reasoned, and it had a destination. She looped her arms around his neck, rose onto her toes, and drew him into a hug. She tried to put that storm of emotions and desires into the touch.

After an awkward beat, he made a rough noise, and his arms came around her waist. Ferocious. When she relived this later, she was going to characterize his embrace as ferocious, but of course you'd expect a Viking's hug to be. He pressed his face to her neck and inhaled. All Nic's nerves, skating down her back and thighs, stood up.

"You don't argue with me when I hug you," she whispered.

So of course he started to. "Is this thank you?"

"No." While she wanted to thank him, she wasn't going to try to take him to bed out of gratitude. "It's that we're both bruised. Under our clothes, where no one else can see, we're like the apples at the bottom of the bin."

He huffed out a laugh. "We're bad apples?"

"No. We recognize each other's hurts."

She let that sit there, between them, the promise of it. The question of it. But she could feel his body responding to her nearness, could feel him growing hard, hungry, giving a preliminary answer.

"We barely know each other." When he voiced it like that, it wasn't an objection, just a statement of fact.

So she offered him one back. "I know you, Will Lund."

She didn't know the name of his third-grade teacher, or whether he thought presents from Santa Claus came wrapped or bare—or even whether he believed in Santa. But she knew his pain. She knew he was kind. She knew that he wanted her. And she was done pretending she didn't want him back.

Which they must have had in common, because with a grunt of affirmation, he kissed her.

She'd missed the taste of him. The surging power. The way his hands rushed up her body, waves up the shore, breaking on her back, her stomach.

This wasn't like their first kiss . . . or their second kiss. There was no surprise this time, just hunger and arousal and need. Gnawing, adamant need.

"You're not damaged," Will managed between frantic kisses down her neck. He pressed his mouth over her shirt, and she boiled underneath.

At the moment, she felt replenished. The parched creek bed full to brimming after the flash flood.

"Neither are you."

She caught his head in her hands and dragged him back to her. Her hips rocked into him, but it wasn't right. She was too short for this, but going into his house, dragging him across the street into hers—it would risk dissolving the spell. She wouldn't chance that. Not when she could feel her libido rushing into every cell in her body, the too-long-dormant hunger roaring back. Not when she'd discovered the just-right taste of Will.

She dropped back onto her heels, kissed his neck for a change. His collarbone.

But that freed up his mouth. "What does this mean?"

His question was reasonable, but this wasn't about reason. It was about the way his thigh felt pushed between her legs. About his hand cupping her ass. About the fresh-laundry smell of his clothing. Why hadn't she known before that fucking fabric softener smelled so god-damn erotic?

She ran one hand down his chest, tracing the undulation of the muscles under the cotton. Wanting to repeat it bare. Wanting to follow the path with her mouth. There was that landscape she was itching to learn.

"What does this mean?" he repeated.

"It means we like kissing each other."

"Nic." Needy. Begging.

But she couldn't name this for him. Didn't want to. He had to figure that part out. "What do you want it to mean?"

She meant the question to be coy, but it came out too direct, too neutral.

"I thought we were friends."

"We made out right here," she countered.

"And then you didn't kiss me again."

Because she wasn't very bright. "You took me to my grandmother's house. Are those things you do with friends?"

"We're on the edge here. And if we . . ."

"Fuck?"

The word—she'd intentionally chosen the crudest one—made his eyes flash bronze. "Right, then we won't be friends anymore."

"You can be friends with your lovers."

"Says the woman whose ex is a scumbag."

"I was being aspirational."

"I'll never be that guy, Nic, but you just ran away from something here. And if this doesn't . . . I mean, I seem to break *everything*. That doesn't mean I'm not—I mean, God, I want you. There aren't words for—"

They didn't need words. She could feel it, the length of his interest. And she was . . . flattered by his tapping the brakes, even if clearly she hadn't meant to. It spoke to his carefulness, with her if not with himself.

If he were trying to make a case against sex, he was doing a pretty bad job. This was more evidence of how it was a good decision.

"It can mean everything, if we say it means everything," Nic interrupted him. "Or we can say that we're friends who happen to be really attracted to one another. It can mean we're taking a risk because we want to. And that we're going to go inside and—"

She could see it, immediately, how they were going to be together. Knew that everything that kiss had promised, that entire filthy book of suggestions, was going to come true. Heat shot up her body, from the spaces between her toes up her spine and out through the ends of her hair. She shivered in anticipation.

"—fuck," she finished. "And it can be that."

"Is that what it is?" If there were a way to x-ray someone's thoughts, some medical test for intentions, his intense gaze would have done it.

"Yes."

For a minute, he watched her, flipped his shield up. Leashed his desire.

His control was arousing as hell. Obviously, whatever argument she'd thought she'd been making with her body wasn't persuasive to him at all. He was only going to act if it made sense intellectually.

"Okay, then."

And before she had a second to revel in her win, she was over his shoulder and he was crossing the yard. Those great legs of his eating up the ground beneath them, while every bit of her hummed in anticipation.

She didn't get a good look at his kitchen before he started up the stairs and then down his upstairs hallway to his bedroom.

She bounced once on the bed before he'd covered her with his body.

"Dreamed about this," she managed between kisses. Frantic, breathless kisses. The contact, the break, the gasp, the struggle with her shirt, her pants, and then finding his mouth again.

Will rolled back onto his knees and was peeling his shirt up. His muscles were lightly scored and perfect, the sexiest anatomy textbook in the world—and she was going to get to touch him.

She skimmed her fingertips over his body. "How are you a vet?" Weren't vets supposed to be basically disembodied, just hands and a head? It would be a shame to dis-anything this body.

"How are you a chicken person?" he asked, returning the favor.

He came over her again, his belly brushing over hers. It was an accelerant, kerosene on the firepit that didn't need it. She would have rushed everything then just for the relief of knowing that they'd done it, that she'd had him, but Will obviously had other, slower plans in mind.

He began fumbling with the clasp of her bra, and Nic could feel gravity find her breasts. It was the swollen, tender point of her cycle. Great for cleavage, not so much for . . .

"Be careful with them." Her voice came out as a shadow.

Will immediately froze. "Careful?"

"Everything's sort of . . . sensitive." She left off *not in the good way.*

He pulled back. He hadn't turned on any lights, and his blinds were still drawn from the night before. The afternoon sunshine was making its way in through the cracks, leaving strips of light and dark across his face.

"Do you want me to put your bra back on?"

"No, I just—" *Wish I hadn't said anything at all.* "They get like this at certain times of the month, and touch is a lot then."

The burning in her cheeks now was self-consciousness, not arousal. She didn't normally mention this to her partners, and when she had, they hadn't normally cared. No one had been cruel, but they also hadn't been . . . conscientious. So she'd just stopped saying anything at all. She had absolutely no idea why she'd blurted it out now, and she wanted the words back.

"Nic." Will cupped her face with one hand, the contact so tender she had to close her eyes. "I'd never hurt you."

"I know."

He touched his mouth to her forehead, to her closed eyes that were leaking stupid tears for some stupid reason, to her own lips. Each kiss lighter than the last, until she was shaking, desperate for firmer touch, for him.

*"Will."*

But just when his mouth fused with hers, a soft *thump* landed on the bed next to them, and Nic found a small face, with too-long whiskers and pale-green eyes, staring at her.

"Hoot, this isn't the time." Will pushed up onto his arms.

The kitten promptly sat down, her tail twitching playfully as if this were her favorite game in the world.

"Hoot," Will said with a growly note of warning.

Nic giggled. "She doesn't seem inclined to listen."

"No, the women in my life don't tend to take direction." He stood up—and his body was perfect. Just absolutely perfect.

He tried to scoop up the kitten, but she'd sunk her claws into the comforter, and he gently prized them free, one at a time, while Hoot meowed in complaint. Nic couldn't stop laughing, which was so much better than leaking tears because she'd somehow accidentally confessed some other vulnerability to him and he'd responded too sensitively.

At last, he freed the comforter from the cat, who he carried to the door. He shut it in her face, and Hoot immediately launched herself at it. The door guttered, but it didn't open.

"Where were we?"

"You were giving directions that no one was following."

"That gonna be a pattern?"

"We'll have to see."

He shucked off his pants—which would've been a *whoa* moment, but Nic was still trying to play coy—before sliding her bra up her arms and over her shoulders and beginning to work the clasp. No one had ever put a bra on her before.

She started to protest. "You don't—"

"For me."

Pushing against his shoulder, she shoved him onto the mattress and straddled him. "And what's for me?"

"Everything else."

Only if Nic were very lucky. Dropping her head, she licked down his neck. The skin there was softer than she would have imagined, and, given how Will was almost trembling between her thighs, more sensitive too.

Gesturing at his response, she whispered, "That was for me?"

"Yes."

She found one flat pink nipple, and she dropped a spiral of open-mouthed kisses around it, closer and closer until she was dizzy, until he was panting. But it seemed to surprise them both when she ran her teeth over it, catching on each of the ridges that had appeared.

Will's hips jolted off the bed, bringing the ridge of his erection precisely where she wanted it.

She lifted her head an inch or two from his body to ask again if his response was hers, but he said "Yes" before she could get the question out.

It was yes when she repeated the same things on the other side and when she explored the inside of his elbow. Yes wasn't an answer at that point; it was a thing they made together—particularly when he shoved her panties over and his fingers skated into her in a single fluid motion.

"This is *mine.*" It didn't feel as if Will was talking about how wet she was for him, or for the one afternoon.

She had to close her eyes against the intensity of how he looked at her when he said it, but that helped mask whatever self-consciousness might have come from how shamelessly she moved against his hand, when she showed him how and where she needed to be touched.

Will was a *particularly* quick learner.

When her spine had melted and she was on her back next to him, shimmying out of her panties and begging him to hurry up with the condom, it no longer seemed so absurd that she'd confessed her discomfort to him. His response felt like being cherished. And because he knew the truth, because she knew that he'd be gentle, she didn't hold anything back, didn't try to protect herself. Because while this might be fucking, it could be honest. It could be caring.

And it *was* caring when he pushed into her. Caring when he cupped her breasts, never squeezing. Caring when his chin tipped up and he moaned, and she knew he was finding release. Caring when she followed him over the edge.

Friends cared, right?

# CHAPTER 21

Will's final appointment the next day was Marilee Hancock's fluffy Akita named Rutabaga. It was an impractical dog for the South, but Will tried not to mention that too often. Up at the front, Marilee presented him with a quiche.

"Baked it this morning," she said with the assured air of someone whose gifts were always appreciated, which of course this one was. It looked delicious.

"You didn't need to do that."

"Of course I didn't. I thought you'd enjoy it."

She'd thought right.

The day before, Nic had pulled out of Will's arms almost immediately after they'd finished—and he'd let her go.

Twenty-four hours later, Will was still stunned. He'd had too much pent-up longing, for her specifically and in general. It had been too long, and he'd forgotten how sex was, forgotten the intimacy, the way her cries would feel like his pleasure, the way his shell would crack and she would slip inside his heart.

She'd tried to skip out with a small wave, but he hadn't allowed that. He'd kissed Nic goodbye so that she'd remember. He'd kissed her so that that night in bed, she'd burn for him. He'd kissed her so that she'd never forget that it could be like this, she could feel like this—and that he was the one who'd made it happen.

And all day, he'd noodled around for an excuse to reach out today. The quiche was it.

He stowed it in the fridge and went to examine Marilee's dog.

Then, before he drove home, he texted Nic:

> Have you eaten?

Who could eat an entire quiche by himself? Ridiculous. He had to share it with someone. It was like an honor thing.

Are you inviting me to dinner? she replied.

> Yes, I'm calling a meeting of the sad friends supper club.

The what?

> It's what I call us in my head.

At least it was the only thing he was going to share with her that he called them in his head.

> I need help eating a quiche from a patient's owner. It's bacon and leek.

He was not above bribing Nic with bacon. After the last few years, he had no shame.

After a few seconds, she replied, I'll bring wine.

> I'll be home in ten minutes.

To kiss her at the door or not to kiss her at the door: that was what he pondered the entire drive. When he got home, Hoot kept him company, attacking a leaf that he must have carried in on his shoe. She crouched down behind the couch, craning slowly around the corner, her tiny butt quivering in anticipation before she pounced. She had too much energy, and she turned a somersault over the leaf. For a second, she lay sprawled on her back, blinking, as if trying to figure out where she was.

Then she promptly attacked the leaf again.

"You're a persistent ball of fluff," he muttered.

Hoot gave him a smug look because she somehow knew she had him wrapped around her paw.

When Nic knocked on the door, he let her in with a buss on the cheek and a hug, but it was the kind of hug that involved burying his face in her hair. It was not the way that he'd greet his sister—and he wanted Nic to know that. They were going to proceed the way she wanted to, and he was trying, desperately, to be okay with that, even if it wasn't at all what he wanted.

The first thing he noticed was that Nic had done her hair, it smelled more of product than it had the other day, and she was wearing lipstick and her full Chick Nic costume. She'd probably been filming, but it felt almost like armor. As if when she was that person, she wasn't the woman he'd made love to.

He tried not to take it personally as he ushered her into the dining room, where he'd hastily set the table and placed the quiche.

"Do people give you food all the time?" Nic asked as she slid into a chair.

"Yes. Quiche is unusual, but jams, pies, and cookies show up pretty regularly."

"And I keep giving you eggs. It's like we all think you need to put on some weight."

"Something like that. Also knitted and crocheted throw blankets. Just let me know if you need any. I have an entire closet full."

She fumbled with the wine. She'd opened it at home and stuck the cork back into the bottle—smart. He produced two glasses from a cabinet, and they clinked.

"Bacchus?" he asked.

"Dionysus. I'm more of a Greek-mythology girl. How have you been?"

The question was as heavy as an eighteen-wheeler. *Since the incredible sex?* But if that was what she wanted to know, Nic was going to have to be more direct. He could be coy too.

"Okay." That about captured the emotional average of the last twenty-four hours.

"No news?"

"None, which probably isn't good. I don't even know what good news would be any more. But no, my friend Frank is playing very hard to get. Have you heard anything more from your ex?" Damn, but he hated that guy.

She shook her head. "Nope. I know the blowup will come, but what can you do? What are you doing? How are you handling the wait?"

*Falling for my neighbor who doesn't want a relationship.* "Just working, cleaning up the messes that one leaves." He shoved a thumb in Hoot's direction. "Trying not to panic. I've done everything I could. I've made mistakes, and it's . . . out of my hands." During his second call with his therapist, she'd talked about the things he worried about versus the things he controlled. Will knew he'd taken whatever actions he could.

Which, incidentally, applied to Nic as well.

"That sounds really healthy."

"You seemed surprised. But I got a therapist."

Her expression fixed. "You what?"

"Decided to stop moping and do something. My therapist thinks I have situational depression."

If he'd worried, in some deep chasm inside himself, whether Nic would think less of him if he admitted he'd gotten some help, the slow, warm joy that blossomed over her features would have destroyed it.

"I'm sorry for the diagnosis, but you seeing someone? That's wonderful. I really mean it, Will, that's wonderful."

He made a noise of agreement and downed half a glass of wine. He might have admitted that he was depressed, but he still didn't like talking about it.

Nic just kept on being excited for him, though. "I hope your therapist helps you see that it's not only you, it's thousands of small business owners in the same position."

"Nah, that doesn't track. Rugged individuals built this country. A whole crowd of mavericks, pulling ourselves up by our bootstraps. Our fates are our own. 'Collective' is a lie."

Nic wouldn't know it, because she'd never met him, but Will was doing a pretty spot-on imitation of his father.

Likely assuming he was sending up people on the news, she laughed. "That story is . . . seductive. I guess it's scary to admit how much in life isn't about what we do, what we have control over, but is this web of connected pieces."

"Blaming it all on the system and the man sounds like a conspiracy thing." Or like socialism.

"It totally does."

"So, yeah, my therapist agrees it's not only my fault, but I guess I can't help but hear my dad and my brother in my head making fun of people who can't take responsibility for their shit." He knew that when his family found out how much trouble his business was in, when Will couldn't hide it any longer, they were going to turn all that criticism onto him.

"See, that—taking too much responsibility—sounds like hubris."

"You and those damn Greeks." Really, so much of what he'd done had been about science and animals and then simply trying to get through the day. He'd never bothered to develop some kind of value system to understand the meaning of life. He'd never needed one before.

Nic obviously had this. "I'm serious. Trying to claim everything you do and everything that happens to you is because of your choices alone . . . baloney on a biscuit, but that seems self-destructive. I love myths because of Granny, sure, but people have told them for centuries because they wanted to understand the world. It's what they care about and fear and know. When the Greeks talked about people offending the gods, they were trying to tell you something. You're basically Icarus-ing yourself here."

If she didn't want him to fall for her, she was going to have to stop saying stuff like that. But pointing it out would be too much, too direct, and he was trying to keep things light. He wanted to let her have the decision.

"Sometimes"—most of the time—"what's happening to me feels so overwhelming, I can't think about the larger picture without completely losing it."

"I get that. I wanted to say . . . to *offer* something. It might not help, it probably won't, but it's silly to pretend I don't have any power because I do. You could appear on my channel." She winced as if suggesting it pained her. "I have no idea if it would make a difference, and there might be consequences. People will suggest that we're together. It hasn't been that long since Brian, and the blowback would mostly come at me, but doing it would get more eyes on your practice. On you."

"On me?"

"Oh, come on, you have to know how you look. There's no point in being bashful." The way she was regarding him, over the rim of her wineglass, was pure fire. Was this about his practice or about them?

He deflected. "What? How do I look?"

"Like an avenging Viking."

He felt himself flush. Bashfully. But he wanted her to keep going. "Is that how *you* see me?"

"It's how you are. All tall and blond and growly." She shivered, and he wanted to do an impression of Hoot: leap across the table and pounce on her.

"Hmm. I sound pretty hot in your head." He said it lightly, but it didn't feel at all trivial. He still thought of her as so unreachable, so far above him. It was impossible, but impossibly flattering, that she seemed to find him as attractive as he found her.

"You are objectively pretty hot, Will Lund." Then her tone shifted back to business. "But that's my point, why not capitalize on it?"

"Capitalize on what? Everyone within driving distance already knows about my apparent hotness."

"It would be a form of advertising, of establishing a brand."

He felt himself bristle. He was all about her telling him that she found him attractive. He was not at all about turning that into some silly advertising ploy. "I don't think veterinary medicine is about *brand*."

"Don't do that. I used to work in marketing, okay? And it's not selling out to know your image makes a difference. I'm not talking about making a logo and a website and redoing your sign and business cards—though that wouldn't hurt—but it would take time and cost money. I am saying that I was going to do some videos about what happened to Camilla, but I held off because your critique . . . stung. Because it was right."

He almost choked on a bite of quiche. "Excuse me?"

"You were right to say that I play a little fast and loose with medical advice. And so if you came on, you could give advice from an actual medical perspective."

Will muttered "What a change" to himself.

"I heard that. Anyhow, you could talk to an audience of hundreds of thousands of people, be a counterweight, look fantastic, and correct whatever I've gotten wrong. Though, again, there will be talk." She sat up and gave a little shrug, leaving the decision up to him. "One of the rules of the sad-friends supper club is that we look out for each other."

"Oh, is it?"

"Yes. And it's just an idea."

An idea that involved them spending more time together in a way that she knew would make it look like they were *together*. An idea that she'd suggested in part because she thought he was hot. An idea she'd offered in order to try to help him.

Maybe she was flashing her cards too.

"We're having a . . . car wash," he admitted. "Next week. The damn x-ray machine is malfunctioning, and we need a new one." He sincerely doubted they were going to raise anywhere near the $5,000 price tag for a refurbished one, but he didn't have any other ideas.

Marsha had laughed herself silly.

"Oh my gosh!" Nic's eyes were bright as Christmas lights. "You have to let me film it."

*"No."*

"You don't have to like the game, but that's not an excuse to pretend we're playing something else. Let me do an episode with you that's serious, but then let me capture something fun. Please."

He wanted to give her anything she asked for in that voice. Anything.

"It won't be ridiculous?"

"I'd never, ever make you look ridiculous. I'm going to do an episode with Helen Washington too."

So it wasn't only about him, but it was about her trying to use her platform to benefit other people. It was thoughtful of her.

"I appreciate it," he said. "I just . . . YouTube."

"Despite appearances to the contrary, it's not my favorite either. But it is the way of the future. And whatever happens with your practice, maybe it's time to admit that you need to join the twenty-first century."

"Hey, we have a Facebook page."

She laughed. "Oh, Will."

But her tone was so fond, he didn't even mind that she was teasing him.

# CHAPTER 22

"You have to try to smile," Nic instructed. They were standing in the very same exam room where he'd berated her. *My, my: how different things are now.*

She'd insisted he put on his lab coat—it hugged his biceps in a way that communicated "star of *Grey's Anatomy*" and not "struggling rural vet"—and she was trying to get him to film a brief introduction of himself before she set up the tripod and she interviewed him for real.

"I *am* trying." His expression was pure stony Viking.

"You're going to frighten the children. See, this is me. I'm a child who loves chickens and is watching the latest episode from my favorite YouTuber and, 'Oh no, who is the glaring man? He's scary.' Unsubscribe." She mimed pressing a button, and then she set her free hand on her hip. "Don't be scary."

Will mechanically raised the corners of his mouth, revealing a foreboding smile—were his teeth really that large?—and Nic sputtered out laughter.

"Not like that! A normal smile." The kind of smile he'd given her that made her bones dissolve, but she sort of wanted to keep that one for herself.

He pressed his palms to his eyes. "This was a mistake."

"No, it wasn't. Let's try again. Forget that I'm filming. Talk to me like we're sitting on your porch." Except hopefully without the massive sexual tension, because that wouldn't help matters and that was between them.

After a few seconds, he dropped his hands and rolled his shoulders. "Okay, okay. I know you're trying to help. I can be . . . less scary."

"Let's get some B-roll first."

"Did you say B-roll?"

"Yup. I don't normally edit much, but I'll make an exception for this episode. Wash your hands." She pointed to the tiny sink.

"You want me to wash my hands? Who would want to watch that?"

"Loads of people. Trust me, I'm a professional."

She made Will wash his hands, put away pill bottles, spin some test tubes in a centrifuge—

"What do you use this for?"

"Science stuff. Come on, I'm a doctor."

"It's poop, isn't it?"

"It's for plasma. Get your mind out of the gutter, woman."

—and type on the computer at the front desk, all while she filmed and they teased each other. By the time they returned to the exam room, he'd mostly relaxed.

"One more time, from the top," she said sweetly. "What's your name?"

He managed a small smile then. An actual one with the right amount of teeth, achieving dangerously sexy and not dangerously shark-like. "I'm Will Lund, and I'm a doctor of veterinary medicine."

That was the line she'd been trying to get him to deliver before. She'd meant to get into the frame with him, but maybe it was better this way.

"How long have you been practicing?" she asked.

"Seven years."

"What kinds of animals do you treat?"

"It's a small-animal practice, so mostly pets like dogs and cats, with some other mammals. There's a large-animal vet nearby, but I get called in occasionally to help with stuff on farms. I rotate through the county animal shelter too."

"And chickens?"

His cheeks hollowed for a second, as if he were trying not to laugh. "While they aren't a huge part of the practice, and I'd never claim to be an expert avian veterinarian, I do see chickens, yes."

Touché. "So tell us, Dr. Lund"—he'd hear the sexy twist she put on that—"what are some of the keys to maintaining good health in your flock?"

"Well, I'm always a big fan of preventive care, because the fewer interventions you make, the better for you and your pets. So that means maintaining a good diet, making sure they have access to clean water, and ensuring their environment is safe. When I do see chickens, it tends to be . . ." His expression went—not scary but thoughtful. "Look, chicken keepers tend to delay coming in until it's too late. Not always, but more often than, say, dog owners do. And they tend not to schedule regular visits when their chickens are healthy for checkups as often as other pet owners do. As a result, we don't catch problems early, when they might be easier to deal with."

Nic was tagged in that remark, and she didn't like it.

"I know not everyone thinks of their chickens as pets," he went on. "But farmers take the care of their animals seriously. They vaccinate their herds and have annual wellness exams. So I don't buy that logic."

His tone was cordial but firm, and Nic couldn't find any fault with what he was saying, even as she knew some of her viewers would resent it. It was hard to face a $500 vet bill for an animal you'd paid $5 for, especially when the vet in question didn't seem to have any particular insight about chickens. Nic didn't like culling her flock, but she understood that that was how many of her viewers addressed any serious medical issues. She'd had more than a few emails criticizing her for taking Camilla in for being egg bound, an incident that easily might have killed the hen.

"So where's the balance?" she asked Will.

"I'm not sure. Some vets aren't experts about chickens, but maybe vets haven't developed that expertise because they aren't seeing a lot of them. Again, preventive care is cheaper than an emergency. If you want good medical treatments for your flock, you have to find a vet and go there. Regularly. Otherwise it won't be there when you might need it."

He was talking, of course, about himself. He and this practice very soon might not be here. Nic wanted to set her phone down and wrap her arms around him, but they had a mission, a mission that—hopefully—would help him. She pressed on.

"You'd advocate for more regular visits?"

"Yes, absolutely."

She asked a few more questions about some of the most common problems she and her viewers ran into, and then she pressed stop and set her phone down.

"See, you're . . . not a natural." She wouldn't lie to him, not even about that. "But you got the job done."

"That's it?" He appeared distraught, as if, now that he'd gotten into the groove, he wanted to keep going, when she knew that he'd hated every minute.

"That's it. I'll edit and drop it in the next few days. Be prepared, a horde is sure to follow. You'll probably get a hashtag and everything."

"#ScaryVet?"

"#HottieMcHotFace is more likely."

"That's clunky."

They shared a smile.

He hadn't said anything about the bank, and they hadn't broached the subject in a few days, but she knew that the clock was ticking and that if a miracle was going to arrive, it had to be soon. She really ought to have swallowed her objections and done this for him weeks ago.

"Have you recorded with Helen yet?" he asked.

"She took a week off for a family reunion—"

"She does that every summer."

"It really is creepy that you all know each other's vacation schedules. Anyhow, we haven't had a chance to film it yet, but we will." Nic kept her promises, and she did want to feature the feedstore. It was special.

"And your ex?"

"Is still being quiet, at least according to my assistant."

"You have an assistant?"

"I hate administrative stuff, and she keeps some of it off my plate. And then I can completely ignore Brian. I really ought to give her a raise. Watching his show merits hazard pay."

"You have an *assistant*," he repeated.

"Hey, you have a technician."

"For the moment."

She did touch him then, setting her hand on his arm. His biceps was firm and warm through the two layers of cloth. "You want to talk about it?"

"Nope. I don't want to wallow in self-pity."

"See, I always do. It's one of the many differences between us."

*Us*: a word without a clear definition. They hadn't slept together since the emotionally overwhelming, completely wonderful library trip. The last week had felt much like the weeks before. They hung out, teased each other, ate food, and drank beer, and between them, the most electrifying tension flowed.

There would be a moment, a catch, whenever they were together. He'd be staring at her mouth, she'd get mesmerized by his hands, and it would all come crashing back: the way he'd tasted, the line of his neck, the force with which he'd moved in her, over her. It made her vision swim, the memory of it. Knowing that she could fall into his arms and he'd catch her and carry her off to his bed—God, that had been delicious—and they could do it all again.

Were they friends? Were they lovers? Had it meant nothing? Had it meant everything?

She could open her mouth and ask him. She'd insisted on keeping things casual, but they didn't feel casual. And if he said he wanted more, then she would jump on board. Gladly. She simply would feel more comfortable if he were the one to press the accelerator. As it was, she felt as if she were standing out there all by herself, the only one . . . feeling all the feelings. Being all needy.

Frankly, she was being a chicken—and not in a kick-ass, peck-at-everyone, latter-day-dinosaur way.

"I appreciate you doing this," he said. "Even if it doesn't . . . thank you."

"I can't make any promises, I'm very niche. But I don't think it will hurt in any way." Even if people did start speculating about Nic and Will's relationship, that would be all upside for him. "And the car wash—"

His cheeks went ruddy. "Is going to be humiliating."

"—is going to be *amazing*. Before this video drops, you should . . . I dunno, set up a website that's not on Facebook. Maybe even one that's separate from the practice, just for you." That way, if the worst happened, he'd already be looking toward the future.

He snorted. "That's not a very Yagerstown thing to do."

"The world is wide. You never know what opportunities might be in it."

She sounded like Brian, but hopefully the only good parts of him: his sense of self-worth and ambition. Say what she would about her ex, and she could say plenty, he did understand that the sky was the limit, and he never sold himself short or had any hesitancy about promoting himself.

Nic never wanted to be as brazen as he was or to use people like he did. But even good people could use a tablespoon of Brian's confidence and shamelessness. At least enough to override the humility that held

Will, and others like him, back. Whatever happened with his practice, Will had to believe that he was capable of great things. Whether it was saving his business or something else, he had to believe he was worth it.

She probably couldn't convince him on her own, but he needed to find that for himself.

"Hey, so, speaking of opportunities, wild question," Will said. His expression had gone stony again, which she knew meant he was uncomfortable. "Are you free on Sunday night?"

"I'm free every night." Other than Will, Emily, and BROODY, Nic knew no one and did nothing in Yagerstown.

"I'm supposed to have dinner at my parents' house, and I thought maybe the sad-friends supper club could provide emotional support. I'm . . . I mean, no pressure, but it can sometimes be a little—a lot—"

He was saying he wanted to introduce her to his family.

This was such a larger step forward, it was basically a hop, a skip, and a jump.

She wanted to say yes. She wanted to say no.

Nic managed, at last, to sputter out, "Yes?"

"Yes?"

She didn't blame him for clarifying. She hadn't sounded certain. "The sad-friends supper club should definitely go to dinner at your parent's house. It won't bug your mom if you show up with a plus-one to a family event?"

Okay, maybe she was trying to give him an out a little bit. Or herself. She didn't know.

"Not at all. She'll probably throw an impromptu parade."

"I love a parade." That at least was true, even if the rest of her insides were an absolute muddle.

Dinner with his family: that merited a wowzer.

# CHAPTER 23

"This is a mistake." But there was no one nearby to hear Will's pronouncement about the car wash.

Kim was waving their first customer—Marsha, because of course it was—down the gauntlet of high school basketball players that she'd dragooned into helping him. If Will Lund needed a few warm bodies to help him run a charity car wash, well, then a few warm bodies he would get. Didn't her cousin's friend's husband coach the team? They'd be there. Jarrod, who owned the gas station, had lent them the pad free of charge. Ella had made the sign—**DOC LUND NEEDS A NEW X-RAY! WE'LL WASH YOUR CAR, GENEROUS DONATIONS APPRECIATED**—and added balloons and streamers.

But everyone could tell Will was in a mood, so they'd let him take charge of the cashbox and the towel-off. It wasn't that he didn't appreciate the help. It was that needing it made him feel like a doofus.

"William!" Marsha said, climbing out of her car. "Isn't this great?"

He grunted, but as used to him as she was, she didn't take it personally. She only patted one of the kids on the arm and handed him her keys. "Be sure to get the windows." She strolled over to Will. "Do you want me to take over the money part?"

"We won't be that busy."

"Sure you will. I put it on every Facebook group and LISTSERV in town."

Will ran a hand over his face. Why he'd agreed to this, he would never know. "Thanks."

"You're welcome." She dug around in her purse and came up with twenty dollars. "Here you go."

"I'm not going to take money from you."

"Of course you are. That's the whole idea of this thing. You definitely won't get that x-ray if you refuse everyone's donations. And look who's here."

Nic pulled her green Subaru behind Marsha's Honda. She hopped out with a wave. Her hair was in pigtails, and she was wearing a fitted gray Chickens for All T-shirt and lime-green shorts so tiny, they might not count as shorts. As she walked over to Will, the head of every boy in the line clicked toward her.

She stopped in front of Will, beaming behind her oversize sunglasses, and he didn't have any choice but to wrap his arm around her waist and drop a kiss on her forehead. He wasn't the jealous type, or at least he hadn't been the jealous type, but Nic had a way of shaking him up like a snow globe, stirring up a blizzard of change inside him.

He glared over Nic's shoulder at the boys who were still staring at Nic's butt. They at least had the good sense to look ashamed, and all but one of them immediately began washing Marsha's car. The lone holdout was still blinking in recovery, but, well, Will could sympathize.

"Hey," he ground out.

Her answering smile was too knowing. "Hey yourself."

"You're going to cause an accident in that getup."

"It's a car wash. I figured the fewer clothes, the better."

Marsha cackled. "I'm going over to the table."

"Take my money first." Nic pulled a $100 bill out of her pocket.

"Well, will you look at that," Marsha crowed as Will said, "That's way too much."

"Which is none of your business," Nic said.

"You can give that to me," Marsha sang out.

"Excellent." Nic popped up on her toes to reach over Will's hand to Marsha, who snapped the bill out of the air.

"Thank you kindly," she called as she went to set up the cashbox at the folding table Jarrod had found for them.

Will would have kept arguing, but it was clear he was being handled. So he turned his attention back to Nic.

"No room for your wallet in those shorts?"

"I've got my driver's license and my phone in a waterproof case. It's all I need." She winked at him and grabbed a towel.

"I don't want you to feel . . . obligated."

"That's handy because I don't."

One of the basketball players pulled Marsha's wet car up in front of them, and Nic attacked the hood with her towel. Her good cheer and effort of course made Will feel frustrated and foolish, so he went to work next to her.

They had a steady stream of customers: the owners of patients, sometimes with their dogs in the car with them, and Will's former teachers and the parents of his high school friends. Emily Babbit came, though it seemed as if it were out of loyalty to Nic rather than him. Will wanted to apologize to every single person because he was in this position, but Nic and Marsha intervened every time he started down that route.

"See, was that so hard?" Nic cooed after he'd reluctantly accepted some money from Nanette.

"Something is hard, Jones," he muttered back. "But we'll have to get home so I can—"

She *tsk-tsk*ed. "Children are present."

"Children who are probably still staring at your butt."

"And you get to sleep well at night knowing you're the only one who's touching it."

Which was something, he supposed.

Over the next few hours, she dried cars, recorded him awkwardly answering Travis's questions about whether goldfish ever got to go to the vet, and charmed everyone in town. All those folks could be forgiven if they kept looking back and forth between Nic and Will speculatively.

"So are you two . . . ," Sami asked. He was the rare person who was brave enough to voice what everyone else was wondering.

"Drying your car, yes," Nic said with a devastating smile. "And Marsha will take your donation right down there."

"I can do it. It's my charity car wash," Will said.

"Nah, I don't trust you not to bargain him down. I'm sending Mr. Hak to Marsha."

Sami chuckled. "I think I better listen to her."

Will was tempted to say *I never do*, but that would be a lie. He did, and almost everything she suggested—while it might make him feel silly or exposed for half a second—had been a good idea. Nic was smart, and she was canny, and she was kind. He would be lucky to have her advice in his life for as long as she felt like giving it.

So he just said, "Good call."

After Sami drove off, Will rolled his shoulders. "You really going to stick around the whole time?"

"What else do I have to do? A flexible schedule is the one influencer perk."

"I'm just saying, you don't have to."

"And I'm just saying—you aren't wet enough to go viral yet."

"Damn, because I really wanted to."

Nic's eyes began to twinkle. "We can fix that."

"Aww, really?"

"I see some hoses right over there, and look, there's a break in the traffic."

"How convenient."

He should call this off, make it clear he was joking. Nic would let it go. Well, he was 90 percent sure she would let it go. But he couldn't seem to step back from the dare of her, and he didn't want to.

He gestured at himself. His shirt and athletic shorts were damp, clinging. But he wasn't really drenched, not like he'd been that day they'd chased her hen in the rain. "You don't think this is wet enough for virality?"

"Nope. Not even close." She began walking backward, away from him, pulling her phone out of her pocket. She fussed with it for a second, presumably turning on the camera, and then she handed it to one of the basketball players. "Hold this for me. Keep it focused on Dr. Lund."

"I think you're full of it, Jones," he called.

"This is my world, Lund. Can I have that for a second?" She asked the kid holding the hose so sweetly, he pretty much bowed as he handed it over. "You sure you don't want to retract your desire to get wet?" she called.

"Never."

With a shrug, she turned the hose on, full blast. She directed the spray to a spot about six inches from his feet. "You sure?"

"Positive."

Then she proceeded to soak him from toe to head. He had to remind himself to stop laughing or else he was going to end up with hose water in his mouth. It was bracing and ridiculous, and he couldn't remember the last time anything had been so funny.

When she finally turned the water off, he pushed his hands back through his hair and shook, feeling like a wet dog. Nic's eyes on him, though: that was reward enough for how on display he felt, how ridiculous. He'd do whatever it took to keep her looking at him like that.

After a beat, Nic retrieved her phone from the basketball player and turned it so that she was on camera. "Well, America, say hello to

Will Lund—and you're welcome." She turned off the video and called out, "Anyone wanna guess how many likes that'll get in the next hour?"

The guesses that everyone shouted sounded impossibly high.

Nic sauntered back over to Will. "Why are you smiling? I thought you'd be pissed that I went through with it."

"Not at all. But . . . well, I know something you don't."

"What's that?"

"This time you aren't wet too." He grabbed her around the waist and hoisted her, laughing, into his arms.

Goddamn, but she felt good there, squealing against his chest, all the soft curves of her pressed up against him. And she was clinging to him, not pushing him away. Even though she knew all of it, every humiliating detail about him, she was still reaching for him.

"That serves me right," she said, tipping her head back so she could look at him. "How are you feeling?"

"Wet." But that wasn't what she meant. "And . . . low, I guess." People had showed up, but when they found out how dire things were and that this little fundraiser, while it might help with the x-ray machine, wasn't going to be enough to save the practice long term, he just hoped they still liked him.

"It's humbling to need help, but it's a testament to how much you've helped everyone here that they want to turn around and do that for you."

He set Nic down and crossed his arms over his chest. He knew that she was right, but—well, he still had trouble trusting it.

"We're pretty much done here." It was more than an hour after the closing time they'd posted, and it didn't look like anyone else was going to show up. "You can take off."

"What are you going to do?"

"Clean up here and then go home and lick my wounds, I guess."

"I know what will help." Nic held a hand out to him, and he took it.

"Your backyard?"

"Hey, you don't have to be so skeptical. Have a seat." She pointed at the Adirondack chairs she'd finally got situated in the corner. She needed to get an umbrella, but the sun had shifted to the front of the house after lunch, leaving the backyard cool and streaked with long shadows.

Inside, she grabbed several towels, two big glasses of iced tea, and a bag of frozen peas, which she delivered to Will. He'd removed his soggy socks and shoes and was stretching his toes in the grass. It should be illegal how erotic that was.

Nic had meant to ask Marsha how much money they'd raised, but she didn't want Will to get any touchier than he already had been. He absolutely hated needing help, and the more everyone in Yagerstown—with the notable exception of his parents—had tried to love him, the more growly he'd gotten. She'd had to spray him with the hose to keep him from combusting as much as anything else.

He shook a finger at the bag of frozen vegetables. "Hey, only my pride is bruised."

"Those are for the chickens."

The flock was crowded in front of the gate, pushing at one another and clucking loudly. "You know what's up, don't you?" She opened the latch, and they trailed her back to the chairs, snipping at one another the whole way.

"Here." She ripped open the bag and removed a clump of peas that had stuck together. The chickens froze—at least as far as chickens were able to freeze—until Nic launched it into the air, and they dove for it. Camilla came up with the pea-and-ice cluster. She craned her head up and began to run around the yard while the others tried to steal her prize.

Nic tossed herself into the chair next to Will's giggling.

"You are a cruel, cruel woman."

"The most fun you can have for two dollars involves a bag of frozen peas and a flock of chickens."

Camilla had finally managed to eat her peas, so the flock was stalking back across the yard toward Nic. She handed a single pea to Will. "Seriously, nothing is funnier than a chicken running."

He glared but then chucked the pea toward the birds. Mitzi dropped her head and barreled toward it, snagging it out of the grass and swallowing it in a single motion.

"Damn. Do they have to do it like that?"

"If they want to be fast." Nic tossed four peas to the chickens in quick succession; then she passed the bag to Will. "Their heads throw off their balance. They've got to torpedo themselves to compensate. The only thing better is chickens running up stairs. They have to shift their weight from side to side and hop. It's absurd and delightful."

Will threw out a handful of peas and, at the ensuing chaos, snorted—which he quickly smothered when she caught him at it. "They're like cartoon characters."

"Why do you think I love them so much?"

Margaret Bourke-White had tired of the hostility, and she picked her way across the yard. Will, because he was a softie, filled his hand with peas and offered them to her. She ate them greedily. When she finished, she hopped up onto the arm of Will's chair, and then she shifted into his lap.

He passed the bag of peas back to Nic so he could pet the hen. "You're better at sowing discord than I am."

"You know how to sweet-talk a girl." She threw out more peas and gestured at Will petting MBW's crown of feathers. "Should I be jealous?"

"Anytime you want to climb into my lap . . ."

Well, that was pretty much all the times.

"I'll just have to dislodge her and the kitten," Nic finished for him.

"Who is also your fault." He cleared his throat. "Thanks for that, she's real—lively."

Nic had to force herself to look away, across the lawn at the small dinosaurs fighting over peas and away from the naked emotion in Will's face. Being with him today, in front of everyone in town, knowing what they all thought when they looked at Nic and Will together, it had made a lot of things seem possible. Heck, seem likely.

*You can try a future on for size,* Granny had said, but Nic wasn't so sure that was true. With Will, it felt as if there were only two options. Either they were going to be in this, all the way in this together, or they needed to let it go. Anything else was going to get one of them hurt.

Nic tossed another handful of peas into the flock of chickens, trying to take her normal joy in their rabid squabbling. But all she could think was, *Maybe Will's right, and I'm a cruel woman.*

# CHAPTER 24

Will flipped the air-conditioning on. He turned the radio off. No, that was too quiet. He turned it back on. He adjusted a vent.

"We don't have to do this." Nic was in the passenger seat beside him, her face screwed up with concern. "We could, I dunno, stop at a restaurant instead. I'd be willing to fake a headache for you. I think I feel one coming on right now, actually."

"Why do you say that?"

"Because you've fidgeted more in the last two minutes than you have in the month I've known you."

He froze, his hand poised above his water bottle. "I want to make sure you're . . . comfortable."

"Will, I'm fine. Are you?"

He shouldn't have invited Nic to this farce. He had no idea what he'd been thinking. If his mother hadn't been so excited when he'd called, he would have taken Nic up on her offer to ditch, but canceling would only create more mess.

He tried to project the confidence he didn't feel. "Yes."

She wasn't buying it, though. "Why are you nervous? Is it about me? Because I charm people for a living. They don't share your absurd prejudice against chickens, right?"

"No. Well, at least my mom and sister don't." They were going to love Nic unreservedly. He had no worries about them.

"But your dad and brother?"

How to put it nicely—which sounded like his mother. "They'll probably think the chicken thing is a little silly," he said, knowing, of course, that he had treated it as silly, "but they won't say that to your face. Most likely. I don't want to give you the wrong impression. You're not walking into a minefield here. My family is . . . I mean, we get along, but only on the outside. They're not ogres."

"There goes my hope for a *Shrek* reboot. You said they're sort of arrogant."

"Luke is, yeah. And my dad follows his lead. They aren't bad people, but they like golf, and they have investment portfolios. And I . . . don't."

That hadn't always bothered him. Those differences had seemed insignificant, trifling matters of personality and not of values. But the less confident Will had become, the more it had seemed to matter, the more sensitive he'd become about it, until it had taken over the relationship.

"Anyhow, just talk to Ella, my mom, and the kids, and ignore the rest." That was what he always tried to do, but now that he said it aloud, he realized how dysfunctional it sounded. "It'll be strained and probably awkward, but then it ends."

Next to him, Nic only said, "Hmm."

They pulled up a minute later, the guaranteed short trip of a small town. Nic preceded him up the walk with a dozen eggs in one hand and a bouquet of flowers in the other, because she'd somehow known a hostess gift would make his mother love her. Because Nic was perfect and would be fine and all the problems centered on him, stalked him really, like a hunter with a stag.

"Jay and Laura, Luke and Kayleigh, Ella and Mike," Nic reviewed.

"And the kids are Noah, Ryan, Abby, and Hannah."

"Got it."

And she did. When he had swung the door open and made the introductions and Nic had shaken all the hands and cooed over all the babies, it was clear she was more at ease with his family than he'd managed to be in the last few years.

"She's a looker," Luke said when they stepped out onto the patio to watch Dad finish grilling.

Will gritted his teeth and did something with his head. He hoped it didn't come across as agreement. Nic was beautiful, but he didn't want to rate her with his brother. She wasn't a Miss America contestant, and it wasn't 1950.

"Is she really a . . . what did Abby call it?" Luke asked. "A YouTuber?"

Abby, Will's older niece and Luke's oldest kid, was sitting on one of the lawn chairs, staring at Nic through the sliding glass door. Nic was chatting with Mom and Ella, telling some story with exaggerated hand gestures, her face elastic and animated. Something in Will's chest tightened, but it felt embarrassing to indulge it in front of his family, so he gave himself a shake and turned back to his niece.

Abby's mouth was open and her eyes shiny with admiration toward Nic. That vaporized when she clicked toward her father. "Yes, Dad," she sneered. "She's a *famous* one too."

Oh, Will was going to have to send his niece a huge birthday present this year.

"How does that even work? How do you do that as a job?" Luke seemed both exasperated and a little offended by any method of generating income that he didn't personally understand. He was brutal on the subject of community organizers too.

"From the ads." Abby had the not-so-patient air of someone who'd been over this and over this, probably on the entire drive to Yagerstown. "You monetize your content."

Nic was the most exciting thing to happen to the monthly Lund family dinner since Mom had started putting the ketchup on the table in the bottle versus in a bowl. In some ways, Nic's presence took the pressure off Will, and he ought to be grateful. Instead, he was tetchy.

"Uh-huh," Luke replied. He obviously mistrusted the entire idea.

"And Uncle Will has been in her latest videos," Abby went on. She turned to him. "You were awesome, but maybe, like, a bit stiff in that interview in your office."

"But the car wash one?"

"I'm going to pretend I *didn't* see that one." Which was probably better for them both. He assumed her uncle basically cosplaying a wet T-shirt contest would be revolting to Abby. "Promise me you won't try any of those dance challenges."

He'd already received some very teasing remarks at the grocery store, and Nic had said something about how the views were good, so he guessed that was positive—not that it was going to help matters. His practice was screwed regardless.

"That's a promise," Will told Abby.

She gave a satisfied nod and then turned to her dad. "He's going to be a star."

"I doubt that." Will had no intention of making any more appearances on YouTube, whatever his niece might think about it.

"He could if he wanted to." Nic slid into the chair next to Will's and touched his forearm briefly.

He liked the moment of warmth more than he'd thought he would. More even than when he'd hugged her at the car wash.

"Why would he?" Luke clearly couldn't fathom any of this. "No offense. It's fine for kids, but . . ." That was classic Luke: suggest something was silly or fishy without ever bothering to articulate why. Nothing sounded more scary to him than the undefined.

Nic shrugged. "That's like dismissing TV as a fad for the youth in 1945. Social media will change, platforms will come and go, but the top YouTubers make as much money as the top TV news anchors, and more people probably watch the YouTubers."

Abby snorted, and Will had the distinct impression she would have offered Nic a fist bump if her father hadn't been glaring at her.

For her part, Nic had only a beatific expression on her face.

Will wanted to laugh. The entire program for these things was that Luke would be vaguely rude about something, his father would agree, his mother would be tense, hoping that the lid wasn't about to fly off, and he and Ella would only roll their eyes because they didn't want to make a scene.

But of course Nic knew and cared about none of that. It wasn't that she was fighting with Luke; she wasn't playing his game, and it was awesome.

Luke, though, was not enjoying it. "So you're encouraging Will to . . . ?"

"I'm not encouraging him to do anything. It's a hard and unpredictable way to make a living. Sorry, kiddo." She directed that bit at Abby but then turned back to Luke. "It's not for everyone, and it rarely works out. As it so happens, though, I think your brother is a totally wonderful vet, and he should keep doing that. Guest appearances on my stuff notwithstanding."

Luke was straining, hard, to keep his mask of calmness in place.

Nic beamed and then said to Abby, "So your mom said you're into lacrosse."

That was as solid a transition as any.

For the next ten minutes, Will watched as Nic made effortless conversation with his niece and his father. He couldn't remember the last time he'd had fun at one of these rather than dwelling in endless dread.

Eventually, they relocated inside to eat.

Luke had recovered by this point, and he and Dad were getting started on their typical domination of the conversation.

They'd covered the fact that there were too many superhero movies and the weakness of this year's PGA field. Will was sorry he wasn't sitting closer to the kids, because—now that they had explored Will's merits as an assistant youth soccer coach—their *Minecraft* discussion seemed far more riveting than the adults' bullshit.

"But what *is* glowstone?" Nic asked Ryan just as Luke said, "It's not just the federal government, though, it's a local issue. Why isn't the economy back?"

Oh hell, Will should've asked Luke about how the sod was doing. He'd much rather talk about expensive grass than listen to his father and brother talk about anything related to money.

"Pure stubbornness," Dad said. Because people were choosing not to spend, not because they had lost their jobs or watched their industries disappear and didn't have any money. No, he thought it was their *choice*.

Will took a swig of water, wishing it were vodka, trying not to think about how his parents hadn't even bothered to show up at his pity charity car wash to buy a new x-ray machine. Not that he'd wanted them—not that he'd wanted anyone—but even still. Their absence had spoken volumes.

"We have a vaccine, what is people's problem?" his brother demanded.

"Jay, Luke," Mom put in warningly. It wasn't that she disagreed; it was that the tone was getting heated, unpleasant. Appealing to politeness was the only chance of shutting them up.

Will downed his water. It didn't help. His stomach was still an inferno.

Across the table, Ella looked at Will and rolled her eyes, but he couldn't join in. Not this time. He was too angry to find any part of this funny, even as a release valve.

Luke ignored Mom and said, "I get why people might avoid some nonessential stuff, like, say, having their dogs' nails trimmed at Will's, but restaurants are still down, like, twenty-five percent, and—"

Will thunked his empty glass on the table . . . and stared at it. What was he going to say? He'd let a hundred comments like that from Luke go over the years. It would be absurd to object now. And besides, where was the lie? Will's business *was* down. It was failing, in fact. On what grounds would he disagree?

"I'm sorry," Nic said, loudly, cheerfully. *Pleasantly.* "I need to . . . acknowledge that. Small-town vets are incredibly important. I mean, didn't we learn what *essential worker* really means in the last few years? The guy stocking the shelves at the grocery store is absolutely essential. As much a part of the public health system as a doctor. What I do is totally silly. Entertaining, maybe, informative, I hope, but unnecessary—well compensated but unnecessary. Will, on the other hand, is clearly essential. One of my chickens was dying last month, and he saved her life. Like, actually saved her. Pets are parts of people's families, and Will cares for them. That's incredible."

She turned her attention to Will, her expression adoring. And while he knew, absolutely knew, that she was putting some of this on in order to make a point to Luke, Will also knew that what he saw there was real. She believed in it, and in him.

"I'm not disputing his knowledge," Luke insisted, "just reflecting on how the market values those skills. It's terrible, really. We can *say* workers are important, but—"

"You clearly thought that logic was silly when it came to highly paid YouTubers," Nic said sweetly. "Maybe the economy is pretty random. Maybe the market isn't some perfect, infallible thing but a representation of some people's values. And pretty screwed-up values at that."

If Nic had insulted one of his children, she couldn't have hit Luke more effectively.

"And this conversation is not conducive to digestion," Mom said smoothly before Luke could respond. "Let's try something else, Jay."

"How 'bout those Bears?" Dad said—and everyone laughed awkwardly, and there was an entire emotionally repressed childhood in an emotionally repressed joke.

Nic was still holding Will's gaze, still telling him that she saw him, that she valued him. Will nodded, hoping she understood, before turning back to his food.

He was so damn grateful that she'd said something, he almost couldn't keep up the motions.

But it wasn't only gratitude he felt. For all that he and Nic had said their relationship wasn't serious, her incursion in this conversation on his behalf was the sunlight finally, finally breaking through the clouds of Will's life. He was a bit numb from the shock of it. From her and how he felt about her and most of all what he wanted with her.

The rest of the meal passed in its normal strained fashion, and after dinner, they cleared the table, drank decaf coffee, and ate some cookies. It was good that he had a lot of practice mindlessly enduring these things because he was able to fake it without blurting out what he'd realized about Nic in front of his family.

When they were making the rounds before leaving, Ella gave Will a hug and whispered in his ear, "I *like* her."

"I do too."

*Like* was the weakest word for it, but until he'd said it to Nic herself, he certainly wasn't going to shout it at his sister, so sure, *like* was going to have to do for now.

Across the room, Luke had gotten his poise back and tried once more to explain himself to Nic. "At dinner, I wasn't saying I think it's right Will makes as much as a day care worker—"

"No, you were throwing out some platitudes about the wisdom of the market and letting us fill in the logical gaps. He's your brother, and he's a hero, literally, daily, to the people of this town." She let that sit there for a second before she added, "It was nice to meet you." She offered him her hand, which he shook mechanically, before she swished off.

"She's, um, pretty blunt," Luke said to Will.

Here was the place where Will was supposed to smooth things over, to make some excuse, or to apologize and make Luke feel better. But Will didn't want to. He'd spent the last ten years never saying anything honest to Luke, and he was done with it. If he took anything away from this dinner, it was going to be a tablespoon of Nic's boldness.

"She is," he agreed. "But, dude, she's not wrong. I don't even know if you're aware of it, but you can sometimes be a bit of an ass about my job. And I don't mean your jokes about how my patients try to bite me. You find lots of ways to mention the fact that I don't make much money and I live in a small crappy house in our small crappy hometown. It doesn't feel super brotherly."

"I do not—"

"You do. Yagerstown isn't what you wanted, and that's fine. But it's what I wanted." It was what Will had given everything for and what he'd fallen short of. His failure didn't make it an unworthy goal, though.

Luke blinked at him. Swallowed. Inclined his head about two centimeters. Which was probably as close to an acknowledgment or an apology as he would ever come.

Feeling light, feeling like he could fly, like he *had* flown, Will said the rest of his goodbyes and met Nic by the front door.

"Ready?" he asked.

Nic's eyes were still heated in a promising way, but it was tinged with softness. Pity, maybe, but his family had bought and had that gift wrapped for him.

"Yup," she answered.

They didn't talk as they walked to his car, but the space between them teemed with the things unsaid. He opened her door and watched the fair skin of her legs catch the glow from a streetlight. She caught him staring and tipped her head.

There were sparks there too. A whole fireworks display's worth. But if he touched her then, if he said anything . . . well, he had no intention of doing this in front of his parents' house.

"Soon," he said.

Will put on the car radio, and Nic didn't object this time. Maybe she felt, like he did, that this was a larger conversation. The drone of the music gave him something to think about other than the patch of skin just inside her knee or the turn of her wrist inches from his hand.

Finally, finally, he parked in front of her house.

"You told my brother off." He pulled his keys from the ignition and set them in the cup holder. The clink of metal against plastic was impossibly loud.

"Was it too much? I didn't mean to 'tell him off' so much as help him hear what he sounds like. I don't think it's intentional. It looked to me like he's gotten in this habit of picking at you, and now it's how he relates to you and—"

Before she could finish the thought, Will undid his seatbelt, closed the gap between them, and stopped her mouth with his.

She tasted like coffee and righteousness. She'd walked into that house tonight and defended him. Gently, very gently, she'd made Luke look like an idiot on his own terms, and she'd called Will a hero. A hero. She'd seemed to mean it too.

So Will kissed her because he was grateful. And he kissed her because she was beautiful. And he kissed her because he knew now that he was falling for her. And he kissed her because once she was so close, he couldn't see why he ever needed to stop kissing her.

"Your house or mine?" he asked.

She laughed, low and throaty. "You're skipping a few steps there."

"It's that or I keep pawing at you in the front seat of my car."

He found her mouth again to make his point, and then he kept kissing her because he'd meant what he'd said. He fully intended to strip her naked, and he didn't care where that happened.

It seemed she didn't either, because she soon removed her own seat belt, too, and slunk across the console into his lap. Which was an improvement because he could feel almost every inch of her then. And what soft, generous inches they were.

But when he pressed her back into the horn and it sounded, dully, he realized that wasn't going to work either. They needed more space, preferably space that was enclosed, horizontal, and soft.

"So . . . your house or mine?" he asked again.

"I have to—to put the girls away." Nic was gratifyingly breathless. One of her fists was cinched around his shirt, as if she wasn't going to let him get away from her. Her skirt was hiked up around her waist, and her hair was a tangle.

It was the sexiest damn thing he'd ever seen.

Awkwardly, he boosted her up and slid out of the car still holding her. He would've carried her up the walk, up the stairs, but she twisted until he set her down. He trailed her to her house, touching her shoulders, her back, her hair. Every cell of the woman inflamed him.

She let them in, and he promptly shut and locked the door behind them. Good, that was good. They were making progress here.

"Bed?" he asked.

"Up the stairs, the only one with furniture. I'll be right back."

But of course he wasn't going to let her out of his sight. "I can get the chickens."

"Well, you know where they live."

He followed her through the darkness of the living room and the dining room, into the kitchen and out the back door. Nic stayed just out of his arm's reach, giggling as he stretched for her.

"Nope, this first. Then that."

At least *that* was on the agenda.

Outside, the chickens weren't in their yard.

"They're already roosting," Nic explained as she opened the gate into the small fenced enclosure. She picked up the feeder, which she must have set in the yard at some point, and hung it inside the coop before locking the door. She let herself out of the run and then latched the gate as well.

The moon was nearly full, and it made her hair glow, caught on her eyes. With her clothing mussed like that, she looked like he'd already had her and was about to do it again.

"You're like some nymph," he told her.

"And you're Apollo."

"He's the sun god?" Will hadn't felt very sunny lately, but he'd take it if it earned her for him. She deserved a god.

Will pulled Nic into his arms and kissed the side of her neck through the curtain of her hair, softness over softness.

Her body undulated in ways that were probably illegal in some states. "Upstairs. Now." But she seemed to be on board with not waiting. All those steps. All that walking. Who could blame her?

He pressed her against the doorjamb. "Or I could make love to you right here. You'd need to be very quiet, though."

He nipped at her collarbone, and she was decidedly not quiet—and decidedly into it.

"*Will.*"

Interesting. "Hmm, as much fun as that would be, I want to see your bedroom, so . . ."

They finally made it through the back door. Nic's hands were under his shirt, tracing erotic patterns over his skin with her cool fingers. There was no need to keep the fabric on, so he stripped it off and dropped it on the floor of her dining room.

"I don't think I'll ever get used to that." Meaning that she thought she'd be seeing his chest often.

If she was certain, if she was here with him, in this tender madness, he'd be more than happy to oblige.

"I don't think I'll ever get used to this." He ran his hands over her torso, gently skimming over her breasts. "Is this okay? Are you sore?"

"Today, I'm perfect."

Which she was. He found the zipper, and her skirt slithered to the ground. "You're so beautiful."

"Ditto."

They were kissing again, then, stumbling through her living room, up the stairs. They broke apart so he could wrench her shirt off, and then it was just the burn of her skin on his and the cool relief when they finally tumbled into her bed.

Touching her made him dizzy. There wasn't up or down. Right and left didn't mean a thing. There was just Nic. The greedy wetness of her mouth. The noises she made when he found the right places to touch her. The certain anchor of her weight beneath him.

His life stood on the edge of a scalpel, and he had no idea which way it would fall. But she took the sting out of the insecurity. He'd still be hungry for her, no matter the outcome. This was the only ironclad guarantee in his life.

He dropped kisses between her breasts, down the swell of her belly, and across the coarse curls of her mound. She made a little surprised gasp every time his mouth left her body. He wanted her to keep doing that all damn night.

Will reached the apex of her thighs. He made room for himself between her thighs before parting her lips with a finger. She was already so swollen and wet, it took every ounce of his self-control not to surge over and into her. But he had other plans.

He buried his face, his mouth, between her thighs. Jesus, the way she tasted: sharp, almost bitter, and then sweet on the finish. Her hips reared up, and she made a high, breathy moan. He licked into her again and again until she was quivering, close. He raised his head slowly, his tongue skipping off her clit last.

Nic's hands were thrown up, clutching her pillow. Her eyes were closed, her body drawn like a bow, her breasts high, her nipples puckered and tight, her knees fallen wide. It was the hottest thing he'd ever seen.

But what had his heart somersaulting in his ribcage was the trust in her position. They'd shed their armor. This was more bare than bare, more real than real.

"Please, Will." She rocked her pelvis. It was too needy to be an invitation. More of a search. A plea.

He fell on her. Sucking, abrading, gasping, thrusting: him on her, her against him. The orgasm that he could feel tear through her a few seconds later felt mutual.

"Condom?" he asked when she stopped moaning.

"Top drawer."

Then there was the sweet relief of sliding into her, of her thighs clasped around his hips, of his name on her lips as she came.

Afterward, when he held her, it felt . . . right. They were mismatched, since he was basically a giant. But it was more that the space he had made, could make, inside his arm was Nic's exact dimensions.

He fell into a rough sleep with one question burning in his head: *What does this mean?*

# CHAPTER 25

The girl clutching the handle of the small plastic critter tote had the most serious eyes Will had ever seen. Brown laser beams that pierced his exterior and could probably see straight into his soul—except her only concern was the fate of her gerbil.

"Can you promise me he'll be okay?" she demanded.

"I can't." Will tried to gentle his tone, to not be—what had Nic called him?—an avenging Viking, but he wasn't going to make a guarantee he couldn't keep. "That is, I can't without lying to you, and that's not fair. I can say we do this surgery all the time on small mammals, and most of them pull through just fine."

The little girl in front of him, Iris Mortimer, had a problem. Steve at the pet store had broken the only cardinal rule of selling gerbils: he'd given her a male and a female, rather than the two females she'd thought she was getting. So now, inevitably, her tank was overflowing with two generations of baby gerbils, and her parents wanted the situation and the male gerbil, Rainbow Dash, fixed.

"Tell me about it again," Iris said. "The surgery."

"First, I'll administer the anesthesia—"

"And that's where the problems can happen. I saw a video on YouTube."

That website again. "Yes, the internet was correct in this instance: the anesthetic meds can cause complications. Rainbow Dash is small, and he's never had surgery before, so we can't predict how he'll respond. If he's allergic, if he'll tolerate it, that kind of thing."

Iris nodded, but her eyes were filling with tears.

*Please don't cry.* "After he's asleep, I'll shave some of his hair and make an incision." Will did manage softness that time, when he was talking about the minutiae of surgery. Nic would laugh her ass off at him. "Then I'll remove . . . what needs to be removed."

He was going to have to practice if he ever had kids so that he could talk about reproduction in front of them without blushing from his chest up and over his scalp. After what he'd done with Nic last night, he'd think he could handle a little clinical anatomy talk, but apparently not.

Iris was poised enough for them both, however. This had stopped her impending tears. "The testicles." She offered the term as if Will had forgotten and she wanted to help him out.

Will shot a look at her mother, who was sitting in the corner of the room, reading her phone. He'd gone to school with Annie, and it seemed impossible that she was old enough to have a nine-year-old.

At the word "testicle," Annie looked up, locked eyes with Will, and gave a little shrug as if to say, *Kids these days. What can you do?* But if your kid's gerbils had apparently been "wrestling" all around the cage, and then about twenty-four days later a litter arrived, Will guessed you had to have a pretty detailed conversation about the birds and the bees.

"Yes," he told Iris. "I'll neuter Rainbow Dash, and then I'll put in stitches to close the incision."

"Those can cause problems too?" She had done a lot of research.

Will wished most of his patients' owners were this prepared. "Yes, but I'll use internal ones that dissolve so you don't even have to bring him back for me to remove them. Then we wait for him to wake up, and, as soon as he does, you can take him home. You just have to make sure his tank is clean and that the—the area is clean. Just keep an eye out."

"I always do," Iris insisted. "And it'll work? Because my parents are not happy about this turn of events." The way she said it, it was clear she was quoting them. The words and the tone sounded far more like Ben and Annie than Iris. "I had to promise to do all the chores forever. Like, more than a month." In the corner, Annie rolled her eyes but didn't look up from her phone. "Except here's the deal, Dr. Lund, you are not getting this part: Rainbow Dash cannot die because it would kill Applejack. They've bonded. They've mated for life. Do you know what that means?"

Okay, Will was officially not prepared for this conversation in any fashion.

He had had deep exchanges with patients' owners before, often immediately before or after putting an animal down.

*Do you believe I'll see my dog in heaven?* Early in his career, Will would try to flip it around, to ask what they thought, but that never satisfied anyone. It was as if they believed that he, as someone who'd been at countless animals' deaths, had some sort of special insight into the mysteries of life and mortality. It was a terrifying trust that people gave him, a terrifying knowledge that they attributed to him.

So he'd fallen back on "I'm sure that you will," which allowed him to avoid parsing his own agnosticism about an afterlife.

*Is she in any pain?*

There, he always said no, though the truth was that he didn't know. Animals hid their discomfort so well, whether out of an evolutionary protective measure, fear of disappointing their owners, or plain old shock. He knew that he did everything he could to make them comfortable, and that had to be enough.

But he wasn't prepared to talk about the depths of gerbil love with a nine-year-old.

"I know." He would never admit this to Iris, as it would seriously hurt his credibility in her estimation, but he'd hastily reread all the pages on gerbils from two different textbooks in preparation for this appointment, and they'd included that fact.

The Romeo-and-Juliet-esque "I'll die without you" part hadn't been in there, but there had been a few lines about how they could form permanent bonds with mates and tank buddies.

"I understand you're worried." He needed to get this back on firmer, less fatalistic, ground. "I'm going to do my best for . . ."

"Rainbow Dash."

"Right. But neutering him is the best solution to your problem, even with the risks. If you do the cost-benefit analysis, I think you'll come to the same conclusion."

Iris rolled her eyes at his attempt to dazzle her with fancy adult words. She looked so like her mother in that moment, he almost laughed.

"You'll take care of him like you would if he was your own gerbil?" Iris demanded.

"I treat every one of my patients like it's my own." He knew he was going to have to fix Hoot as soon as she was old enough.

This at last seemed to placate Iris.

Behind the plastic window of the carrier was a layer of wood shavings and a large gray-and-white gerbil. Rainbow Dash stood on his back paws, his tail curled around his feet, regarding Will with an air of distrust. Will was going to earn that.

He sent a wordless apology to the gerbil.

"Do you have any more questions, Iris? Annie?" Will knew that it was important not to rush this part, the preoperative check-in. It was good customer relations, but it was also important for Iris to be comfortable with this and with him. Even if she had to switch to another vet after his practice folded, he didn't want to put her off the veterinary medical establishment permanently. She needed to feel as if her worries had been heard and addressed.

But all Annie said was, "Nope. What time do you want us to come back?"

Iris's eyes widened as if she couldn't believe her mother's callousness, but of course she was lucky that her parents would even consider a fairly expensive surgery for a rodent. Most people in Yagerstown wouldn't, which was at least 10 percent of Will's business problem.

"How about four?" he said. "We'll call once the surgery is done. But Rainbow Dash should've woken up by then, and we'll have had a few hours to observe him."

"Excellent." Annie went to the door and opened it.

Her daughter did not follow her. She was still rooted in the exam room, staring at her gerbil.

"Iris," Annie called.

"Remember: life partner." If Iris had wagged her finger at him, Will wouldn't have been surprised. With one more longing sigh in the direction of the critter tote and one more warning glare at Will, Iris finally followed her mother.

Out in the hallway, Annie said, "We need to find the world's smallest bag of peas."

Iris's confused response floated back to the exam room, and Will smiled, thinking about Nic's chickens chasing frozen peas around her lawn. Then he leaned down to look at the gerbil.

"What's it like to mate for life, um, mate?"

But of course Rainbow Dash didn't respond.

Will knew what it meant to love someone. When it came down to it, he loved his family, which was why their criticism stung. He'd loved some of his ex-girlfriends, and that love continued to exist in some ossified form in the museum of people who he used to be.

That was the problem for gerbils. If Rainbow Dash disappeared, Applejack would be stuck in perpetual mourning until the grief took her. Will's reasoning had gotten him past heartbreak, but maybe he had been using his brainpower to stop himself from experiencing some feelings at all.

Take Nic. Two days ago, he wouldn't let himself love her because he knew—well, he'd thought—that wasn't what she wanted. Sure, his longing was there, water under a thin shell of ice on a frigid January morning, but if it wasn't going anywhere, then he wasn't going to shatter the crust with his boot.

Except then she'd stood up for him, and the shell had cracked. All the tenderness and feelings had come rushing out. It had been there when he'd moved inside her, written as if in neon on her bedroom walls.

He was falling in love with Nicole Jones.

Would it be gerbil love, forever love? He couldn't say.

But it was the most fragile, new, and hopeful thing in his life, and he wanted to tend it and see what might bloom.

# CHAPTER 26

The knock came on an otherwise normal afternoon. Nic was uploading a new episode and answering emails, but those routine tasks were weak distractions from the memories of the previous evening—and the previous night.

She'd been almost radioactive with rage at Will's family, which had dissolved into fervent affection afterward, in the dark. As if she could somehow convince Will of his worth with her body. She couldn't say whether she'd succeeded, though she had proved to herself that she was falling for him.

This was the meaning of "hoist with your own petard," wasn't it? She'd never been clear on that one.

What was clear was that she and Will were going to have to stop pretending this was meaningless. She'd told him they could choose a label for what they had, but you couldn't choose your feelings. They popped up in you like daisies and spread over your heart before you had a chance to decide how you felt about them. Falling for Will before Nic had healed entirely *was* a terrible idea, but she'd already done it.

The shock of that realization was probably why, after the knock, she ran to the door automatically, only to find Brian and a woman that she didn't recognize on her doorstep. The woman held up a phone.

*Oh. Shit.*

Later, Nic would wonder why she hadn't shut the door in their faces and gone back inside. What were they going to do, force their way into her house and broadcast themselves committing a crime? This wasn't sedition at the Capitol. No, Brian had shown up wanting a scene, but she didn't have to give him one.

When it had started, though, she'd been so confused she'd stood there blinking for a good eight seconds before asking, "What are you doing here?"

"Nic, I've been so worried." And the thing was, it sounded true. Anyone who knew him only from the internet and heard him say those words in that tone would've believed him too.

But his fake concern, and the realization of what he was trying here, made anger shimmer, rainbow bright, in Nic. It was the previous evening with Luke all over again: the sharp realization that the man in front of her was a bully and the equally powerful recognition that she didn't have to take it.

Will's brother had cowed him—his entire family, really—into warped normalcy, which she'd been able to disrupt because she wasn't under his spell. Brian had done the same thing to her for years, and she could be as strong now with him as she had been with Luke. She could take herself back from him.

Nic stepped out onto the stoop, forcing them back, and pulled the door closed behind her. She didn't owe his viewers a glimpse of her front hallway.

"You have to stop doing this." She didn't sound baffled. She sounded as strong as she felt. "I'm not in trouble. I'm not having a breakdown. We broke up, I moved across the country to get away from you, and now you are stalking me."

*Let this be live.* If it was live, then that word, that label, would have gone out to however many viewers. Many of them wouldn't be willing to hear what Nic was trying to say, but maybe some would. This was not okay.

Nic kept advancing, and Brian and his friend kept backing up. The woman shot Brian a look that said she hadn't bargained for this and didn't like it.

"You're not in my life anymore," Nic went on. "That's a good thing. I didn't invite you here. I don't want you here. Please go, this is scary."

Fear was there, too, along with the anger. She hadn't given him her new address, and she also hadn't given it to Rose for exactly this reason. How had he found her? She should've started a livestream of her own, but her phone was inside, next to where she'd been working. All she could do was hope that Brian had made the mistake of broadcasting this to the world.

"*Nic.*"

How many times had Brian used that tone with her? Often when trying to get her to change her outfit "because it would photograph better" or do something again, pretending it was the first time "but with a bigger reaction." She couldn't believe she'd ever fallen for this vocal version of cheese out of a can.

"Nothing you could say would change how I feel about this," Nic told him.

"We've never really talked since we broke up."

"You accused me—falsely—of hitting on your best friend. You destroyed my oldest friendship in the process. And honestly? That's the tip of the iceberg. You lied to me and manipulated me and disregarded my feelings over and over again. Once you dumped me, it was like I came out of a fog or something. Brian, I truly hated every minute I spent with you. I hated how you made me feel, how you belittled other people, and who I was with you. And you." Nic turned her attention to the woman with Brian.

Her eyes were glued to the screen of her phone, trying to keep the shot together, with Nic in the middle of it, as Nic walked them right out of her front yard.

"I don't know you," Nic said to the woman. "I don't know if you're dating him. But if you are, leave now. I promise you're already in too far, and it's going to sting when he cuts you loose, which he'll do when it most benefits him."

Nic turned back to Brian, who was, of course, smiling. But it wasn't his charming smile. It wasn't his faux-concerned smile. It wasn't a smile of confidence or control. It was a smile he'd plastered over genuine fear and probably nausea. He looked more than a little green, and Kermit had been right: it didn't look as if it was easy for him.

"I see what you are," Nic told him. "It took me years. It took way too long, and I'll have to live with the shame of that forever. Go away, you pestilent worm."

Nic took three more steps, until Brian and his companion almost fell off the curb into the street. She knitted her arms over her chest, and she felt . . . good. Holy cow, she actually did feel better. These weren't the words Brian had wanted her to say. He'd probably had a monologue of his own prepared, something he and the woman had probably bounced around ideas about—not written down, just some spitballing, you know—that he'd planned to railroad at Nic. He'd wanted a moment. He'd wanted her to cry. He'd wanted her to apologize.

And she'd refused.

Instead, she'd said exactly what she needed to, hopefully to him and the internet. She could've done cartwheels across the lawn, and once they left, she probably would.

Except the neighbors might be watching—oh crap, it was good Will was still at work. This would set him off like a rocket.

"Scoot," she told Brian and the woman, nodding to a rental car that was parked across the street and was undoubtedly theirs. "You aren't welcome here."

But in the sick, uncertain pause that followed, in the moment when Nic thought perhaps she'd not only gotten out of this but had won, Will's Jeep turned the corner.

"Oh no," she whispered to herself.

She truly was a magnet for disasters.

The call had come at the close of an otherwise normal day. Will had finished with his cases and appointments and was putting notes into patient files—Rainbow Dash's operation had been successful, and Annie and Iris had just picked him up—and he was thinking of texting Nic to see whether she wanted to have dinner, maybe talk about where things stood between them, when his phone rang.

Later, he'd wish he'd taken a moment and paused. Wasn't that always the case? You wanted to hear news, and, when it came, you wished you could go back to when you didn't have it.

But as he typed, he answered the call almost without thinking.

"Hello?"

"Can I speak to William Lund?"

"This is he." The formal words would have been awkward in his throat at any point, but now, they downright hurt. This was the bank. Whoever was in charge there had decided his fate.

"I'm Douglas Smithson."

"Where's Frank?" Frank at least had been sympathetic to Will or had faked it very well.

"I'm calling about your request to defer the deed of trust payments on 27150 Route 74, Yagerstown, Virginia." He didn't explain about Frank's whereabouts. It was like there was no longer any Frank.

"Yes." Will's pulse was going in his fingertips with the deafening *rat-a-tat-tat-tat* of a jackhammer.

"I'm going to turn on the recorder now."

Oh God. The guy was turning on the recorder because he thought Will was going to react badly and they wanted a record of this conversation, of the news being delivered. They were declining.

Will's head began to throb, and his guts tangled into a volvulus. The guy read some statement filled with fancy words and empty platitudes, but the message was clear: *No.* No, they would not give Will a break. No, they wouldn't help him help his staff. No, they wouldn't help him save his business.

Last night, Nic had convinced him for two seconds that he wasn't a failure, but here was the actual, certified, institutional truth: he was a loser.

After the guy had finished, Will managed to say, "I see."

"Is there anything else I can help you with?"

Will almost laughed. The question implied that the man had been helpful to begin with, that anyone or anything could help Will, when of course they couldn't. He was fundamentally and incontrovertibly fucked.

"No."

He stared at his phone for a long time after he hung up. This was when Marsha would have come in, found some excuse to chat, and made him tell her what had happened. Then, somehow, magically, she would have put a positive spin on it and tried to cheer him up.

But now, there was no one to even notice. Kim had left for the day, and Will was almost done. His family still didn't know how perilous things were, and after last night, it was clear they didn't really care. He wasn't in the mood to confess all this to his parents, to have them be outwardly kind while Dad cringed inside that his son was a failure and Mom couldn't believe he was making things so uncomfortable.

Nope, there would never be a good time for that particular conversation.

The only exception was Nic. For weeks now, she'd listened and tried to help him. Hell, she'd even stood up for him. She still liked him, she was still attracted to him, despite everything.

Not for the first time, she was the only person he wanted to talk to. Later on, he'd have to tell Kim; he'd have to tell everyone. But today, the only person he could share his raw pain with was Nic. Because he cared for her. Loved her. The idea was a compass heading, pulling him across town, back to her.

Except when he turned onto his street and he found Nic, her arms clenched across her chest, with her ex and some random woman standing in the middle of the street holding up a phone, everything crumbled. Again.

Will immediately pulled over, put his Jeep in park, and jumped out. "What's going on?" he asked.

Nic radiated tension, and her elbows were razor blades, slicing through the air.

He stopped a few feet from her. He wanted to offer her some kind of physical support like she had for him the other night, but she seemed close to spontaneous combustion, so he kept his hands to himself.

"Brian stopped by," Nic said, summing up the obvious.

"I see. And you are?" he asked the woman.

She was blonde where Nic was chestnut and tall where Nic was short. Maybe Brian had been trying to change directions.

"A friend of Brian's" was all she said, without pausing in her filming.

Will was certain all this was going to make an appearance on YouTube, oh, shortly.

"I think we've said about all we have to." Nic's words were as sweet as antifreeze. "So I'm going to head inside—"

"But the vet just showed up." Brian smiled at Will, and all Will could see was how perfectly his fist would fit in the other man's mouth. "We haven't met, but I was a huge fan of your appearance on Chick Nic. Is that going to be her thing now, having all her boyfriends on?"

Will had no intention of taking that bait. All he wanted was to get this guy away from Nic. Everything was going wrong today, but he could do that. "She asked you to leave, and so—"

"Nah, Nic loves a good scene. Loves to get loud. Take it from me. After all, I do know her *very well*." The way he said it was obscene, and Will saw red.

His blood had been fizzing since he got off the phone with the bank, and this guy was practically begging him to unleash that anger. It would be so easy, so satisfying, to burn up the last bit of his credibility whaling on Nic's ex.

Nic dug her fingers into Will's arm. "He's not worth it," she whispered.

Her hand was cool on his skin, and Will tried to focus on the feel of it, but it was an ice cube tossed on the desert sand, and he burned through whatever poise she was trying to offer him in an instant.

She turned her attention back to her ex. "I don't want to see you again. Ever."

Brian shrugged. "Have it your way." He was obviously relishing every single second of this, and he didn't mean what he'd just said. He was going to keep doing this when he needed a boost in viewership or he was bored. If Will didn't end this now, he was going to keep harassing Nic forever.

"Go," Will told him, trying to put a promise in his voice about what would happen if Brian didn't.

Brian didn't move. The woman didn't move. Nic didn't move.

"Now," Will added.

"Or what?" Brian was mocking him, and something in Will crumbled.

Nic must have felt it happen, felt the restraint inside him cease to be, because she tugged his arm so hard, it startled him.

"*Inside*," she hissed. "That won't help."

She pulled him back a step. Rotated until she was in front of him and set her free hand against his chest. She began pushing him. "Inside," she repeated.

"Hey, now, he still has things to say," Brian called.

But this wasn't totally about Brian, not anymore. Nic and Will were both exhaling clouds of rage that butted up against one another. Nic frustrated with him for God knew what reason, Will livid with her because she wouldn't let him tear her asshole ex limb from limb.

They backed up her front walk like that, in an angry waltz, until she managed to open the door and to shove him through it. Then she closed the door behind them and leaned up against it, as if she was worried he might try to bore back outside.

"Why did you do that?" he asked. "That guy has to be taught a lesson or else he's going to keep doing that to you." That might be the last good thing Will could manage to do.

"I had the situation under control, and I don't want you to go to jail for assault."

"You did *not* seem to have it handled," he said, because she hadn't. Her eyes flashed. "What's your problem?"

"Today, everything."

And wasn't that the truth?

# CHAPTER 27

A cyclone of emotions twisted in Nic: anger at the years she'd wasted on Brian, joy at having told him what he was, and exasperation at Will for materializing at exactly the wrong moment. He'd made Brian's appearance so much worse.

"What the hell are you doing?" she asked.

"Your ex showed up and threatened you." Will was pissily incredulous that she was even asking—and still as volatile as jet fuel.

"Thanks for defending me, but his goal was to make me look like a drama queen." There was a core of good intention to what Will had done, but the outside was rancid, like a poisonous M&M.

"What was I supposed to do? Ignore him?"

"You could've checked in with me and then stood there glowering, trusting that I had it handled." That would have been perfect, actually. Come to think of it, why hadn't he given her the benefit of the doubt?

"The other night, with my family, you didn't just sit there."

The two situations weren't analogous. "You're still going to see your brother at Christmas and whatever, so I was rude to nudge him to be less mean. I didn't burn any bridges or risk getting arrested. We're not going to have a relationship with Brian, but that doesn't mean you can start a fistfight with him."

"I wouldn't have *started* one."

She didn't know if Will meant that he would have waited for Brian to throw the first punch or that any fight would have begun and ended with the same swing, and she didn't care.

"You're making me feel like an after-school special. Violence isn't the answer." Public humiliation was a much better way to deal with Brian, and she'd achieved that. "I said what I needed to."

Her words weren't going to matter to most of his fans. They were going to hate Nic more than they ever had. This was going to generate a landslide of nasty mail and problems for Nic and everyone else associated with Chickens for All—and they'd just dug out from the last go-round of abuse.

Nic understood why hens pecked each other in times of stress.

"What happened to you?" Nic could tell Will had had a disaster of some kind. She began flipping through all the possibilities.

Oh. "The bank?" she asked. "Did they get back to you?"

"Yup. And what do you know, they only offer deferral when they think there's a chance a business will recover, and mine doesn't qualify."

There it was. Under all his bluster, that was hurt in his eyes.

*Oh, Will.* She reached out and took his hands, which were still balled into fists. The man was going to splinter into a thousand pieces if he didn't relax. "I am so sorry. That's terrible."

He shook off her touch. "Maybe I did want to kick that guy's ass, but you have to admit, he had it coming."

She really didn't, so she ignored Will's attempt to change the subject. "I was fired, early in lockdown, and I felt . . . it was awful."

"Yeah, it sucks."

Which had been what she was saying. "I know. I'm on your side here. The rest of this is a distraction."

"From me being a failure?"

"You're not a failure."

"I'm going to have to close my practice. That's the definition of failure."

"No, that's brave, that's—"

"My only option."

"But accepting that and moving on takes courage."

He couldn't see it. She wasn't certain whether he was even seeing her standing in front of him. He was barely making eye contact.

"Standing up in this town after everyone knows, when they're all pointing and laughing, will be *very* courageous." Will could be cutting when he was angry. That dry wit that she liked so much when he was teasing stung now. He sent out verbal strikes like cracks from a whip.

It reminded her, more than a little, of Brian.

Trying to ignore the parallels, she said, "Failing publicly is awful. I know because I've done it."

"It's not the same."

Sure, among other things, he wasn't a public figure, and this wasn't playing out on the internet. "No one in Yagerstown is going to mock you." Where had that idea even come from? "Everyone here loves you." She'd seen it at his car wash and the farmers' market, with the librarian and the patient's owners who literally invited him into their home because her grandmother once lived there. "You're the one who keeps them outside. Why is that?"

"Because they wouldn't like me if they knew the truth."

The only person who hadn't seemed to like Will was . . . his brother.

Okay, so now that she'd met his family, she could understand how Will could want love but not be confident he was going to get it. His sister aside, that had been one cold house. Nic had wondered why they hadn't come to his car wash, but it hadn't surprised her after she'd met them. It was no wonder he shoved people away before they could reject him. That had to be an easier path than living with Luke. So in response, Will had marooned himself on a desert island, convinced that no one could ever want to join him there.

Nic tried to let go of the last bit of frustration she had with Will. His day was worse than hers, even, and that was saying something. He was at emotional DEFCON 1 here. Will needed to understand that she cared about him. That no matter what, she was going to keep on caring about him.

Her feelings, well, she wasn't worried about those. She knew how she felt about him, and that wasn't going to change.

But Brian had rubbed her face in her bad decisions this afternoon. Making herself vulnerable had not proven to be a good choice in the past. Which had been precisely why for weeks, she had held off and hesitated. Despite that, though, she'd fallen for Will. It had been inescapable, like gravity or taxes or hens molting in midwinter.

Even still, it scared her from the roots of her hair to the tips of her toes to do what Will needed from her here. Exposing herself again was a risk.

*Please, please be worth it.*

"Will, *I* know what happened, and I . . . I'm falling in love with you."

She looked into his angry face, ripped her feelings out, and set them in his hot hands. Feelings that were so new, the leaves hadn't hardened yet and the stalks were still tender green. It was terrifying to *have* feelings like that after living in a barrel roll for years, in which down was up and up didn't exist.

But Will was different. Right?

The way she felt about him was different.

This time was going to be different.

Except he only stood there, his posture knotted and angry, not saying a single fucking thing.

"Did you hear me?" she whispered.

One second became two became ten, and across the hallway, Will . . . was clogged. She knew—hoped—that that was love in his eyes, but fear was there, too, and fury and confusion. Those last three were unmistakable.

That putrid stew of emotions flashed over his face, around and around, until he finally stammered, "You don't. I'm a failure."

The light that had been shooting through her chest guttered. "No, you aren't. You aren't your practice or your bank account or the letters after your name."

"I'm not trick-or-treating. The lab coat isn't a costume."

"Sure, but you can't act like this one terrible moment blots out the rest. It's not the end of your story, it's not everything you are." He was his family, the people and animals he cared for, and—her. He could be who they were together. "We all stumble, but everything I've been through in the last year tells me we can all have something better."

"I tried that."

If Nic could deal with the fallout from Brian, if she could rebuild her life, if she could be willing to trust someone again, anything was possible. If Will really believed that he couldn't change, that none of them could, he wouldn't have started therapy. More to the point, he couldn't be a healer. He knew that people could get better. He had to know that.

If he could just admit how he felt, how she knew that he felt, Nic was certain they could work it out.

If.

"So you were trying," she said. "Why?"

For a moment, they stood there, breathing heavily, almost curving into each other. *Please let him unbend, accept this, love me back.*

But when he snapped back up to his full height, his expression was pure avenging Viking, and she knew that wasn't how he was going to play it. He was going to keep smashing.

"Because I was falling for you." Except he almost spat the words out as if they tasted foul. "But I've realized it's hopeless. *I'm* hopeless. There's no better for me."

His words crashed over her. Once again, she'd fallen for the wrong man. Stupid, stupid Nic, making the same mistake all over again.

They'd spent a month not being able to avoid each other and then not wanting to. She'd thought they were hurtling toward something epic. Something real. Something for forever.

But his rage had annihilated it. He'd pulled up the drawbridge to his island. He wasn't going to let her or anyone else in. Not now, and not ever.

"I see." Except she couldn't see anything. Her vision was blurry with the tears she wasn't going to shed in front of him. She needed him to leave. Now. "I—I'm sorry about the bank's decision." She pried her front door open. "Let me know if you . . . if you need anything. But I think we should take a break. Sort some things out on our own."

His throat worked, and for a second, she wanted him to apologize right then, to tell her again that he loved her but to say it right this time. It wasn't something to shout; it wasn't something to throw in her face or to use as an excuse while he isolated himself again.

But he had said it himself, hadn't he: he didn't believe in change.

Maybe he was right. He hadn't been so different from Brian in the end. Nic had wanted, so badly, to believe that this place and this man weren't like the ones from before. That had obviously been wrong. From here on out, she needed to remember that and keep her guard up. Exposing yourself was always a mistake.

She pointed to the door again. Will watched her for a few seconds, so seemingly resentful about what she'd made him feel, before stalking outside.

The sun was almost blindingly bright as Will stumbled down Nic's front walk. He stopped at the junction with the sidewalk and turned back. He looked as wiped out as she felt, his eyes vacant and his shoulders fallen.

A beat passed, and then Nic shut the door in his face as her tears began to flow. She didn't owe him the evidence of how he'd shattered her heart. She'd already given him everything, and it hadn't been enough.

# CHAPTER 28

The day after he'd lost it at Nic's ex, apparently while live on the internet—and received a steady stream of texts from seemingly everyone he knew asking why he hadn't broken "that creep's nose" and congratulating him on his new girlfriend—Will told Kim that he was going to have to close.

After all, besides Will himself, she was going to bear the most significant price for his failure. She deserved to know before the rest of Yagerstown.

Kim was calm and apologetic. "I'm sorry."

"No, *I'm* sorry." God, the sheer volume of apologies he needed to make would crush an elephant. "I'm the one who failed."

Kim wrinkled her nose. "Nah, you caught a bad break. And I was offered that groomer position at the PetSmart in Roanoke. The money's fine. I'll be fine. But what are you going to do?"

He had absolutely no answer to that question.

After Nic had told him that she loved him and he'd responded by having a volcanic hissy fit when he should've admitted that he felt the same way, he'd spent the night staring at his bedroom ceiling, chewing on his mistakes. He had a lot to digest.

He'd really never had any plan beyond "become a small-town vet." His entire life was someone else's backup plan. He'd assumed his own success, or at least that he and his dreams were failure-proof.

Nic had tried to tell him he didn't know the end of his story. But all he could see right now was the darkness, even though he knew he'd put himself there. He was alone because he'd scared off anyone who might have wanted to join him in the damn cave.

Nic, good Lord, Nic. In that moment yesterday, she'd offered him everything. She'd stopped him from making a terrible mistake and kicking Brian's ass. She'd pried the truth about what had happened from him when he hadn't wanted to give it. And then she'd offered him her heart. She'd looked so beautiful, so brave, telling him how she felt.

He should've fallen to his knees. He shouldn't have cared about anything other than what they'd found together. Without meaning to and almost by accident, Will had shown Nic the most vulnerable bits of himself. She'd seen him at his worst, and for some reason, she'd still cared for him. All she'd wanted was for him to trust her in return, and he hadn't been able to. It made him sick to his stomach. He wasn't sure how he was going to find the words, or if they even existed, to apologize to her.

"And probably grovel." Groveling was guaranteed.

Kim snorted. "Good luck with that."

He was going to need it.

"Things haven't been good at work since before the coronavirus. I kept it to myself because I was embarrassed," Will admitted to his stunned parents, sitting across from him. "And then I didn't tell you because I'd been quiet for so long. It would have been . . . unpleasant to bring it up. What happened is not pleasant. But I can't keep it to myself any longer."

Mom looked stricken, Dad as if he didn't understand.

Will spit it out: "My practice is failing." He tried to breathe through the biliousness, the pressure in his skull.

His parents were still blank. Still processing.

Will tried not to focus on how the next Lund family dinner was going to be an absolute clusterfuck. Too bad Nic wouldn't be there this time to help take the edge off.

Then Mom raised a shaking hand and asked, "Are you sure?"

God, so much of this was perversely funny. Yes, Will was sure that, now that the bank had declined to defer his payments, he was going to have to close his practice. That wasn't something he would be confused about.

"Yes." But even though he kept the snark to himself, he wanted to text Nic. Missing her was like a sickness.

Next to Mom, Dad was still absorbing what Will had said. Finally he nodded. "I'm sorry."

The words almost seemed to confuse him, but at least he wasn't shouting at or blaming Will. Will had not been looking forward to that part.

"I am too." He should have included that when he'd talked to Nic yesterday. He was mad—clearly—and he felt like a failure—obviously—but he was also goddamn sorry.

"I would've expected this from Luke. He's always making rash decisions," Dad said, surprising the fuck out of Will. It wasn't that Dad was wrong; it was that Will had assumed his dad admired those qualities in his other son. "But you've always been so solid. So conservative." From his dad, this was a high compliment. "Your business didn't recover?"

"No. People buying so much stuff on the internet has not been good for me. We were in the hole for so long, and things didn't . . . any rebound now is too small and too late."

The yelling was bound to begin at this point. Dad was never going to accept that. Will almost wanted him to shout, to get it over with.

But there was no bellowing. Instead, Dad sat with Will's explanation for a minute. Shifted in his chair. Tapped his lip thoughtfully.

Mom's attention kept shifting between Will and Dad, as if she would be willing to physically hurl herself between them if necessary, probably shouting *Get along*, as if civility were their problem.

"You did your best," Dad finally said.

Will took each of the words separately, then tried to string them together. *His* best? His *best*?

He'd never thought his father would ever say those words to him. It was one of those things he wouldn't have even wished for because it seemed impossible. Like wishing for Superman to come to your birthday party.

Dad thought he was steady . . . and that he'd done his best.

Will was grateful the chair had arms to clutch. "I wasn't sure you'd see it that way."

"Of course we do." Dad was aghast.

Except the honesty thing went both ways, didn't it? They had to lance these boils, every one of them. "It hasn't always felt that way, which is why I didn't tell you sooner."

His parents exchanged a look.

"You mean Luke's silliness." Mom was trying to clarify. She couldn't assemble the pieces of this.

But even incomplete, this was the closest they'd ever come to acknowledging their second son's bullying. Apparently all it had taken was Nic standing up for Will and then his business failing for them to see the truth.

"Yeah. But it wasn't just Luke." Will shifted in his chair. "I mean, I love you guys. I do. But the last few years . . . I felt—I mean, I was—a little bit of an outcast." Within his own family.

His insides were compressing into a singularity that would surely swallow him up at any moment. It would be such a relief to collapse into a black hole at this point.

After a fucking eternity, Dad said, "Luke was always more like me. I've always known . . . how to talk to him. To relate to him. You didn't need me so much." His voice creaked; it was unused to speaking these silent family truths. "That sounds like an excuse. It is an excuse. What I really mean is I'm sorry. I should have been the one to tell Luke to knock it off, I shouldn't have left that to your—"

"Friend." It wasn't what Will wanted from Nic, but after what he'd done, he'd be lucky to salvage that.

"—Nicole. I owe you many apologies."

"Mm." Will didn't want his parents to castigate themselves, and somehow, *sorry* felt inadequate. He still hadn't processed what Dad had said. It still was too jarring, too fresh that they'd admitted that everything Will had seen and felt for so long was real.

"I wasn't honest, and I let things slide I should've spoken up about," Will said. It wasn't as if he didn't have regrets too. He'd come to think that some of it was his fault. He'd permitted the nitpicking to go on for so long, Luke and all of them had ceased to think of it as wrong. It just *was*. It had taken seeing it through Nic's eyes for Will to find the power to object.

"We'll—we'll do better," Dad said.

Which was probably all they could really hope for anyhow.

Everyone screwed up. The goal was to see it and then do better. So simple, that, but so powerful.

Dad sort of reset himself, pushed his shoulders back, cleared his throat. Got himself sorted. The moment was over, and it was almost a relief, actually.

"Is there anything we can do to help? We have some money saved." For all the crap Dad had said over the years about success being the inevitable result of hard work, this offer, and his sympathy, seemed genuine.

"I appreciate it. But things are over, and I do need to get going." He had more people to inform, and he had this entire shift in his relationship with his family to ponder. At least it would be some distraction from how he'd broken things with Nic. "But I'll see you soon."

His father didn't hug him, and he didn't say he was proud of Will, which was maybe a relief, because then Will would have known that the foundation of the earth had actually been ground into powder and blown away. They could only handle so much change at once.

As he drove home, Will was certain Nic was responsible for the change, at least as much as he was. She was perfect, and he'd driven her away like the buffoon he was, the one he'd wanted so desperately not to be.

# CHAPTER 29

After three days of it, on Friday Will flipped the sign on the door to CLOSED early and drove himself home, where at least he could hide out without anyone bothering him. Hoot met him at the door with a shrill meow.

"What are you complaining about? I'm not even late."

But she followed him around until he'd fed her and then as he heated up his own dinner and did some laundry. He tried not to think about how almost everyone in town had stopped by, bringing him food, offering support. The amazing part was that it didn't even feel like pity. They were crushed *for* him, commiserating *with* him. Even his therapist had been on his ass during their latest session about how this was no one's fault. Everything Nic had said about the system had been right.

Later, Will poured himself an iced tea and moved to the porch. He positioned his chair so he didn't have to look at Nic's house and ache, and he let Hoot out. He didn't approve of outdoor cats, as a rule, but the screens were all secure.

Hoot sat under his chair for a good ten minutes until she felt confident enough to stalk out, hugging the walls and moving stealthily, except for her tail, which was twitching with excitement.

At least one of them was having a good night.

And then, when he was watching his brave kitten and moping and *not* aching, his phone sounded. He scrambled for it, hoping to see Nic's name, but it was only Owen, his vet-school friend. Saw you on YouTube.

It wasn't clear whether he'd seen Will on Chick Nic or on Brian's show. Neither was good.

I'm so good at the socials, he wrote back. Even though they hadn't spoken in a while, Owen knew him well enough that he'd pick up on the sarcasm.

And then Will's phone rang.

"Hey, man, it's been a while." Owen sounded cheerful, but then again, he probably hadn't been kicked in the teeth by love this week, so it was easy to be.

"It has." Will honestly wasn't certain when they'd spoken last.

"So you're treating chickens now?"

It had been on Chick Nic, then. "Occasionally."

"Gotta love those flocks. And you're getting wet for charity too?"

Damn it. It had been funny in the moment, but Will was going to regret that one. He could only hope Owen didn't ask about Nic. "Sometimes."

"And the woman, what's her name—"

Nope. They weren't going to do this. "You doing a lot of clinical stuff?" Will spoke over Owen. He had the impression Owen had moved into the business side and didn't see patients anymore, poultry or otherwise. Hopefully his question would change the direction of this conversation.

"Nah, all acquisitions and management."

When most people thought about vets, they pictured private practices like James Herriot's or Will's, but the truth was that big corporations like Peticine, where Owen worked, were gobbling up those kinds of little practices constantly.

The back of Will's neck tingled. "How's that going?"

"Like gangbusters."

Will pressed the half-full glass of iced tea to his temple. When Will had bought the practice from Dr. Sinclair, he'd turned down Owen's offer for Peticine to corporatize the practice. Will didn't like the idea of taking orders from some MBA who didn't know or particularly care about animals. His margins were already small enough that the idea of forking over whatever percentage to some overlord who added no value made Will want to chew tinfoil.

But beggars couldn't be choosers. Beggars didn't get to have objections, even reasonable ones.

"And I saw that you're having some trouble," Owen said.

Hoot sprawled out at Will's feet. She'd adjusted to the porch, and her posture suggested that she considered herself the queen of all she surveyed. She looked up at Will and blinked contentedly.

Selling the practice would mean giving up control, giving up on one dream. But in exchange, Will would be able to keep Kim and Marsha's jobs and take care of animals. It mattered to the people of Yagerstown whether they could access veterinary medicine here or whether they had to drive twenty minutes down the road.

"Yes, I am. I might be open to selling, in fact." The words *hurt*, but Will spoke them anyway.

Owen laughed. "Is this still a social call?"

"Not entirely."

There was a beat, and then Owen said, "We had wanted to move into the area. Let me razz you about all the beefcake shots on YouTube, and then we can do that."

"Perfect."

Will could give up his pride. He didn't need it anyhow.

# CHAPTER 30

Nic contemplated going out of town the day after Brian ambushed her and she and Will fought, but she hadn't been able to find a single decent-looking beach or mountain rental. Okay, so everyone else was making up for the vacations missed during quarantine, but she needed to get away from her almost ex—actual ex? She couldn't figure out what precisely Will was to her.

But without an exit strategy, she stayed home. Literally stayed home, as in hid behind her curtains trying to bandage up her pride. Again. It had an annoying symmetry with how things had ended with Brian.

The more time she spent in her own head, though, the more she couldn't decide whether she'd overreacted. Will had been having an epically bad day, and the alarms in her head were on hair triggers. Maybe it had been a one-off, a fight that didn't necessarily indicate what their future might be like.

If he still wanted a future with her. If she could forgive him. If he even asked for forgiveness. If she could grant it.

Her insides were a dark chasm, and like in the myth, she simply didn't know what was going to float out of it: the Nemean lion or hope. All she'd wanted was for Will to be different, to be worth it. It was almost too scary to think *different* might be a mirage.

The fallout from Brian's charade did distract her. He and his new girlfriend had been livestreaming the confrontation, and Nic's words had gone off like a concussion grenade in the influencer community. She'd turned down most of the interview requests, but she had posted the blandest video ever where she'd fed the girls different treats and talked about the herb roof garden. It hit a million views in a few hours as everyone watched and rewatched it, searching for clues into Nic's mental state.

Which delighted her. Come on, she was allowed to be petty this once.

But more than a few of the viewers were also searching for another glimpse of "the handsomest vet in the world," which gave Nic heartburn.

Will was handsome. Handsome and unable to see the truth about himself, handsome and determined to be alone. If she should have seen that Brian was a sociopath, she should have seen that Will was isolating. She couldn't save him; he had to save himself.

Late that night, her phone sounded with its text alert. She wanted it to be Will. She absolutely didn't want it to be Will.

It was Rose. Are you still up?

Nic called her immediately. "Hey."

"I saw Brian's latest."

Of course this was still about him. Everything for the rest of time was going to carry the faint whiff of eau de Brian.

"Nothing good ever comes after that sentence," Nic said.

"He showed up at your house?" Rose's tone was different, as in normal. Concerned.

"Oh, yes."

"And the hot vet—"

"My neighbor." While she was thrilled that Rose wasn't shouting at her, wasn't being cold, Nic also wasn't willing to discuss Will with her. Frankly, there was no one in her life right now with that level of clearance, except maybe the chickens, and they had no questions about Will. Chickens were wonderfully discreet in that way.

"That's some neighbor," Rose said, voicing the thirst of a nonzero portion of the internet.

"Yeah, he's . . . anyhow, you were saying?"

"It was really crappy of Brian to do that."

Nic pulled the covers up over her arms; she was starting to get chilled. And maybe confused. This was everything she'd wanted from Rose months ago. Why was it coming out now?

"Are you okay?" Rose asked.

"I don't know what that even means." And it was true. Nic was simply too muddled, processing too much, to pick specific emotions out of the pea soup in her soul. "I mean, I'm physically okay. But I'm not sure I'll ever get over what he did to me—and to us. You were my best friend. I would never, and I do mean never, hit on—"

"I know."

"You . . . know?" Nic looked at her phone for an instant and then pressed it back to her ear. This was truly happening.

Rose let out an endless ashamed breath. "I realize how this is going to sound, and it's probably hard to believe after how I treated you, but I have said and done so many things in the last six months that I regret. I looked up one day and said to Tony, 'Who are we?' It's been even harder for him, he and Brian were so close for so long, but it—he is not okay. The way Brian treats people is not okay."

No, it wasn't. "How did you . . . I mean, what finally changed?"

"Brian didn't pay Tony for some contracting work. Or there was some confusion and—no. *No.* He completely screwed Tony."

Nic knew how you had to remind yourself of the truth sometimes with Brian. How reality became a column of sand, pouring through your fingers the second you tried to grab hold of it.

"You know that cabin he bought?" Rose asked.

"Up in Shasta Lake?" Nic hadn't had a chance to visit it in person before the breakup, but he'd told her all about it as he'd researched various properties and developed his plan, and she had seen pictures. It was going to be his next big project.

"Yeah. So he'd asked Tony to do the work when he first bought it, but Tony said he doesn't like to do business with friends. Then there was some blowup with Brian's contractor—probably because he wasn't paying that guy, either—and so eventually Tony offered to finish the work because he had a hole in his schedule."

"What happened?"

"Well, Tony spent weeks on the place. He had to have a shower retiled three times because Brian didn't like the tiles he himself had selected, and then there was some dispute about the kitchen cabinets. You can imagine."

Yes, Nic could. Brian was the very definition of persnickety.

"I've been a contractor's wife for years. I'm used to the complaints, both from the clients about the work and from Tony about the clients. And it seemed like pretty normal stuff, if maybe more . . . exacting than normal. But fine, whatever, it's Brian's money, it's a high-end job, he has standards. Okay."

Rose drew one of those long bracing breaths that Nic had heard her take a thousand times—before giving a speech in tenth-grade English class, before she walked down the aisle to marry Tony—and a wave of déjà vu hit Nic.

"I thought they were going to get through the job with their friendship intact. Except when the work was done and Brian finally signed off on it and sent the check, it was a third of what they'd talked about. It didn't even cover the crew's wages and materials, because of course Tony was giving him a break to begin with. And when Tony asked him about it, Brian said, 'But what about the cash?' and it was like, 'What cash? You never gave me any cash.'"

There it was. "He was lying?"

"Yup. I swear, up until that moment when he was trying to convince Tony he'd already paid him when we knew he hadn't, Tony was still on his side. Still convinced even after weeks of haggling that it was a mis-understanding. He wouldn't let me so much as bitch about Brian. But as soon as Tony pressed and Brian realized the jig was up, he totally turned poisonous. Said he'd paid less because the work was substandard, accused Tony of cutting corners. He even said some of the crew was stealing from him—and Tony's had the same crew for years. He loves those guys. So he and Brian had a huge fight. It wasn't even about the money, really. It was more the betrayal. I don't imagine they'll ever talk again."

Nic exhaled. None of that surprised her in the least, but she hated that it had happened. That Tony had lost his best friend, that Brian had no loyalty to anyone and an absolute willingness to screw anyone for anything if there was the slightest upside for him.

"He has the most incredible ability to convince you the sky is green even when you can look up and see it's blue," Nic told Rose. "Believe me, I know how even months later, you go outside and see the sky, and some part of you goes, 'It's so green out today.'"

When those moments happened, Nic still felt sick to her stomach. She wasn't certain whether she'd ever get his voice all the way out of her head. He was going to haunt her forever.

"You don't have to be kind," Rose said. "I would understand if you want to yell at me."

The familiarity of that stung too. "I don't, actually. I was and am hurt. Twenty years of friendship, and you still took his side like that. But I lived it, too, I know. I know how he can be. I'm only sorry he hurt you too." Which was the truth. Yelling at each other would be exactly what Brian would want, which applied to both Nic and Rose's friendship and Nic and Will's relationship.

God, she was going to have to ponder that later. Brian hadn't shown up at her house hoping to sink whatever she and Will had been build-ing, but she was certain that he'd see it as a bonus if he knew that had been the result. She didn't want to give him that, even as she didn't know what to do about Will.

"So that's what happened," Rose said. "How we woke up."

"I'm sorry, but I'm glad you got out."

"What are you . . . up to?" Rose asked. "It feels weird that I don't know."

It was exceedingly weird. All of this was weird.

"Pretty much the same old. I bought a house." The words were that first time you went jogging again after months off: tight, almost painful.

"I was looking at your feed. It's *cute*."

Another stab, there. "You should come visit." It sort of didn't feel like Nic's house because her once—and future?—best friend had never seen it. "It's almost all set up now."

"And you're in your grandma's hometown?"

"Yes! I even went to her house." Nic winced. Thinking about that day necessitated thinking about Will, and she couldn't do that without literal, physical pain yet.

He'd been so kind, and she'd wanted . . . God, she'd wanted. She'd fallen for him with nothing held back. She knew that he loved her, but he'd still pushed it and her aside. If the problem had been one of feeling, it might have been easier to accept than whatever apple-of-discord mess they were in.

"What? No way. How did you swing that?" Rose, of course, had no idea of the larger context.

"You know my neighbor, the vet? He sort of knows everyone in town, so he arranged it." *And then he screwed my brains out.*

"That was nice of him." Rose's tone implied that it had been more than nice of him, which of course it had been.

"Mm-hm."

"And is he doing any other *nice* things?"

"That's a longer conversation," Nic finally said. She simply wasn't quite ready to let Rose all the way back in. "But it's late here."

"Ack, East Coast time! I always forget."

"No worries. But"—and here Nic tried to pack as much sincerity into her voice as she could—"I'm glad I called."

"Me too. Have a good night."

Nic tried to get comfy again, but her brain was whirring now. She texted Emily to see whether her eggs she was incubating had hatched.

We have pipping! was the almost instant response.

So a few days?

I'm up now and hopeful.

Of course Nic called her. "Are you livestreaming it?"

"I don't think anyone wants to watch a bunch of eggs under a heat lamp when absolutely nothing is happening but something might happen."

"I actually think that's the definition of the internet."

Emily laughed. "No, I realize I'm being ridiculous, but I guess I'd rather be ridiculous and sleepy tomorrow than risk missing it."

"I get that."

"How is Will doing, since I have you on the phone? And don't act like it's nothing. Everyone can tell something is going on there."

If Nic struggled with whether to trust Rose enough to let her back in, this was a different calculus: Were she and Emily close enough to talk about Nic's love life?

*The only risks that pay off are the ones you take,* Granny had said. But she probably wouldn't have seen this as a risk. You feel something, you say it, right? Nic had known Emily for years online. Now they were just adding another dimension to their friendship.

"I don't know how he's doing," Nic said. "We sort of . . . *broke up* is a strong phrase. What do breakups look like in your thirties when you're not, like, officially dating in the first place?"

"Oh, Nic, I'm so sorry. I wouldn't have asked at all, but he was clearly so smitten. Are you sure you broke up?"

Nic briefly summarized what had occurred.

"What a doofus," Emily pronounced. "Look, I've known him for-ever, and I—like everyone in town—thought he was moments away from proposing at the car wash."

"Things weren't like that." But Nic had hoped they might be. Someday. Maybe. "It was more as if he and I were"—*sharing midnight confessions and falling in love and hurting each other*—"flirting. And now we're not."

"That sucks."

"It does. But hey, I bought some interior shutters, and I'm going to put them up tomorrow so I can't see his house any longer, which is very healthy."

Emily giggled. "I'm all for decorating, but that's not how flirtations usually end."

They'd been expensive shutters too. "I shouldn't be surprised. It was my first attempt at a relationship after Brian. Of course it was going to be a disaster. Now that that's over, though, I'm ready to meet Mr. Right."

A lie that smelled of chicken shit baking in the August sun. Nic would never be ready for Mr. Right. All she wanted was Dr. Viking, and he wouldn't let himself have her.

"Well, it shouldn't be too hard to find someone perfect in a town of five hundred people."

Nic snorted. "Yeah, I wasn't really thinking about the dating scene when I picked out the house." Though it had turned out to be plenty deep. "Very shortsighted of me."

"Thank God for the internet. You can probably have a better man delivered."

"If not, I see start-up potential."

As Emily guffawed, relief settled in the vicinity of Nic's stomach. This was what she'd been missing. When she'd opened up to Will, it had been, at least in part, trying to fulfill the Rose-shaped void in her life. But with Rose back and with Emily, the void no longer existed. Except maybe a new rent had opened up inside Nic, one that was distressingly similar in contour and dimension to a certain surly veterinarian.

"Okay, well, I'll let you get back to the great egg watch."

"Huzzah! I'll text you if there are any developments."

But the next morning, it wasn't a text from Emily that Nic woke up to. It was one from Will: You don't have to answer, but I'm sorry and I miss you.

Something about the simplicity of it lodged in Nic's chest. She'd been expecting something like this because eventually, he was going to return to reason. She'd told him that he didn't know the end of his story, but the truth was that she didn't know the end of hers either. Could you predict the future based on the past?

She'd distrusted vets because one once had patted her on the hand and told her not to worry. That had been an absurd overreaction. Then Brian had been the literal worst. But that didn't mean another sociopath was out there waiting to wreck her life a second time.

Nic peeled back the curtains and regarded Will's house. He wasn't evil or destructive; he just didn't believe in himself. That was an area where she had no power.

Because what she knew now absolutely was that she *had* power. She could stand up to Luke and to Brian, and she could tell Will how she felt. She could heal things with Rose and have a new beginning with Emily. She could keep chickens and help others embrace that, too, if they wanted. She could inspire folks, like with BROODY. And she wasn't going to let anyone take that from her.

So she didn't respond to Will. He was on his own journey, and he had to do this part alone, but she did email Lylia.

> I have a few thoughts about the future of Chickens
> for All. Let's schedule a meeting.

Because that was what she had control over.

# CHAPTER 31

The next two weeks shot by in a blur. Owen fast-tracked the acquisition, and Will quickly received, pondered, and then signed the contracts from Peticine. With a few swipes of a pen, he went from owning a veterinary practice to being a peon.

A hundred other things needed to change—their website, their interior decorating, not to mention everything about the business-management side—but none of those were his responsibility any longer. He'd become a lowly cog in a vast machine.

The upside was he was able to retain Kim and to offer Marsha her job back, but the latter laughed in his face. Or, well, into her phone.

"I love being retired, and you cannot tempt me back," she'd cackled.

"You've been retired for, like, three weeks."

"And I've had a ball every minute!"

He wished he could say the same. After his first conversation with Owen, he'd sent Nic another text: I'm selling the practice to Peticine. You were right about everything. I miss you.

And she'd replied, That must have been so hard to do, but I'm glad it worked out. Miss you too.

But then it had been radio silence.

She could miss him and not be willing to forgive him. That would be understandable. He knew that part of what he'd done wrong was treating her as if she couldn't handle things, like he didn't trust her judgment. So he didn't want to push against her boundaries now. He was going to give patience a shot for once.

He did leave a bag of organic scratch grains for the chickens that he'd found in the practice's storage room on Nic's porch. He'd considered adding a bouquet of flowers, but that had seemed like too much. Too overly romantic a gesture. So he'd just added a sticky note with one sad letter *W* scrawled on it and hoped it would be enough, that she'd see what he was really trying to communicate.

Nothing said, *I'm epically sorry, please forgive me* like organic scratch grains, right?

In the days that followed, he spent more time at his parents' house and played basketball at the park to stay out of Nic's hair. He threw himself into the full practice schedule for the Rumbling Puffins—who managed to score two goals in their next game. He even rolled his grocery shopping into a trip to Rocky Mount so as not to run into Nic at the store.

The missing her, it was palpable. Only those words from her text, Miss you too, had him at all hopeful. The way it had felt with her hadn't been on just his side. It had been real, and it had been shared. The waiting was hell, but he could get through it. His therapist kept reminding him that if he'd learned anything, it was that he was tougher than he'd given himself credit for being.

One afternoon, Owen called to tell him that they'd be replacing his sign with one that was "appropriately branded," whatever that even meant. After a moment of indigestion, Will decided to drive to the Tinee Giant to grab a six-pack of beer and drink a toast to the old sign, to the idea it represented.

He'd known this tangible change was coming. He might as well mark it.

Beer acquired, he drove back to the clinic, flipped open the tailgate of his Jeep, and cracked a bottle open.

"Bottoms up." Feeling foolish, he literally lifted his bottle to the sign. To his dream. A dream that he'd failed to achieve, yes. But he had managed to run this place for seven years. He'd treated hundreds of animals, volunteered at the shelter, and supported his staff. Those were achievements of a sort, and they weren't cheapened by the fact that he hadn't been able to do them forever.

That was what Nic had meant. His fingers itched to text her, to tell her, but he was waiting, respecting her, so he didn't.

As he sipped his beer, a truck came down the road. It was Helen Washington, probably heading home. When she saw him, she slowed and then pulled into the lot.

"Hiya, Will. What are you up to?"

"The sign's coming down soon," he explained. "I'm saluting it, I guess."

He felt vaguely foolish as she watched him for a few beats. This was precisely why he'd kept everything to himself, trying to avoid this feeling. But it hadn't stopped the inevitable. It had only made him lonely.

Helen was probably trying to decide whether she should be concerned.

"Do you want a beer?" He held up the rest of the pack. It wasn't as if he was going to drink any more before he had to drive home, and he liked Helen. It would be good to have the company.

"Sure." She parked and spent a few minutes fussing with her phone before she got out and joined him. "I had to text Rhonda, tell her I'd be late."

He offered Helen a bottle, and they clinked.

"I'm glad you're not closing," she said after taking a long pull from her beer.

"If it could've been anything else, I'd have done it. I'm sorry that I couldn't keep it local. I know that everyone—"

"Understands. Things change. This is just one more piece. You did the best you could."

Which was so much more generous than he deserved.

"It makes me nervous," he admitted. "They could shut this location tomorrow, and I wouldn't be able to do a thing about it." He had no more agency. He'd traded it away.

"If you got through the last few years still thinking you have much power over, well, anything, I have a bridge someplace to sell you. We're all just ants on someone else's hill."

"I know you're right. But I . . . yeah." He gave her a sad smile. He wanted to believe in what she was telling him. What Nic had tried to tell him. What his therapist kept saying to him. But it was hard to accept, if only because it made him feel small, diminished.

Maybe there was a kind of freedom in that. He had let go, stopped pretending he could do everything, be everything, for everyone. It could be enough taking care of animals. That was the part he really liked anyhow.

For a few minutes, he and Helen drank in companionable silence. At least until the quiet was broken by another car. This one pulled straight into the lot, and Marsha climbed out.

"You're having a party, and you didn't invite me? Me, your office manager from the beginning of time?"

"I'm not having a party." Or if he was, he'd meant for it to be a private affair. "Did you do this?" he asked Helen.

"Of course I did. You were sitting here pouting, all lonesome and stuff."

"I wasn't pouting," he protested. "I was reflecting." Honestly, it had felt like a moment of growth for him. It had been a lot less self-indulgent than the moping he'd been doing at home.

Helen and Marsha weren't buying it.

"Then we'll reflect with you," Marsha said. "Give me one of those beers."

"Yes, ma'am."

Marsha launched into some colorful story about her grandkid, and by the time it was over, Kim and her boyfriend had appeared, and they were followed by Sami, Nanette, Ella, Carolyn from that chicken-keepers group, Emily Babbit, and then Will's parents. Apparently Helen's wife had the number of everyone in town.

"How many people did Rhonda invite?" Will asked.

"A few." Helen's smile was mischievous.

It was a good thing Sami had brought more beer, some pretzels, and—

"A cooler? You brought a cooler? What if the cops show up?" Drinking in public was illegal, wasn't it?

Sami chuckled. "Darryl and Benny are cool."

Then there was Lurene with a platter of deviled eggs—"I'd already whipped them up for cocktail hour"—and just when Will was growing really flustered, because this was too much, too kind, the car he wanted to see but had been afraid to hope for crawled into the lot: a dark-green Subaru with the prettiest driver in town. The person to whom he owed the biggest apology.

Nic parked and got out. He hadn't so much as seen her for two weeks; he'd forgotten how shiny her hair was. In the falling light, she almost had an aura, smudged gold shimmering around her, but her movements were tight, her smile pasted on. She wasn't certain whether she would be welcome, or she didn't really want to be here.

Helen nudged him. "Go talk to her."

It was probably fairly obvious that he'd gotten up to greet everyone except Nic. But the things he had to say to her weren't for public consumption.

Emily went over to Nic, and they shared a few whispered words. Then Emily shot Will a dirty look. Okay, so she definitely knew what had happened—and he deserved every dirty look she might ever want to give her. It warmed him, knowing that Nic had allies here who were already so devoted to her.

Will didn't feel like the man who'd almost pounded Nic's ex two weeks ago before pushing her away. In some ways, he was much smaller, but he hoped he made up for it by being more honest. He'd finally admitted that he couldn't do everything for himself, and he was letting everyone see the truth.

It was what she'd wanted for him and what he had needed to do to be worthy of her.

But in order to say that to her, he had to get everyone else out of here. That would require some public speechifying, not his favorite task in the world. But there wasn't anything he wouldn't risk for Nic anymore.

He hopped up on the tailgate of his Jeep and held up a hand. The crowd—because they were a crowd at this point—stopped jabbering.

"Hey, everyone, this is . . . thank you." Will's heart was going like a kick drum in his chest. "If you didn't hear, the sign, it's, um, coming down soon, and I just wanted to take a second to process it. I'd been feeling like I'd crashed and burned here, with this. With having to take the buyout. I'd tied myself up in knots about whether it was the right choice. Maybe I was tempted to demolish a few things—"

"You should've hit that guy!" Sami called.

Will winced. It was incredibly good that Nic had held him back. He needed to thank her for that.

"Anyhow, I've tried to think about it another way. To see what I did accomplish and to know that I did my best." He locked eyes with Nic. Hers were shiny, soft.

In his chest, hope unfurled, warming all the parts of him that had been cold. She was willing to listen to him, at least.

"So thank you for coming and, um, celebrating the seven years I helmed this practice. It's not winding up how I wanted, but . . . well, someone once told me I don't know the end of the story. And she told me that I wasn't alone. So it's fitting that you're all here." He was surrounded by the community Nic had had to point out to him, the one he hadn't been able to see. "What I should say, then, is, Here's to the next chapter." He held up his bottle.

"Hear! Hear!" Marsha shouted, raising hers.

"Hear! Hear!" everyone else echoed.

But while he was grateful, so grateful for everyone who'd come, Will couldn't tear his attention from Nic. He saw as much as heard her "Hear! Hear!"

Sami cleared his throat. It took Will a second to realize that it was directed at him.

"Should we relocate to the Red Room?" Sami asked. "Really get this party started?"

Will had the sense Sami was trying to help him out. "Yeah, that sounds good. I'll meet you there." He had no intention of doing that, however. He was going to make oh so many apologies.

"I'm going home," Helen said loudly.

The hubbub started up again, and there were a few minutes of confusion while everyone untangled their stuff and said goodbye and loaded back into their cars. Will hugged his sister and his mom and promised he'd call them the next day, and then he went and closed up his tailgate.

Nic held back, just like he hoped she would, until his parents, the last to leave, pulled out of the parking lot, and he and Nic were alone at last.

"So," she said, "how have you been?"

"Um, it's been a confusing two weeks." He'd been overwhelmed, exhausted, ashamed, and grateful. He'd yearned for her. The number of things he needed to say were so numerous, it was like trying to pluck a single mite from a mangy dog.

He knew he was the dog in this scenario.

"How's Hoot?" Nic asked.

"Good. Not destroying so many socks. She misses you." *We both do.* "I'm glad you're here."

"I'm glad Nanette had my number. I've been wanting to . . . talk. But I think it took until today for me to be ready."

She was holding herself carefully, and Will tried not to read anything into her posture. He'd wanted to make his case. This was the time.

"I get it," he said. "I've wanted to hear your voice fifty times a day, but I was trying to give you space. I didn't want to show up at your house until I knew you wanted to see me." What Will absolutely did not want to be was anything like Brian. "I don't think I appreciated what your ex was really like until I saw him in action."

"That was the worst Brian has ever been. But . . . it was also the worst I've ever seen you."

Will flinched, but he knew that his behavior had warranted her censure. "I said this over text, but I need to say it to your face: I'm sorry. I was so angry that day, I was almost trying to demolish my life. It was almost as if I wanted you to dump me."

Her eyes were serious as she nodded. "I can see that."

"When you said that you loved me, or could love me, I was happy . . . relieved. Because I knew I was falling for you, too, and I'd been worried you still thought things were casual. But with what the bank said, with my failure, what I heard loudest in my head was *no*. That no, you couldn't love me. That no, I didn't deserve it. It felt like a cosmic joke on me. So I shoved it away, which is what I always do."

"I could see what you were doing and why."

She'd seen everything. "That's because you've always known the truth about me. From the very first day, it's been scary, how you know me. Because I can't hide from you. I can't even hide the things I'm embarrassed about from you. It's difficult to believe anyone could know all those things about me and still care. But that is something I need to fix about myself, and despite what I said that day, I *am* trying to."

It was still hard for him to believe that change could happen, that he could shift his luck. But what did he want to do? Sit around sulking for the rest of his life because he might fail again? He'd hit rock bottom here, and, as far as he could tell, he was still breathing. He would prob-ably fail again at some point, but that didn't mean he couldn't get up off the dirt.

He wasn't certain what else he could do or say to prove it to her, but maybe that was the point. He'd made his case, and she had all the power now.

She pushed her hair behind her ear, looked at the ground, and swallowed. Will was shaking, at least inside, but he kept his mouth shut. This was her turn.

Finally, she said, "That's a very good apology." When she looked up at him, the sunset was reflected in her eyes, which seemed appropriate, since she seemed to contain the whole of the world just then.

"I'm coming out of this relationship where Brian would fight with me or tease me or badger me when I felt or said something he didn't like until I retracted and told him I saw things his way. It got to where I didn't want to have the fight, I didn't want him to wear me down, so I would just not disagree. I can't—I won't—go through that again. When you said no, that I didn't love you, it felt like that was what you were doing. Dictating to me."

"I wasn't trying to tell you how to feel that day—I have no idea what I was trying to say, honestly, it was basically a verbal Hulk smash—but I understand how it sounded. Again, I'm sorry. I'll repeat it as much as you'll let me. I didn't—I don't—feel like I deserve you, Nic Jones. And if you never forgive me, I'll regret being an ass forever. Because that last day, I'd been coming to tell you that I loved you. I'd just had the worst news of my life, and you were the only person I could bear to share it with."

His intentions had been good. What he'd done next, that had been where he'd swerved off the road and crashed in the ditch.

"All these other people"—she waved her hand around the parking lot to indicate everyone who had just left—"they want to share it too."

"I get that now. But even if I'm not alone, even if other people can know that I'm not . . . perfect and still like me anyhow, you're the only one inside my armor. Just you." He wasn't going to let himself think he was all alone again, but he also wasn't going to pretend that he didn't trust Nic more than he did anyone else.

"That makes me sound pretty special." Her tone had lightened. Gone almost, almost flirtatious.

"You are."

"I'm realizing that myself, but maybe I haven't always been. With you, these past few weeks, months, I've gotten up off the mat. I had let that rat of a man weaken me and confuse me. I'd lost sight of what mattered. I have a voice. I can use it."

Which sounded so very good to him.

She tipped her head to the side. "Do you know the story of Psyche and Eros?"

"Nope." It had to be a good sign that she was telling him stories.

"Psyche is this beautiful girl, so of course Aphrodite is mad at her."

"Have you ever noticed gods and goddesses are the worst?"

"Hush, you're missing the story. Aphrodite's jealous, and she sends her son to shoot Psyche with an arrow so she'll fall in love with a monster, but Eros becomes infatuated with her instead. Except she's cut off from everyone else, condemned to this horrible fate, right? And so she jumps from a tower."

"Always cheerful, the Greeks."

For a second, it looked as if Nic might smile, but she was focused on something here, trying to communicate something important to him. "She's caught by the West Wind, who takes her to Eros's palace. She doesn't know who Eros is because he always comes to her in the dark. That's where they reveal their true selves to one another. Where they really fall in love."

Will had fallen for Nic in the dark of his porch, where they'd, almost by accident, whispered who they really were. Once he'd known who she was, who she really was, there had been no way not to love her. He was done trying.

"What happens next?" he asked.

"The usual stuff. They're torn apart, there are trials and pain and all that jazz, but then Zeus makes her a goddess, so they can reunite and marry as equals."

"They get a happy ending?"

"One of the only ones in all those myths."

*Our ending can be happy.*

After another pause, she tapped her toe against the gravel. "I'm terrific." She said it like it was a challenge, a dare.

"You're smart and hardworking, you run a chicken empire, and you look phenomenal in the rain." He'd run out of breath before he ran out of ways to tell her she was amazing.

"I always look phenomenal. You'd be lucky to have me."

"I'll never take that for granted again."

Her eyes flicked over his face, searching for . . . something. Evidence that he meant it, probably. Will would have stayed in the moment forever, because it meant she was weighing this, weighing him. After a few seconds, her posture relaxed, and Nic looked more herself than she had during the entire conversation. More like the woman he loved.

"How have you been, really?" she asked. "Are you okay with how things worked out?"

"It's going to take some adjusting, it's a new role for me. But I think it's going to be good." It was almost a relief, being able to spread the responsibility out. Not having to take everything on himself. But the relief of her forgiving him, if she forgave him, would be even sweeter. "It happened because of you, you know. A friend from vet school saw your show, and he reached out."

"I'm glad it helped."

"It was everything. You've always tried to give me everything." And like an idiot, he'd pushed her away.

"You meant that stuff, about waiting for the ending? About seeing what you'd done?"

"I did. Even if you can't forgive me, Nic, you pushed me to be better, and I will always, always be grateful. And grateful you bought that house." Pure luck had brought them together.

"When I moved here," she said, "I was holding it together but just barely. I was literally running around in the rain chasing a bird, for crying out loud. You helped me rediscover my center, by taking me to Granny's house and then by giving me another shot at . . . at love. Love that wasn't slick, wasn't public. Love that was tender but fierce. I was able to stand up to Brian because I'd stood up for you. I was Psyche, alone in the dark. And if you can let me care for you, if you can feel worthy of that, you could be my Eros."

She set her hands on his shoulders, and he could take a deep breath for the first time in weeks.

"Telling people the truth, seeing that they didn't care, that they weren't judging me, I realized I had wasted a lot of time," he told her. "I got hung up on some pride thing, and you were what pushed me forward. What saved me."

"I'm pretty sure we saved each other."

Her smile started slow, but that was what made it real. It wasn't showy, it wasn't Chick Nic, it wasn't for everyone else. It was a spark they would breathe into a fire, together.

"What I'm saying is I can forgive you." She made a wry face. "I mean, where else am I going to find a Viking vet?"

"Denmark."

She was laughing when she kissed him, which felt like good luck.

# EPILOGUE

It had been a typical Sunday. Nic and Will had made the long trip to Roanoke for a Target run. Such drives were fraught because Will's musical taste was basically guys with guitars—country or rock—talking *around* their feelings, and hers was more girls with guitars flaying their hearts for you, but, as with everything, they made it work.

"Hannah likes her," he'd said, pointing at the radio.

"Everyone likes Taylor Swift. *You* like Taylor Swift."

"She writes really clever songs."

"Damn right she does."

After she'd forgiven him and he'd settled into his new role and Rose had come to visit Yagerstown, Nic and Will had established a routine. A real life. His work, hers, dinner usually at her house, long evenings talking—among other things—on the porch, falling asleep in one of their beds. It had been languid and lovely, and a year had vanished in seemingly the amount of time it took to make a lasagna.

Truly, Will had adjusted fine to selling his practice. He seemed relieved, even, to have less responsibility and to be able to concentrate entirely on animal care, which was what he loved the best. The change seemed to have mellowed him, and he'd never once shifted into Hulk-smash mode again. He shared his community with her, the one that he hadn't realized he'd had, the one they'd grown together.

Like today, when they hit the grocery store and he'd even remembered her favorite kind of "that tasteless and overpriced soda water," plus he'd grabbed an extra case of the flavor he always drank when he thought she wasn't looking. On the way back, they'd stopped at Helen's for some chicken feed, and after a long chat, Nic had thought it was time to head home when Will had said, "We need to make one more stop."

"Sure." Nic wasn't paying much attention to their route. Instead, she was not very secretly playing with her engagement ring, a white gold band sporting a princess-cut diamond cuddled by sapphires. The stones had come from a pendant and some earrings of Granny's. Nic had had the ring for three weeks, though who was counting?

She twisted it back and forth in the midsummer light, throwing sparkles over the car seat, which was completely silly and juvenile, and she was going to stop doing it by the time they got home.

He'd proposed during their first vacation together. When Nic had realized the one-year anniversary of Will signing his practice over to Peticine was coming up, she'd wanted to recognize it somehow. She'd offered Greece as an option—she could imagine Granny saying, *You take that fine man to Greece, or else I'll never forgive you*—but Greece could wait. So they'd gone for something a bit more modest: five days hiking the Appalachian Trail in Tennessee and southwest Virginia followed by one night at a superexclusive spa because she wasn't going to climb mountains and sleep in a tent unless there was a facial, a massage, and a ridiculously large bottle of champagne at the end of it.

As they'd stood at McAfee Knob, overlooking the impossibly green valley below with the hazy blue mountains along the horizon, he'd said, conversationally, "So, you given any thought to marrying me?"

She'd felt herself starting to smile. "Some."

"I don't have a ring, I should warn you. I figured I'd just lose it. But"—he gestured at the view—"I can't imagine a better setting."

Except she was looking at him. "You and me, forever? It's all I ever think about."

She licked her lips. "Me too."

His smile was pleased and relieved and so, so sexy. "Good. When we get back, we can pick something out, and I'll do it right, get down on one knee with roses, the whole thing."

"Nah. I don't need any of that stuff. I just need you."

And he'd kissed her then—the cliff be damned—and it had been perfect.

Now that Will could take vacations, Nic fully intended to kiss him on the edge of any number of cliffs, especially since Nic had expanded the Chick Nic brand while taking on a different role. She wasn't on camera every week anymore. Emily, who was watching the hens while they were away, was doing videos and running forums directed at chicken advocacy groups and rooster-inclusive flocks. Helen had started an affiliated channel about independent feedstores. Even Will had done a miniseries on avian medicine, and he now had a full-blown cult following. Chickens for All had become much more than Nic had ever dreamed it could be.

"What am I doing this for?" she'd said into the dark of Will's bedroom one night.

He'd shifted beside her. "I can't answer that."

"I know." Which she appreciated. "But it doesn't seem real until I say it to you."

He'd gathered her close then, which was what she'd really wanted. To know that he'd sit with her until she had the right answer and that he'd support her unconditionally. To know that when she leaped this time, he would be there to catch her.

Changing her role to brand manager had felt like putting Brian truly behind her. While Will had worried he'd never leave them alone, that final conversation had been so humiliating for Brian, he'd never uttered her name in public again, at least as far as she knew. Entire days went by sometimes where she didn't think of him once. The nightmare had finally faded, leaving only a sheen of scum behind.

The best things that had come out of the Chick Nic years were the community and the chickens. Well, and Will.

Will turned his Jeep into a neighborhood, and Nic let her hand drop. "What's out here?" She'd learned Yagerstown well in the last year, and she wasn't aware of any businesses in this part of town.

"I have to grab something at the Wallaces'."

The people who owned Granny's old house. Oh, well, it would be good to see it again.

Will parked on the street and hopped out.

"Are you sure they're expecting you?" Nic asked. No cars were parked in the driveway. The house stood still. Airless. Almost . . . vacant.

"Yup." Will marched up the front walk and then pulled a set of keys out of the mailbox.

"*Will*," she hissed. "What are you doing?"

"Who knew you were so jumpy? You'll kiss me on the edge of a cliff, but you won't engage in a little breaking and entering?" He shot her a hot smile before unlocking the front door. "Come here."

When Nic extended her hand toward him, her fingers trembled, but Will gave her a certain squeeze and drew her over the threshold.

Their steps echoed over the wood floors, as there were no rugs. No furniture. No pictures on the walls. Curtains still framed the windows, but they were out of place, given how the rest of the house was a shell.

"Where are the Wallaces?"

"Gail took a job in NoVa, and they cleared out this week. They were going to put it on the market, but she called me first and asked if we wanted to buy it."

"You bought Granny's house?" Nic's voice reverberated off every hard surface, upstairs and then down. Shock and excitement and . . . shock ricocheted around them like verbal buckshot.

Will shook his head and curled his free hand around her neck. "Nope. I wanted to see what you thought first."

Since they'd returned from their hiking/engagement trip, they'd been getting caught up on the work they'd missed. Will had been swamped with appointments and Rumbling Puffins practices, and Nic had had a flurry of virtual meetings. While the engagement had never been far from her mind—hello, gorgeous sparkly ring winking on her finger every minute of every day—the wedding itself or what their lives might look like afterward hadn't rated.

They'd celebrated with his family, with whom Will had found a tentative détente, and with their little community of friends. But they hadn't talked about whether he'd sell his house, she'd vacate hers, or if they'd just continue to sleep at one or the other every night. What had mattered was knowing that they belonged to each other now. The rest was just . . . details.

"I could buy her house," Nic whispered.

"I'd like to think *we* could, but yes."

Nic took a few steps, keeping her hand linked with Will's. The dining room seemed huge without a table in it. There was a scratch down the chair rail, she'd have to touch that up—

She was already thinking of it as hers.

"Is it big enough for us?" she asked.

"Four bedrooms, though one is kinda small. I figured we could use it as an office, or—" He stopped.

They hadn't really talked about whether they wanted kids much, but she'd brought orange slices and Rice Krispies Treats for an after-game treat a few months prior, and the way he'd looked at her while she'd been distributing the snacks, warm and questioning, hadn't been hard to decode. She hadn't wanted to say anything. It had felt like one of those glycerin soap bubbles that float out of the sink when you're doing dishes: too fragile to even call out about because they could pop in an instant.

But she'd felt the knowledge of it when he'd made love to her that night. The way his fingers bit into her hips, the rough tenderness in how he'd moved over and in her. They were forever. They were going to grow a family together and then grow old together. They were each other's missing other half.

"A nursery?" she supplied for him.

"*Nic.*" He was across the space between them in seconds, and then he was kissing her insistently, softly.

As always, though, it didn't stay soft for long. His thigh worked between hers, her back hit the wall, and his hand was moving under her shirt, over her side.

"We can't do that here," she said between kisses. "It's not ours yet." She was pretty sure it would be rude to have sex in a house you were only considering buying.

"Gail said we should look all around, get all the info we needed." He used that seductive tone she had trouble resisting, which of course he knew.

Nic giggled and slipped out of his hold and then back a few steps. She needed the length of the living room to be between them if she was going to make a good decision here.

Will, looking sexy and tousled, leaned against the wall. He crossed one of his long legs over the other and gave her major-league bedroom smolder.

"There will be lots of time for that," she told him. "Later."

Those Viking bronze eyes of his flashed. "So that's a yes? You want the house?"

She walked to the stairs and twined her fingers around the newel post. There were ghosts in this house. Welcoming ones. Ghosts of the past, of belonging, and of the future. She was going to make friends with them all.

"Yeah. Yeah, I do. It feels . . . like coming home."

"I'm glad."

"I don't mean the house, you ding-dong." Though . . . it was partially the house. "I mean this." She gestured between them. "*This* is home."

"You're the only home I'll ever need, Nic Jones."

Okay, so she totally made love to him on the stairs then, but at that point, they'd basically taken the house. Just like that, it had become theirs, another step on the journey they were on together. Always together.

# ACKNOWLEDGMENTS

In June 2020, I was in my backyard hammock, stressed out of my mind (as everyone was) about COVID, trying to find something to read on my Kindle. What was the right book for that moment? I wondered. While my hens made soft chicken noises nearby, I decided to write the perfect hammock romance. Okay, so I hadn't finished a full-length manuscript in four years, and I was epically, seemingly unmovably, stuck. It was a reach goal.

I started drafting, stitching together bits of stories that had been in my mind for years, casting them through what we'd all been living with, our unstable collective mental health and the almost culture-wide gaslighting. I didn't know whether I could finish the project, and I certainly didn't think anyone might ever want to read "the chicken book" even if I did. But if I was going to quit writing, I wanted to go out with something that I liked, something that felt like me.

I would never have written this book without the friendship and encouragement of Genevieve Turner. We met online in 2012, and she's been the best critique partner and friend ever since. She's also one of the more patient people on earth because I have been a *mess* the last few years and she didn't abandon me. Plus she's an evangelist for chicken ownership, and I have my flock because of her. The chickens I have known and loved are/were Honey, Maddie, Moana, Dorcas, Zelda,

Hester, Prudence, and the late Camilla. You are delightful lawn dinosaurs, and I have appreciated your zaniness and eggs.

*Chick Magnet* would not have seen the light of day without Olivia Dade. She has been my most enthusiastic, supportive, and hilarious cheerleader since 2015. She has done more than anyone else to help me rebuild my fragile self-esteem and to convince me that I might be able to have a career writing romance. She is inexpressibly dear to me.

Olivia also introduced me to Sarah Younger, who has been an amazing and strategic agent, protective of me and ambitious for me in the best ways. Even in moments of rejection (of which there were many), she's a ray of sunshine, and she finds the greatest chicken and veterinarian TikToks.

I'm so grateful to Lauren Plude and everyone at Montlake. From our first conversation, it was clear that Lauren *got* this book, and I was totally on board with her vision for it. Her edits were impeccable, and she's been such a champion for *Chick Magnet* and for me. I'm grateful for Ruth's mental health sensitivity read, and for Elyse, Megan, and Patricia fixing my many, many errors. Any remaining typos are my own darn fault.

I must recognize Miranda Dubner, who was a wonderful word-count accountability buddy when I was drafting; I would not have finished writing this without our DM chain. Jenny Holiday beta read an early (weak) draft of the book, and her notes were invaluable. Liz Lincoln and Sue London were such an important support network when I was querying and in submission, and I would have had any number of breakdowns without them. Ruby Lang, Zoe York, Stacey Agdern, Kristi Yanta, Therese Beharrie, Mia Sosa, Namrata Patel, Kristen Callihan, Alyssa Cole, and Allie Parker answered my questions about agents, editors, and pitching and were so generous with their expertise and time. Skye Warren's 2020 Romance Author Mastermind conference was a revelation, and it helped me clarify my goals.

Closer to home, I would not still be writing without my husband, who hasn't questioned why I spend untold hours with my manuscripts. He got on board with my backyard-chicken dreams, and he's always willing to talk through characterizations and plots when I'm stuck. I believe stubbornly, relentlessly in happily-ever-afters because of him.

I'm grateful for my children, whose tender hearts, endless curiosity, and easy belief in me are inspirational. I hope they love this book . . . someday when they're older and Mommy's penchant for dirty words is less upsetting. I'm also grateful for the support of my parents—even when I write books steamier than they'd like.

In closing, *Chick Magnet* is in many ways a love letter to the various vets and vet technicians who've helped our pets over the years. I am so appreciative for the knowledge, kindness, and care you've given my dogs, cats, gerbils, and hens. There is a veterinary mental health crisis in the country, and I've tried to write about this phenomenon as respectfully and accurately as possible. Please get help if you need it. You are so important.

TURN THE PAGE TO SEE
A PREVIEW OF EMMA
BARRY'S NEXT BOOK,
*FUNNY GUY*

# CHAPTER 1

"Do you think it's true?"

If the woman in line behind Sam Leyland was trying to whisper, she wasn't good at it. Of all the bougie coffee shops in all of Williamsburg, Sam had had to pick this one, where apparently people didn't know how to mind their own business.

"I mean, he can't still think frozen cheesecake is fancy," she went on. "That's just—not possible."

"Could be," the equally whisper-challenged man responded to her. "Maybe. Some of it."

"Should we say something? Or—"

The couple dissolved into laughter, and it took every ounce of the self-control that Sam famously did not have to point out they were *already* saying something. The juncture to not say something—the place where they could have all stared at their phones or the floor with the air of exhausted irritation that generations of New Yorkers had cultivated on teeming subway platforms and buses—had passed. Sam should've waved at it as it flew by.

But these people—loud and annoying as they were—hadn't started things. That fault rested with Sam's ex-fiancée, who was cooing her latest single, "Lost Boy," over the loudspeakers about how Sam was such a child. Which . . . fair.

The next time he dated a pop star, it was going to be someone less talented. Someone whose latest single was less likely to top the Billboard charts with its "instantly iconic" video. And he was going to be sure to keep his secret pain buried good and deep, somewhere no one would ever find it again. Like maybe onstage in his act, where everyone just thought he was being ironic and didn't ever suspect he was telling the goddamn truth.

The bit about drawing the cool *S* on his sneakers while his piece-of-shit parents had fought in the next room that had gone viral and established him as the "voice of a generation"—had any generation needed "a voice" less?—every word of it had been true. The bits about paying for Slim Jims at the 7-Eleven with pennies, about flunking out of college, about blowing his *Comedy Hour* audition and then getting the gig anyway: all true. And none of it had felt funny while he'd lived it.

*Do you think it's true?* The words of the woman behind him echoed in his head. Of course it was fucking true. All Sam ever did was tell the truth.

The couple continued to giggle as the line clicked forward one more person. Sam closed his eyes and wished it all away. The loud gossips. The too-catchy song. The pouring rain that had driven him to stop here for coffee rather than at his regular place.

It all sucked, but he hadn't done anything in his life to enable him to complain about his luck. He'd had way more good breaks than he deserved—he knew that for sure. Part of what kept him hungry was the knowledge that he should never have escaped Ohio in the first place. It wasn't gratitude—hell no—but it was a belief that if he stopped moving, he might sink. He was going to sink someday, but every day he didn't was a win.

At last, Sam arrived at the counter.

"What can I get for you, man?" One thing that service workers in New York City could always be counted on for was to never, ever be impressed with you. Sure, Sam would bet he was the most famous person to get coffee here this morning, but still, the kid didn't even blink. Impressive.

"Grande Red Eye with dark roast." Sam handed the kid at the counter his credit card. "And I'll pay for the order of the couple behind me too."

"Oh, no. Don't start that." The kid wasn't going to say *please*, but his eyes were wide and desperate. He was just staying on this side of begging. "It's obnoxious."

"It's not to be polite. I promise. It's not going to start a chain."

"If you say so." Not only was the kid not impressed with Sam, but he was also actively hostile.

Sam stepped to the end of the counter to wait for his drink. Up at the front, the world's loudest whisperers just couldn't believe that that guy from *Comedy Hour* had bought their caramel-macchiato-with-whip bullshits. They, of course, did not bother to extend the gesture to the people behind them—because such was the world.

It was stuff like this that made Sam unapologetic and kept him angry. The only differences between Sam and these two were that he. didn't pretend and that he got to say his piece on national television. Deep down, the three of them were the same, and it was only a complete lack of a filter that kept Sam from being like everyone who complained about how rude he was.

Before the couple had managed to make their way down to him, the barista handed him his coffee. "Have a nice day."

"It won't be." After last week—seriously, how could Salem have not bothered to text him a heads-up before she'd dropped the song? They'd been at least talking about a wedding—there was no way that today could be anything other than sucky.

The whisperers at last arrived. The woman was all fluttering eyelashes and fake kindness. In the morning, you could put on polite or you could put on rude. Sam just happened to think it was more honest to pick the second one.

"Are you Sam Leyland?"

"In the flesh." All of this would be so much more awkward if it were a case of mistaken identity—and it was about to be really awkward.

For one second, Bree's face flashed before him. His best friend since kindergarten, Bree was the conscience he didn't have. Her brown eyes would be serious; her red hair would bounce around her shoulders as she shook her head. *Don't do this,* she'd say.

But even if she were here, he'd barrel into it anyhow. It was his nature.

"That was so nice of you," the woman was still gushing, "paying for our drinks."

"You didn't have to do that," the man added.

"I know I didn't," Sam said, pointing out the obvious. "I did it so that I wouldn't have to feel too bad when I told you you're assholes."

The woman gasped. The man seemed to be legit speechless. Ten seconds prior, the coffee shop had been all noise and bustle. The hiss from the milk frother. The *ting* from spoons hitting mugs. The bubble of coffee percolating. The low-level roar of conversations and the city outside. All it took was Sam being Sam, and the place went dead. Just fucking silent.

He knew he didn't have any special powers, but honestly, he could be forgiven if he forgot. It really did seem as if he'd made this happen.

Anyhow, he was in it now: he had to finish it.

"Look, I'm not saying 'I'm a person, can't you see my humanity' or anything like that." Jesus, he'd never be so absurd. "Just, for fuck's sake, don't talk about someone when they're standing sixteen inches from you. Have you no shame? Point and whisper from across the room like a good WASP. Or just text your friend. Everyone else was. Hey, you, sir—no, not you; you're reading the *New Yorker* so you'll pretend you don't know me—that guy." He pointed to a man of about twenty-five who was staring at his iPhone without blinking and trying to ignore Sam's rant. "You, were you texting someone about me?"

A beat. Then the guy looked up and nodded sheepishly.

"See? And there's no shame in that." Sam didn't blame him at all. "But don't talk over the song." Sam pointed at one of the speakers. "It's a good song. Hell, I love hearing all about how I have daddy issues and that's why I can't commit—because I don't believe anyone can truly love me. It's great. It's like therapy, but I didn't even have to pay for it and the entire world gets to listen in."

The woman's eyes were huge, like the moon in that good-night book Sam's mother definitely hadn't ever read to him. The man was going red in the face, as if he were trying to decide whether he wanted to get in the first fist fight of his life.

Right, it appeared that Sam had made his point.

"So yes, I bought your coffee. But it wasn't a nice thing." Sam didn't really do nice. Not for anyone other than Bree. "And for the record, frozen cheesecake was and remains the shit."

After a silence long enough to watch *Titanic*, the woman managed to say, "You . . . are an asshole."

"Oh, absolutely. I never said any different. Enjoy your coffee." And with that, Sam headed back out into the rain, only to be reminded how awful wet dirty pavement could smell. It was as if everything that got ground into the sidewalk every day had somehow aerosolized into the worst air freshener smell imaginable.

Which was actually a pretty good idea for a sketch.

A relatively painless subway ride later—forty minutes and only three people shouted "You're that guy" at him—Sam emerged in midtown Manhattan. It was Friday at the end of a hiatus week, and Sam had to take some publicity photos and tape some promo spots—which was the kind of stuff he absolutely hated. He knew that it was necessary and that the bozos who thought he was good looking until he opened his mouth and ruined the illusion were central to his career, but he'd rather eat cold SpaghettiOs than take pictures.

He supposed that someone else, someone more sentimental, probably got tingly walking up to the studio where the most famous sketch comedy show in American television history had filmed for the last fifty years. The guest hosts were sometimes saying crap like "Do you know that so-and-so worked here," but the thing was, Sam did know, and he still didn't care.

He'd been aware of *Comedy Hour* when he was a kid, but it had mostly seemed stagnant and boring to him. Sure, he was standing on the shoulders of giants and whatever else he'd be expected to say at the next Mark Twain Prize dinner, but as far as he was concerned, comedy spent too much time looking backward.

What got Sam up in the morning was some kid on TikTok right now writing material that was fresh and could be distributed immediately, whereas Sam had to wait all fucking week. He worried all the time about his big paycheck making him slow and complacent. You had to be a shark in this business. Never stopping. Never satisfied.

Sam rounded the corner and found more people than showed up for the average Mets game. Camera flashes started going, and Sam almost, almost flinched. Someone had tipped the press that he would be coming in. Sam was roadkill here, and they were the vultures.

"Sam! Sam!" one of the "journalists" shouted. "How do you like the song?"

"What do you want to say to Salem?"

"Did you really hate your father?"

"Why did you yell at everyone in a Brooklyn coffee shop?"

The hullabaloo continued, but Sam managed to slam a hard expression on, the mask he used not to crack up when Roxy and the rest of the cast were really on. If his mask wouldn't crack when someone was being hysterical, it ought to be enough when someone—many someones—were being awful.

He wished he had a hat and some sunglasses, but that would make him feel like an even bigger phony. All he could do was to push down the sidewalk, counting his steps and the breaths moving in and out of his lungs while they screamed at him.

Screamed the *truth*: that was the worst part. Sam was a broken piece of shit. Salem had certainly been right about that. He didn't deserve the life he had, and he'd probably wreck it sooner or later. That was the only thing that was going to even the scales.

The door to the studio opened, and one of the security guards, Derek, waved him in. "Sorry about that," he said, once he managed to get the door closed behind them. "I called your agent."

Sam probably had about thirty missed calls from Riaz. This was what he got for not checking his phone. "I was on the subway."

He scrubbed a hand over his face. He deserved this. He should've anticipated it. He'd practically ensured it for showing so much of himself to Salem and by blowing up this morning at those coffee jerks. But facing the consequences of his decisions—bad ones, neutral ones, angry ones, stupid ones—all he could manage to feel was tired.

He'd been in places like this so many times, and he didn't want to sleep in this particular bed. His own mind wasn't a great place to be in the best of times, and this wasn't the best of times. He'd made sure of that.

"You be sure to go out the back door," Derek said. "And don't go in the front door of your building neither."

Christ, he was right. Sam's apartment would be mobbed for the next few weeks.

"Thanks," Sam said. "I'll stay with a friend for a while."

Bree's was the only place where things made sense anyhow.

# ABOUT THE AUTHOR

Emma Barry is a teacher, novelist, recovering academic, and former political staffer. She lives with her high school sweetheart and a menagerie of pets and children in Virginia, and she occasionally finds time to read and write. You can visit her on the web at www.authoremmabarry.com.